C[illegible] TO HARM

An absolutely gripping British crime thriller full of twists

JUDITH CUTLER

Fran Harman Mysteries Book 1

Originally published as *Life Sentence*

JOFFE BOOKS

Revised edition 2024
Joffe Books, London
www.joffebooks.com

First published as *Life Sentence by*
Allison & Busby Ltd in Great Britain in 2006

This paperback edition was first published
in Great Britain in 2024

This book is a work of fiction. Names, characters, businesses, organizations, places and events are either the product of the author's imagination or are used fictitiously. Any resemblance to actual persons, living or dead, events or locales is entirely coincidental. The spelling used is British English except where fidelity to the author's rendering of accent or dialect supersedes this. The right of Judith Cutler to be identified as author of this work has been asserted in accordance with the Copyright, Designs and Patents Act 1988.

Cover art by Nebojša Zorić

ISBN: 978-1-83526-567-3

For Frances, and all the unsung heroes and heroines who are carers

CHAPTER ONE

'So here you are, Elise, on an ordinary ward at last. I wonder what it's like for you after all that time in Intensive Care. For any other patient it would be a promotion, wouldn't it? A step nearer to returning to the world. But for you, my dear, it's definitely relegation. They've given up on you, haven't they? It's no longer a simple coma, with a hope of ultimate recovery: it's Persistent Vegetative State. Of course, some people think it helps to have a label for an illness . . .

'I hope they're still caring for you properly. You must be turned regularly, or you'll get sores. Of course, any other patient would have physiotherapy to make sure that pneumonia didn't set in, and to stop your poor limbs contorting as if you'd had cerebral palsy. And what have they done for you? Given you splints!

'Your poor face. Anyone else would have had plastic surgery for all those hideous scars. And you'd certainly have had false teeth: you might even have used some of the compensation you'd have got to have those terribly expensive implants.

'At least your hair's grown back. Mostly it's a grey stubble, but there are two white streaks either side of your forehead that make you look a bit like a badger.

'How thin you are now. When I first came upon you, you were quite plump, with the sort of flesh that says you eat the wrong things. So it was natural that you should lose weight. One day — we have to

face it — they may stop feeding you altogether. Oh, not just like that. There'd have to be all sorts of legal arguments, I'm sure. But sooner or later someone will decide they need the bed you're occupying and ask to stop treating you. Or someone might even think it's kinder to you to let you die.

'Except that technically you are dead, aren't you? Your heart and body may work, but your brain doesn't.

'All the same, I'll say what I always say when I kiss you goodbye: I'm sorry, my dear. I wouldn't have had this happen for the world.'

CHAPTER TWO

She jerked sharply awake. Where was she? And what was that noise? Had she fallen asleep and crashed the car?

No, it was someone rapping on the driver's window.

God knew what time it was. She hadn't dared drive any longer, that was it, not without a coffee and some fresh air, and before she'd done more than cut the ignition she'd fallen asleep.

She must have dribbled, and probably snored too. But it was the trickle of saliva that troubled her most, an outward and visible sign that she'd not been in control of herself while technically being in control of a vehicle.

'You all right, miss?'

It was a traffic cop, his dayglo jacket fluorescing in the headlights of the cars still using the car park, even at this hour of the morning. Yes, it had been about midnight when she'd pulled off the M3, into Fleet Services. Which was where she must be now.

She heaved herself out of the Saab. 'I've had a long drive, officer. Thought I'd take a break. And before I got anywhere near my KitKat, there I was, sending my pigs to market.'

Nodding without sympathy or humour, the young man — he looked about eighteen — dodged back to his Range

Rover and came back fitting a mouthpiece to a breathalyser. Thank goodness her parents' Devon bungalow was Dry. Capital D. She blew as if to clear the last cobweb from her brain. And then, damn it if she didn't start a flush. Right from her belly up into her hair it went, the night air blessedly sliding on to it like ice cream on to hot chocolate sauce.

'That seems to be all right,' he said, tacking on 'miss' as an almost insulting afterthought as he registered this symptom of her age. 'I suppose this is your vehicle?'

Without speaking she reached for her bag, stowed in the rear foot-well, out of sight of casual predators. She always practised what she preached when it came to crime prevention. Her wallet held her driving licence and a photocopy of her insurance certificate. It also held her police ID. Chief Superintendent Frances Harman.

His double-take was almost comic. 'You're a—? Sorry, miss. I mean ma'am.'

'That's OK — you were doing your duty.'

Another dayglo figure slid into view. 'All right, Gazza? Hey, it's Ms Harman, isn't it? You won't remember me, ma'am . . .'

She might in better light. She played for time. 'You weren't in Traffic then.'

'No, that's right. It was my first big operation in CID, ma'am. Back when I was based in Kent. Operation Rooster. Those child murder cases all across the south. Ken Burbage, ma'am.'

She clicked her fingers. The clouds in her head began to clear. 'That's right! Ken! Some clown had put you on permanent tea duty. But you were far more useful than that.'

'Thanks, ma'am. The way you pulled that case together: you should have seen it, Gazza — we were getting nowhere fast. Then Chief Inspector Harman—'

'Chief *Superintendent*, guv!' Gazza hissed.

The other officer's eyes opened a gratifying fraction. 'Then *Chief Superintendent* Harman came and pulled it all together.'

'Not just me, Ken. It was a team effort. I don't think any of us saw our families while the search was on.'

'Which was why I left CID, ma'am. The wife — *my* wife put her foot down with a firm hand, you might say.'

Fran laughed. Ken probably thought it was at his weak joke. In fact she was enjoying his swift correction of a term she'd never allowed. *The wife*, indeed. 'And now you're an inspector: but what are you doing out and about on a night like this?'

'That's what you taught us, ma'am — hands on. And you told us to do no harm — you said we should be like doctors, and take a Hippocratic Oath. I didn't even know what that was back then. And then you talked about having to put ourselves in harm's way, but not unless it was vital. And about apparently harmless questions.'

Yes, she had made punning jokes on her name, hadn't she? In those days. These days, she didn't seem to have many opportunities for jokes.

But Ken was still reminiscing. 'No job too small, you always said. And when I left, you said the most important thing as you went up the ladder was not to lose touch. So though I'd rather be tucked away in the control room, I make a point of putting myself on the roster from time to time.'

'Despite your wife?' Fran managed a grin, which he returned.

'She understands. So long as it isn't too often.'

'Quite right.' Much as she enjoyed catching up with the men and women whose careers she'd helped, Fran was trying not to dither in the cold night air. She was saved by Gazza's radio crackling into action. 'You take your shout and I'd better go and get a coffee. I've got a long way to go tonight.'

'Back to Kent, ma'am?'

'That's right.'

He pulled a face. 'Safe journey, then. And watch out for the speed cameras near the M25: we're having a special purge.' Then they waved each other off, the night having become the better for their encounter, at least as far as Fran was concerned.

With luck the next leg would be an easier run than the first half of her journey, the M20 delivering her to within ten miles of her Kent home. For some reason no one had ever had the sense to put a decent road all the way from London to Exeter. Hapless holiday motorists heading for the South West had the doubtful privilege of being able to stare at Stonehenge from their traffic jam on the A303, encouraged by the news that in a few miles time there would be a minute stretch of dual carriageway, just long enough for one wheezing caravanette to overtake another. Inexplicably, travel back tended to be marginally quicker, but there were still endless miles of road with solid white lines confining you to the safety of one carriageway, with absolutely no overtaking. Until Fleet, the only loos were at Happy Eaters, a food chain more optimistic than accurate in its title, as far as she was concerned. But then, she was rarely happy going down to Devon, and more than usually serious on the return journey she was on now. She'd had her stint in Devon, for this dreary October weekend at least.

She bent gingerly to retrieve the *Observer*, zap the Saab's locks and stagger painfully towards the services, stiff and unsteady, she had to admit, as an old woman: not the spectacle she wanted to present to underlings, even those from the past. Fancy young Ken ending up an inspector. And he might go further yet.

She missed her step on some uneven paving and yelped, clutching her back. It was always worse after a weekend with her parents. Half of her brain dismissed the pain as psychosomatic; the other half reasoned it might be simply a result of her unremitting activity. Although she had long since insisted on paying for a gardener, her parents contrived to fall out with him, and with each one in a long succession. One had planted too early, another too late. One left the lawns too long, the other clipped them too short. Now they could both complain to her that she never achieved enough in the short time she was with them. Short! It seemed like an eternity.

The same sort of problem applied to the domestic help she'd employed. Now, however, that had been imposed upon them despite their protests, thanks to the intervention of social services. It was rightly official policy, of course, that the hapless help could clean only the rooms her parents used, not the guest room, which was inches deep in dust each time she arrived. As for Meals on Wheels, or whatever the name of its trendy reincarnation, her mother had insisted that she had produced good home cooking all her life and she didn't see why at her age she should put up with stuff the council saw fit to feed to pensioners. In any case, her gall bladder and Pa's high blood pressure meant they couldn't eat half the meals anyway. Ma waved aside any suggestion that the meals could be adjusted to meet their dietary needs. Nor, for some reason, was either of them prepared to countenance ready meals, be they ever so low fat, from a supermarket. It had to be home cooking, which meant, with their other daughter Hazel safely ensconced in Stornoway, that it had to be Fran's cooking — Fran, who at home so rarely raised a pan in anger. Perhaps she should have enjoyed the stint simply because it was different, but when she cooked for herself, it was never bland pap.

As Fran queued for the till — as always, she was surprised that so many people were in transit at one o'clock on a Monday morning — she tried to recall a time when her mother hadn't complained about Pa's attacks on the garden, or he hadn't moaned about the over-cooked and watery substances passing as meals. Now they could both round on her for whatever reason: sometimes she thought it was simply as a change from bickering with each other. But lately she feared that her mother carped if Fran spent time with her father, and he if she indulged her mother. Their possible return to second childhood was the thing she dreaded most.

She fumbled the change: the sooner she got some caffeine inside her the better.

There. Just her and a coffee and a newspaper in a clean, well-lit place. A scene straight from Hopper.

She could ignore the lads in the smoking area high on something or other. Just now she didn't want to know what it was. She had to grip her chair to stop her strolling over and scrounging a cigarette, though. Just at the moment she couldn't see the point of eschewing life-shortening pleasures. A short life and a merry one let it be. No dwindling into old age, please!

If only it were just a day down there. But her parents demanded more than that. Every other weekend. More than that. Every weekend. More than that. It was pound of filial flesh time.

The coffee was thin and bitter, once you got past the heat. She refolded the paper and reached for her ballpoint.

The more she stared at the Everyman crossword, the less sense any of the clues made. Even the quick crossword was impenetrable. Except for one answer, which leapt at her: *inexorable*. Then another: *sacrificial lamb*.

Enough.

She used the loo and set off into the night. At least now she had the system perfected. Back in Lenham her bed would be ready. The washing machine would deal immediately with everything she'd worn in Teignmouth, so the mustiness she'd brought back — her parents abjured open windows on account of draughts — wouldn't get a chance to permeate her home. The morning's clothes, down to pants and tights, were hanging just inside the wardrobe. Even the instant coffee stood poised beside the kettle. As for breakfast, the canteen staff knew exactly what she wanted and how she liked it. Sorted.

* * *

Back in Maidstone the next day Fran was looking at her complexion in the ladies' room. Oh, yes: this was Monday morning in spades. She fished in her bag. Over the years she had learned to use make-up not just for prettification but also for disguise. She could appear as sombre and professional as the most misogynist judge might require, or if M'Lud preferred fluffy women she could do that too. She might have spent twenty-three hours of the last twenty-four on a case, but in her make-up pouch was a clever concealer that would hide bags under the eyes from all but the most searching gaze and blusher to impart at least a modicum of colour. This morning she was speaking first to representatives from Domestic Violence Units from across the country about appropriate means of intervention. Perhaps they'd be more interested in what she said than the accuracy of her mascara. And she'd spoken about domestic violence often enough to be able to sound convincingly angry even in her sleep. It wasn't just women who were victims. Men could suffer too. Children, it went without saying. And old people. They were often victims of household bullying . . . Could she imagine ever being driven to violence against her parents? Those who'd bred her, nurtured her — and now whined at her like overtired children?

Perhaps that was their problem. Her mother and father were just tired. As she was. Whatever the outward appearance, her brain was like the potatoes she'd mashed by the saucepan load yesterday, for the shepherd's pies she'd batch-cooked for their freezer, after she'd mown the lawns and done a brisk autumn prune of the twenty-seven elderly rose bushes, all of which ought to have been uprooted and burned. She'd had to take the garden refuse to the recycling centre, its ridiculously limited opening hours producing long queues.

And now she wanted to sleep. God, how she wanted to sleep.

But instead she had a second meeting, this one with colleagues from neighbouring forces, including the Met, about tackling cross-Channel crime. How on earth could she get through it? The preparatory glossy documents, couched in the sort of language no human being had ever yet spoken, had defeated her even when she was at her most alert. And although insomnia and she were old friends, especially lately, the day after her Devon weekend was always the time she most craved sleep. It would have to be extra-strong coffee instead. And then she'd simply have to wing it. So long as no one asked her to take minutes, she might just get through.

* * *

'Harman's just not doing her job, Turner,' the Chief Constable snapped. 'Not up to it. Goodness knows what she's playing at.'

Mark Turner had had his hand on the door, ready to leave the Chief's office. Now he came back to stand like a naughty schoolboy before the Chief's desk, drawing a deep breath. 'With respect, sir—'

'Have you seen her recently? She always used to be a credit to the force, and now she's scruffy, hair all anyhow, great bags under her eyes. You're her line manager: do something.'

'I wouldn't have thought she was any less presentable than many of our male officers of the same age,' Mark Turner objected.

'It's worse if a woman lets herself go.' The Chief Constable realised what he'd said and slapped a guilty hand over his mouth. 'Only don't tell her I said that: she'll wave every equal opportunities document there is over my head.'

Mark didn't laugh. 'And rightly too, sir, if I may say so. Actually, I've thought for some time she doesn't look well, but you don't discipline a colleague for ill health. I'd have thought it might be more worthwhile enquiring whether we're not simply asking her to do too much. She already had a post in crime; she only took on policy development as a temporary measure when Field had his heart attack. If he's not able to return to full duties, Personnel ought to find a proper replacement.' He felt inexplicably angry. Then he realised he should direct the anger against himself: he was, after all, the one to whom Fran reported, and he should have done something about her work overload weeks ago. And he'd noticed she looked more exhausted than simply tired, but he'd never asked why. Being too busy himself might constitute some sort of excuse, but it was only that. He had time to do the urgent jobs, and enough outside work to see what he could of his family. Not that they needed him so much, now they'd flown the coop. Why had he not asked her out for a comradely drink, a meal even? No, best keep to the matter in hand, pushing the point even further. 'In fact, I'd have thought if we didn't take some work off her shoulders she could start a grievance procedure—'

'For God's sake, she's a police officer, not some pen-pushing civil servant!'

'We seem to be both, these days — especially Harman, the way the Home Office changes policies every time the wind blows from a different direction. She takes the brunt.'

'Except that she doesn't. Not recently. She's been sending substitutes to these meetings of hers. Or, worse, apologies. No, I'm not having her carry on like this. Sort it, Turner, will you? And quickly.'

'I'd like to find out what's going wrong before I jump in with both feet, sir.'

'It's an order, Turner — in case you hadn't noticed.'

'Sir.'

ACCs (Crime) were not permitted to scuff furiously along the corridor, slamming doors and cursing under their breath. Even as he did the grown-up, management equivalent, striding with a file at a furious angle under his arm, Mark laughed sardonically at himself under his breath. The Chief was well within his rights, and it was Mark's duty to obey. Perhaps he was so angry because when things had been so bad for him, when Tina was dying, Fran had simply taken over what parts of his jobs she could do. No questions. She had simply done it. There were days when he'd been afraid his in-tray would buckle, but he'd get back from a scampered lunch with Tina to find Fran had emptied it. She'd written up reports, minutes, anything she could to maintain his veneer of efficiency. Not because she'd wanted anything, just because she was a decent woman.

He'd known her from their rookie days: at one point it had looked as if her career would outstrip his. But when a quirk of fate, or perhaps some residual sexism, had seen his rising slightly more quickly, she'd shown no malice, allowed no backbiting. She'd been a good friend.

And now he had to bollock her.

Like hell he would.

* * *

'Fran!'

She stopped and turned, the sagging tissues of her face managing to pull themselves into a smile, which even reached her eyes when she saw who had called to her down the corridor. Invitingly holding open the door to his office was Mark Turner, a man whose seniority sat very lightly on his shoulders. His warm smile — though his eyes, which missed little, in her experience, were more searching than usual — was like balm.

'How do you do it, Fran? You always turn up as bright as paint meeting after meeting, and, just when everyone's going to sleep, you come in with just the right comment.' He was already busy with his electric kettle. 'Green? Lemon or jasmine?' He'd told her he'd taken to green tea when Tina, his wife, had been diagnosed with cancer. It was supposed to act as a preventative, and, though it hadn't worked for Tina, dead these three years, he'd kept up the habit, eschewing coffee and the sort of tea every police canteen in the country seemed to serve as next door to poison. So long as green tea came with its own quiet shot of caffeine, who was she to argue?

Well as she knew Mark, kicking off her shoes as she collapsed on to one of his comfortable chairs didn't seem appropriate. Especially as, even when he had a visitor as senior as her, there was a constant stream of interruptions from officers, and clerical and other support staff.

It was restful to watch him make the tea, silhouetted against the light through the vertical blinds. He'd lost weight since Tina's death, and had the neat belly and buttocks of a man who spent time in the gym.

Did she find herself slumping a little less? At least she didn't put her head down on his desk and snore. The very thought brought her out in a damned flush. Why in hell did this have to be happening to her just when she least needed it? A couple of years ago she'd have sailed through it all. A couple of years hence, retired, she should be able to cope with anything.

Or nothing. In two years' time, she could be a full-time carer. In fact, in only *one* year's time she could be a full-time carer. Technically, having put in her thirty years' service, she could retire as soon as she'd served her notice. This year.

As if reading her mind, or more probably because he was the same age and must be facing the same decision, Mark asked, without preamble, 'What are your plans for retirement?'

Caught off guard, she said, absentmindedly taking the mug he was offering, 'The day I'm fifty-five it has to be Devon. My parents.' She grimaced.

He raised an eyebrow, more senior to junior officer than she liked, as if she'd just made a crass suggestion in a meeting.

'In fact,' she continued, the decision making itself even as she spoke, an insidious idea she'd rather have swatted away before she articulated it, 'I thought I'd pop into Personnel one day soon to talk about paperwork.'

'You mean you've not already calculated to the last penny how much you'll get?' He contrived to make raising his mug an ironic gesture. It sloshed as he rapped it down with more force than necessary. 'Come on, Fran, you can't just slide away. You've got a job to do here.'

'Which can terminate when I reach fifty-five.'

'We all assumed — hoped! — you'd carry on working till you were sixty. Maybe you'd want to cut down a bit on the active side — certainly drop that extra work foisted on you when Field was taken ill — and concentrate more on planning and development . . .'

She wrinkled her nose. 'Seems a bit like agreeing to play for a non-league club after being Arsenal's striker.'

'Nonsense. You've got an excellent reputation — national.'

Head on one side, she asked, 'What are you not telling me? Mark, has someone grassed me up for skiving the odd meeting?'

'Not your meetings to skive: Field's meetings.' He stared at his mug with what looked like embarrassment, though it could equally have been irritation.

'They have. Hell. Well, they'll have to find someone else to cover everything when I go,' she said defiantly. 'And you? We started on the same day, after all.'

'Keeping my options open,' he said, finishing his tea quickly. As soon as the conversation got halfway interesting, it was over. But he seemed to change his mind. 'Tell you what, why not have a drink one evening? Make it a meal — save us both cooking.'

'Or microwaving a ready-meal,' she agreed.

He produced his diary. 'Next Monday?'

She had the presence of mind to shake her head firmly. 'Mondays aren't good. I've started to spend the weekends with my parents, you see.'

His eyebrows shot up. 'Every weekend?'

'For the time being.'

'Retiring down there's one thing . . . Are they ill or what?'

God, what happens when they're ill? 'Just old and frail.'

'So you go—?'

'Friday evening, and come back Sunday evening.' She said it flatly, as if there wasn't a round trip of some four hundred and fifty miles involved.

'But Monday evening—'

'I don't get back from Devon till the silly hours. Sometimes I don't even start back till Monday morning. All I want is bed when I get home on Monday evenings.'

To her amazement the simple word raised possibilities she'd never thought of. Did they raise them in him? He didn't laugh with embarrassment or suggest another evening. In fact, he was letting the silence grow.

So it was left to her to break it. 'Tuesday's altogether better for any activity,' she declared. The pity of it was, the thought of sharing his bed involved simply a realisation that to do so would spare her an alcohol-free evening and a drive back in the dark. Passion? Her libido had been dormant for years. Why should it wait till the menopause — could this really be the first time she'd spelt that word out to herself — to rear its interesting head?

'Next Tuesday, then. No: sorry — I've got a meeting in London. How about the Thursday of that week?' He wrote with a flourish in his diary, still a paper one like hers. She'd once bought an incredibly expensive palmtop and forgotten how to extract vital information after a particularly traumatic weekend in Teignmouth. She'd retrieved it eventually, of course, but then panicked that she needed back-up. At last it had seemed simpler to abandon sophistication altogether.

All the possibilities hanging almost visibly between them, she was relieved when a token tap at the door was followed by the entrance of the Chief Constable, in full fig. Was it her imagination, or did the Chief lift an interrogatory eyebrow in Mark's direction? If he did, Mark gave no indication of having seen anything.

After smiles and fine words all round, she made her exit.

CHAPTER THREE

'Piss off. Just piss off out of it. I told you, piss off. Just piss off out of it!'

'Dear me! You shouldn't have to put up with this, Elise! Really! You'd think someone would have a word with her. I'll have a look to see if there's a nurse around and ask.

'But you can't hear, can you? You can't tell whether she's yelling obscenities or reciting poetry. But others can — I'm sure it's upsetting for them. Excuse me one moment.

'There. A waste of time that was. The charge nurse says she's not in her right mind, as if that were the great medical diagnosis of the century. Dementia. Nothing they can do about it except wait for her to die. I suggested more morphine, since she seems to be in so much pain, but he says the pain's largely psychosomatic, and any more would kill her — which would be a mercy but which would cause all sort of legal difficulties. Nurses have been charged with manslaughter for less, he said.

'What's that? No, every time you clutch my hand I think you mean something, don't I? But if I remove my hand — thus — you clutch thin air with equal passion.

'Passion! If you want passion, you should see the effect D.H. Lawrence is having on my first-year students. If you ask me, he's positively dangerous. My sister tells me that for years she felt she was a freak because she didn't feel as Lawrence insisted women felt. Honestly! Ha, ha! Oh, dear: it seems wrong, doesn't it, to laugh aloud, just as if

I were safe in the SCR, when you're as silent as the grave and she — there she goes again, that poor woman with Alzheimer's. Pray God I'll go before I get like that.

'Can you feel this, Elise? If you can, give me one squeeze for no, two for yes.

'Yes! Yes, you squeezed then, quite hard. Again, Elise — one for no, two for yes!

'No: I imagined it, didn't I? Let's try once more. One for no, two for yes.

'Not a sausage. Nothing.

'Look at the time: it's time for my remedial class. Oh, yes! I'm doing remedial English with students taking an honours degree in English! There's not one of them that comes on the course without an A at A level, but ask them to spell, to frame a sentence, to structure a paragraph . . . As for sustaining an argument throughout a three-thousand-word dissertation, they can no more do that than— than you can take up your bed and walk.

'I must go. I'm sorry, my dear. But I really must run.'

CHAPTER FOUR

'I hoped you'd speak to me before you went to Personnel,' Mark said quietly, but tapping his desk with palpable irritation. 'I thought we'd agreed— Oh, do sit down.'

Fran felt her jaw set. She tried to relax it. Friend he might be, dinner date for this week, indeed, but while still on duty as they were now, the hierarchy still operated. She ought to have warned him that she meant to put in her resignation. The fact she hadn't was interesting in itself. Even she realised that.

'Fran, you are at perfect liberty to take your pension the moment you reach the appropriate date and run off to retire in any place in the world. We both know that.' He sat opposite her, forearms on his desk, leaning forward as if he were dressing down a raw recruit. 'But I'm not convinced that you should, especially if your destination is Teignmouth. No. Put it another way. I'm absolutely convinced you shouldn't "retire" down to Devon.' The quotation marks floated between them and disappeared. 'Down in Devon you'll become what you're absolutely not qualified to be — a geriatric nurse. And for a pretty short time.'

'We don't know that. They may go on for years.' Her head went back like a defiant teenager's. After another shattering weekend she couldn't lay her hand on her heart and swear she hoped they would.

'I don't know which would be the worse scenario,' he said reflectively. 'Do you? To retire down there, selling that lovely cottage of yours, I presume, to be their unsung drudge for ten years, by which time you'd be too old and too worn out to think of doing anything except dwindling into old age yourself. Or to retire down there and find them both dead within a year and you with twenty or thirty years on your hands wondering what the hell to do with yourself. Those are the options, Fran.'

'I'm sure I could find all sorts of things to do down there,' she countered.

'I'm sure you could.' His smile was dangerously affable. 'You could join the Ladies' Luncheon Club, be a red-hot committee member for every organisation going, arrange church flowers and have your garden win prizes.'

Even to her own ears her laugh was rueful.

'Exactly. Now, it's clear to me you can't carry on as you are. Your job demands a hundred and ten per cent of your time and energy, and the most you can offer is about fifty. No,' he overrode her, 'please don't try to tell me otherwise. I'm saying that as your senior officer. As a friend I'm telling you you're burning out before my eyes. I want to transfer you from your present positions in both Policy and Crime — God knows why Personnel thought you should continue to fulfil both roles, when it was supposed to be a very short-term measure, and why, despite my official request, they've changed nothing in a whole week. I suppose,' he conceded with a grin that made him look absurdly boyish, 'it was because until recently you were one of a handful of officers who could take on both and succeed brilliantly.'

'I'm loath to lose either,' she snapped.

'You don't have an option. Let me make that clear.' As if to soothe her ego, he added, 'And, I repeat, you should never have been asked to try in the first place, in my opinion. No one should. No, you'll leave both with almost immediate effect and take on a project answering directly to me.'

She nodded. She had to listen, after all, when he spoke in his official voice, however angry and resentful she might be. Angry, resentful and tired.

'It's a case we've had on file for some time,' he continued, with a smile aimed to placate, even charm her. 'Almost a dead file. But not quite dead. And it's suddenly become urgent.'

Through the haze of fatigue she heard words that intrigued her. She straightened. To her intense irritation, Mark stopped, and got up to switch on his kettle.

'Unless you'd rather have a blast of coffee?' His hand moved from his tea caddy to hover over his percolator. 'No? Green? Excellent.' While he waited for the kettle to boil, he reached across to an ivy geranium on his windowsill and removed a dead leaf, dropping it in the waste bin. To her amazement he bent to retrieve it, putting it in another bin. 'I mustn't mess up the recycling, must I? Here — is that strong enough? Good.' Sitting at his desk again, he burrowed in his desk, producing a tin of expensive organic biscuits.

Was this what being a widower had done to him, reduced him to this sort of old-maidish domesticity? Or was the term not 'reduce' but 'elevate'?

She smiled and took a biscuit. It was very good. Ah, the rush of sugar!

He patted a thick file. 'You can see a lot of effort's already been put into this. But not enough — you'll see that we're no nearer to solving it than on the day it happened.'

'Who was the victim?'

'A middle-aged woman. Found in the undergrowth just off a lay-by on the B2067, northbound. Nearly two years ago.'

'Two years? Well, it's the old twenty-four-hour syndrome, I suppose. If you don't start getting results straight away, it may take months to get them.'

'Quite. And often matters are allowed to drift, and it's just another unsolved crime and you hope you can pin it on some con already doing time for something else.'

'So what's different about this one?'

He laughed. 'Is it the tea, the biscuit — here, have another — or the challenge? You already look a different woman.' He took a sip of his tea. He might use mugs but they were bone china, as good as she used at home. 'What's different about this one is that the charge may soon change from assault and aggravated rape to murder.'

'*May* change?'

'The victim — we only know her first name, which is Elise — is in what they call a persistent vegetative state. PVS. The medics have been treating her all this time, and now they want to pull the plug on her.'

Her voice was sharp. 'Is that for medical or budgetary reasons?'

He raised a placatory hand. 'Simply humanity, from what I gather. The courts are involved. Elise will be allocated a lawyer whose job it is to fight for her life, such as it is, while the hospital authorities will argue that withdrawing food will permit Elise to die naturally — which technically, apart from the fact her heart's still beating, she's already done. Did at the time of the assault.'

A little silence fell.

Fran broke it. 'Why me?'

'Because I want to assure the court that we've done all we possibly can. By putting you in charge, with your reputation, not to mention your rank, I'm demonstrating that. Of all the officers at my disposal, you're the best for the job. But because the case is pretty nearly cold, some of the urgency has gone out of it. After all, to put it brutally, Elise isn't going anywhere, and the courts take forever in these cases anyway. So if you need to dash down to Devon at short notice, you needn't feel so guilty. You won't be inconveniencing two teams — and let's face it, no matter how well you cover, currently your work has to be delegated to people who aren't paid to do it. It might look good on their CVs if it's official, but if it's a favour for you, it wouldn't get on their CV.'

'I take your point. You've been very patient so far,' she added, wishing she could fire up and deny the implicit accusation.

'Not me. Your teams. And they've been as loyal as you could wish. But at least now some of them will get promotions, albeit temporary, until your future is settled. One way or another.'

'I've got to do it, Mark.' She realised the ambiguity. 'Devon, I mean.' And then realised it was only she who'd registered any ambiguity in the first place. So she was interested in Mark's proposition.

His face stern, he said, 'You have to work out your notice. With luck, you'll have sorted out the case by then.' He played with the rough edges of the file. Suddenly, grinning like a schoolboy, he looked up. 'Tell you what. Give yourself a fair chance. Pop into Personnel and put your departure date back a month or so.'

As kind a dismissal as she could wish for then. But as she got to her feet, she asked, 'How did you manage while Tina was so ill?'

He blinked. Perhaps she'd been wrong to equate a wife with elderly parents. Or perhaps she was presuming too far. But at last he said, 'I did a lot of tap and acro.' He mimed frantic juggling. 'And like you I found people more than ready to help out here. How many meetings did you go to in my place? How many interview panels?'

She shook her head: that was nothing. She opened her mouth, then shut it.

'Go on,' he invited.

She wrinkled her nose, the question was so crass. 'You didn't think of resigning to spend more time with her?'

'I took a lot of unpaid leave, as you may have to do, but somewhere, deep down, I knew that however hard it was, after she'd gone, I'd need a job. This job. God Almighty, Fran. What would I do otherwise? Work part-time in the Cancer Research shop? I'd have died for that woman, but I have to live for me now.'

Their eyes locked. In an instant, their uniforms disappeared.

Was that why he'd asked her out for dinner? Not simply because he felt sorry for her?

But it was his quasi-official voice that suggested, 'Is Thursday still all right for dinner?'

All she could manage was a nod.

* * *

'It's your mother. She's been taken to hospital. You'll have to come straight down. Now.'

'Pa — I—' *I have a date with my boss in half an hour; it's been arranged for days; I'm so looking forward to good food, good wine and—*

'I said, she's in hospital. Your mother. You'll have to come now.'

'Pa—'

'I can't hear a word you're saying.'

Damn him, he'd switched off his hearing aid. She never knew whether it was intentional or accidental. It sure as hell prevented arguments. As did putting the phone down on the stream of questions she needed answers to.

What was she shaking with? Anger at having the evening aborted? Or fear that what she'd been afraid would happen was at last coming to pass? That her mother was dying, which would leave her to work out what to do with her father? Or, deep down, that her mother wouldn't die, that she'd had a stroke and would become a vegetable and she'd have to drop everything here and go to Devon immediately. Now. Before she was ready. Before she'd inured herself to the prospect of leaving behind everything important.

What could be more important than your mother? Or your father, for that matter? Wasn't it her duty to care for them both without complaint, just like hundreds and thousands of women all over the world did? She might be a career woman through and through but she was also their daughter.

Just now the only imperative must be to get down there as quickly as possible. She must tell Mark. Phone or face to face? The latter would be more courteous.

* * *

'But you're going straight off? Just like that?' Mark sounded concerned rather than angry. He got up, putting his hands on her shoulders to press her into a chair.

'These days I keep an emergency bag in my car.' It included a foil blanket, too, the sort serious walkers carried, in case her father locked her out as he sometimes did. With his hearing aid on the bedside table, all the knocking and ringing and shouting in the world wouldn't raise him. 'It's always on the cards, isn't it, one of them being taken really ill. And hospital sounds like really ill. If only Pa had said which one.' Yes, he was much more forgetful these days. 'It could be the cottage hospital, if it's a minor problem, or, if it's serious, acute care at Torbay or Exeter hospital.'

'We'll find out.' Another kind smile. She found herself liking 'we'. 'What about work?' That was his territory, after all, and he was entitled to ask. There was the small matter of her in-tray, not to mention how she'd cope on her return.

'I'll take a day's annual leave,' she assured him. 'Two, if necessary.'

'Holiday entitlement? You should ask Personnel for compassionate leave,' he frowned.

She nodded acknowledgement. Almost to herself she said, 'There's nothing here that can't wait till next week. If there is, they can email or phone. It's happened before.'

'At least come and have a bite in the canteen. Half an hour. It's not a matter of life or death.' Grimacing, he reconsidered his words. 'Oh, my God, I'm so sorry: it could be, couldn't it? But you mustn't try to drive all that way without eating. Come on. Please.'

She hesitated. Should she be irritated or touched by this excess of concern? Heavens, she rebuked herself, the man knew first hand all the pressures on the healthy that the sick could exert. He was just being kind. Did she wish it were more? Why, after thirty years of undemanding comradeship, were her hormones choosing this inopportune moment to hope it was?

'You'll be able to get some bottled water and a couple of decent snacks to eat en route.' He smiled persuasively. 'To spare yourself the delights of Burger King or whatever.'

She found herself smiling back. After all, she told herself, she could just as well call social services and the surrounding hospitals from the canteen as from the car park. 'Give me fifteen minutes to sort out my desk. I'll meet you down there.'

* * *

Mark had been busy. 'Your mother's in the Royal Devon and Exeter,' he said, as he greeted her at the canteen door, fifteen minutes to the second later. 'They won't give me any details because I'm not family. But I also got the number of the duty social worker. She did speak to me.' If he was in ACC mode people tended to jump when he told them to. Her only surprise was that he hadn't persuaded the RD and E to do a Western roll. 'She assures me that your father's care worker will settle him for the night and switch his personal alarm on so all he has to do is press it if he's taken ill too. Here — the hospital number's programmed.' But he must have seen how much her hand shook. He thumbed the pad and passed it across. 'So you can have a sensible meal and take your time. Let the M25 clear a bit. And remember those speed cameras on the first stretch of the M3.'

The hospital switchboard stayed resolutely engaged.

At last she got through, only to find the ward line busy.

'My betting is that she's got another urinary tract infection,' she said, seething with exasperation. 'They make her doolally — or, in hospital speak, confused. For a short time, she's as bad as if she's had a stroke. But a couple of days on antibiotics and she's back at home ruling the world again.'

'So why the haste? Why not wait till tomorrow morning and see?' He shook his head as if apologising for something.

She wasn't sure what it was.

Why not wait? Unbidden, a fantasy presented itself in which the evening they'd projected culminated in his bed.

Why not? Why not have the pleasure of waking up to the sound of breathing, to warmth? Because she wouldn't have the willpower to sneak away at three for the drive to Devon? She made herself say, 'Whatever happens to her, there's my father. They're like two playing cards, Mark. Neither can stand up on their own, but if one props the other — they can, just.'

'Couldn't a neighbour—?'

She snorted with ironic laughter. 'The only one they're still on speaking terms with is stone deaf. They've had terminal rows with everyone, from the folk next door to three of the four GPs in the practice. No one visits them who isn't paid to.'

'There's no one else in the family?'

'My sister. Hazel. They used to have huge rows with her too. But she fell in love with a Scottish clergyman, a widower with three children, and moved to a manse in Stornoway. Since she can't get down at the drop of a hat, she's been rehabilitated. They speak of her with a sigh as their special girl. Girl! She's ten years older than I am. I was the afterthought, you see. The surprise. Or the nasty shock.' She'd never thought of it like that before — the horror of finding yourself pregnant when you'd resolved not to be. They'd never spoken of their joy at having a late baby so she presumed there was none.

He looked at her steadily. Then, to her amazement, he got to his feet. 'I'll walk down to the car park with you, shall I?'

* * *

It was in the car park that she saw him at seven forty on the following Monday morning. She didn't tell him she hadn't been home first: there was no need to go, since she kept an emergency kit here, too, fresh clothes and a complete set of toiletries and make-up. Somehow she'd make it through the day on the few hours' sleep she'd snatched before setting out at four in the morning. She could always resort to the last refuge of the exhausted — a Do Not Disturb notice on her door and ten minutes with her head down on her desk — across her lunchtime.

'You've had a rough time then,' he said. It was a statement rather than a question. He must have caught her with the sun running unforgiving fingers over her face.

'Things have been easier. But the good news is that both my parents are back in their bungalow.'

'Both? Was your father . . . ?'

'Don't ask!' But as they fell into step, she found herself saying, 'I was right about Ma. It was an infection, and as soon as I reminded the medics they got her on to her usual antibiotics and she was lucid again within twenty-four hours.' She managed to censor the details, much as she would have loved to pour everything into sympathetic ears. 'But it was clear she couldn't go straight back home, and social services baulked at the amount of care Pa'd need if I left him on his own, so I had a brainwave. I fixed them both respite care in a nursing home — I even secured a double room. Fine. The ambulance transferred Ma, and I managed to shoe-horn Pa into my car and deliver him. Friday, that was. On Saturday morning I mothballed the bungalow, went to check they were OK, and set off home. I'd got as far as the first Happy Eater when I had a phone call from the nursing home: Ma and Pa had decided that after all they didn't like the place so they'd booked a taxi and got themselves home. So would I go back and sort them out.' If only she could have rewound the words or at least said them in a less bitter voice.

'So you were nearly halfway back here and you had to turn tail back to Devon?'

'Correct.'

'And nurse them through the weekend?'

'They slept a lot,' she said, in exculpation. 'I shopped and cooked — to replace all the food I'd thrown away,' she added. Hell, as if he could be interested in such detail!

For a moment he looked unsure of what to say. At last he managed a smile. 'I haven't had breakfast yet: would you care to join me?' It sounded more like an invitation than an order, no rank involved.

Through the haze of fatigue she groped for the right words. Girlish enthusiasm would be wrong; neither did she want surly acquiescence. In the end she choked back a yawn and nodded. No point in pretending she had energy for anything more. Except a spurt of optimism when he put his arm round her shoulders and gave what might have appeared to any watching officers an encouraging squeeze but to her felt like a promise of support. Comradely support, she told herself.

That, even more than coffee and a full English breakfast, did much to revive her. A quick shower and she might feign positive alertness. Mark seemed inclined to linger over the meal, talking HQ gossip. The easeful comfort of it all. If only she could put her head down and sleep.

But Mark, smiling, was urging her to her feet. 'That case you said you'd take on: you'll be wanting to see your new office and meet your colleagues, no doubt. I'll walk down with you, shall I?'

CHAPTER FIVE

'Elise! Elise! This is really important! You must wake up. You must make a sign! You MUST. You're not trying, are you? Damn you, try this!

'My God, it's left a mark. Right here on your cheek. You can actually see the mark of my hand. What if anyone sees it?

'On the other hand, the ends might justify the means. If the new, minor pain wakes you, wouldn't that be morally acceptable?

'Have the doctors tried recently?

'I'm sure that when you were first brought in, when you were in Intensive Care, they'd done all they could to bring you out of your coma. But now they've got other urgent cases to deal with, other matters of life and death. I suppose I shouldn't blame them if they concentrated their efforts on them.

'That doesn't mean, though, not for one minute, that they should neglect you. The nursing staff — what few there are of them — certainly don't: they do their very best. At least I'd like to believe they do. After all, you need round-the-clock care. I'm sure they would be first rate — if only they had enough time.

'I have to do this, my dear. I have to. I don't like doing it, but if no one else will, then it has to be me!

'Oh, my God. I didn't mean — I really didn't mean . . . Such a vivid mark . . .

'At least shaking you won't leave a mark. And that might be just as effective.

'Anything to get you out of this damned state.

'No. Nothing. Nothing except a stain on my conscience as big as the stains on your cheeks.

'Oh, Elise, my dear. I'm so sorry. So very, very sorry.'

CHAPTER SIX

'What do you think of it?' Mark asked, standing on the threshold of her new office, just off the main CID one, as excitedly as if he'd given her some rash present. And in a way he had, Fran noted, amused and touched, despite wanting to do nothing more than sink into the fine new office chair in the fine new office with her name on the fine new door and go to sleep. Then she looked again at the nameplate: Detective Chief Superintendent Harman. That was quick! She laughed out loud. Mark must have moved mountains to get Personnel to change her designation so quickly.

'Think! Wow, Mark, this is a dream office: carpet, this blond wood furniture!' She explored her new kingdom. 'Blinds that work. Lovely new computer. The furniture and equipment budget must have taken a real battering!' she teased. Presumably this would become the new Chief Super's office when she left — she'd feel guilty if he'd requisitioned all this especially for her. No, the room had probably needed renovating, and she'd leave so little mark on it her successor would assume all the work had been for him or her.

He looked more bashful than apologetic. 'I'm afraid I couldn't wangle full-time staff for you. With Martin that wouldn't have been a problem, but we've got this new chief superintendent starting next week, remember . . .'

She wouldn't rub her face in an effort to recall the arrangements. But she could almost hear the grindings in her brain. Frank Martin, the old DCS, had been spirited away to the Home Office, that was it, leaving a vacancy that had remained unfilled for a month or so. And he was being replaced by — 'Someone Henson? Ex-Met?' she queried. For some reason she'd not been on the selection panel. Perhaps she should have been but had had to make one of her unscheduled dashes to Devon.

'The same. You'll have to negotiate with him for officers as and when you need them, I'm afraid. But remember, you always have my authority to make demands.'

'Until I've thoroughly absorbed the contents of the file, I shan't need anyone. After that, one bright DC should suffice. Mark, this is terrific: thank you.'

He looked embarrassed. He opened his mouth to speak, then seemed to change his mind. 'I hope you don't mind the smell of paint.'

'And new carpet. And — yes, good old-fashioned window polish. An olfactory feast.'

They laughed. But he sobered quickly. 'Look: I haven't been able to cover all the meetings you were scheduled for this week — would you mind putting in an appearance? Just so we can update whoever takes your place? *Both* your places?'

'Of course not. So long as I can doodle on my blotter and steal all the custard creams and be generally demob happy.' She added more seriously, 'I won't let you down, Mark. I can guess who put his neck on the line for all this.' She gestured.

'I'm just sorry it took me so long to get all that pressure off you. Why didn't you tell me how stretched you were, Fran?' He dropped his voice so that as well as reproachful it might almost have been tender.

How long had her standards been slipping so obviously? But she didn't want to bring attention back to herself. 'I bet it was you who got the bollocking for my mess up.'

He didn't deny it. Instead, awkward as a green boy, he asked, 'How about another shot at dinner? What's a good evening for you? Tomorrow?'

What should have been a maidenly blush but turned into a full-scale flush reddened her cheeks. 'Lovely.'

'Excellent.' He hesitated. 'Look, I've got a meeting in five minutes. I'll book a table and call you with the details.' Closing the door behind him, he escaped.

Fran sat heavily in her new chair, staring at nothing. Why should a simple evening out be causing them both so much stress? Because it was the first time she'd been out for anything approaching a date since an abortive evening with— she could barely remember the man's name! Clive Richardson, that was it. At the time, he'd seemed a very desirable bachelor, the first even to interest her since she'd lost Ian, the OU tutor with whom she'd hoped to share the rest of their lives, to his heart attack. Even now she knew she mustn't think about Ian. It'd be better to turn her memory to Richardson. She'd met him, a businessman to the tips of his BMW Seven Series, at some fundraiser for the Police Benevolent Fund, and though neither might have expected to find any rapport with the other, they'd found themselves agreeing to meet for dinner. They'd been walking through the front door of the restaurant of his choice when her mother had phoned. Pa had had a heart attack.

'I've got to go down to Devon,' she'd told Richardson.

'Now.' The simple word had meant they'd never see each other again. And she'd never looked for a relationship again.

So why was she even thinking about Mark as more than a friend? Damned hormones. She smashed the flat of her hand on the wall. Time for a coffee. But that was one thing he hadn't requisitioned for her — a percolator. At least that was a task she felt up to managing. She'd nip out at lunchtime and buy one.

Meanwhile, she made her way through the general office to the water dispenser. Some of her colleagues were young men and women she'd prepared for promotion exams: they flapped cheery but still respectful hands as she passed. Which should she pick as her dogsbody? Someone who needed a bit of confidence to develop his or her potential: there was plenty of time to sniff around a bit.

Back on her pristine desk lay something reassuringly battered: the Elise file. If she immersed herself in that, keeping her head as clear as pure water would make it, she might manage not to speculate on why Mark had gone to so much trouble. And why, despite the sort of snub she'd had to give Richardson, he'd asked her out again. No, she was jumping ahead. They were just mates, giving each other a break from solitary domesticity.

Back on safe, familiar territory, she made notes as she went.

On the evening of February 26, nearly two years before, a patrol responded to a 999 call from a member of the public, Alan Pitt. He had found and attempted to resuscitate a woman he'd found in the undergrowth near a lay-by on the B2067, between Hythe and Tenterden. There were severe head and thoracic injuries; there was also evidence of a vicious rape. Unfortunately Pitt's activities had badly contaminated the crime scene; for some time he'd been a major, indeed, the only serious suspect. But at last forensics had appeared to confirm his story that he'd simply pulled over to take a call on his mobile, and decided the road was quiet enough for him to relieve himself in the hedge and had heard faint groans, which he'd investigated. As he tried to help, the woman had uttered two words: 'Poor Elise.'

By the time she'd reached the William Harvey Hospital in Ashford, the woman was deeply comatose. She had never recovered consciousness.

Elise, then. And you'd have expected that someone, frantic with worry for a sister or lover — she wore no wedding ring, nor was there even a tell-tale furrow on her finger to suggest a thief might have tugged one off — would phone to report her missing. But no one did. Anywhere in the country. She didn't match the description of any missing persons on the official list, though her age distinguished her from the runaway schoolchildren and disaffected young adults. Nonetheless, the first thing Fran would do the next day was to ask one of her new minions to double check. Middle-aged women — the medics thought she was about sixty — tended not to disappear of their own accord. There was a lot of publicity, but her facial and head injuries had been so severe that even if photographs had not been an intrusion into her misery, no one could have recognised her. They'd done a computer-enhanced impression, but Fran never felt those to be as successful as the physical reconstructions in clay and she wasn't surprised that there'd been no response.

Clothes? Hairstyle? Age? Fran would have liked to add make-up to her list, but doubted if anyone would have registered with that when they were dealing with life-threatening injuries. She added it anyway.

The file was, of course, a mere summary of what had been done — the day-to-day log of actions taken and the reasons for taking them. Somewhere there would be bulging dossiers clamped into box files, and tagged and bagged forensic evidence. But they would have to wait for tomorrow. Because, for all her good intentions, not only had she forgotten to nip out at lunchtime for her percolator, she'd forgotten all about lunch, too.

Monday evening was for washing, remember, and sleeping. And wondering what Tuesday evening might bring.

* * *

Tuesday morning brought a canteen breakfast, together with the news that Mark would have to cancel their evening because a Home Office minister had taken it into his head to announce a new initiative without consulting the police first, and all over the country people like Mark were going to have to chase figures that simply didn't exist for a plan that was at best quixotic.

Was she disappointed or relieved? Her main emotion was relief that she could have an early night and an extra couple of hours' sleep.

Wednesday had had a similar fate, Mark still number-crunching fictitious figures and she pulled on to an interview panel for some training post because another senior woman had gone down with flu. If asked, she would have been hard put to say which was more frustrating, the delay in her social life or the fact that she still hadn't even seen the Elise crime scene. Her notes of the interview were scrawled over with her attempts to remember the rhyme about the Wise Men: who, what, where, why, when? Were there any more? Who would have wanted to kill a woman like Elise? What had they used? Where had they actually attacked and raped her? When had they done it? And — which was where the rhyme went wrong — above all, why? Or was 'who' more important? Her mind had hamster-wheeled its way through five promising candidates and one exceptional one, who was finally appointed as senior trainer in equal opportunities. Not quite a wasted day, then. Especially as, in the midst of it all, she'd made a decision about which of the CID team she'd ask for. A young man called Arkwright. Some time ago she'd found herself talking to him in a stalled lift: even though the engineers had got it unjammed almost immediately, they'd decided to cheer themselves in the canteen before they returned to their respective domains and duties. Tom Arkwright, a graduate like most of the new wave of recruits, had a parent problem too: his dad had cancer, which he found himself telling her all about. She felt she could have told him about her parents without it going any further, he had that sort of innocent gravitas, but she hadn't wanted to burden him. When she saw him behind a mound of filing, still hard at it at a time when most of his mates had knocked off, she decided to rescue him.

'I still seem to be spending all my time in committee rooms, Tom, so I want you to be my legs. Legs with initiative, please. There wasn't any record of Elise's assailant's

DNA at the time of the assault, but that doesn't mean he hasn't attacked since and no one's bothered to tie up details. And double check with other forces in case there's been a prison confession they've forgotten to pass on. Anything to ID her, Tom — you have free rein. OK?'

* * *

On Thursday morning, Fran and Mark entered a solemn pact to let nothing interfere with what Mark referred to jokily as a decent meal. At six thirty p.m. precisely both would religiously switch off their mobiles and change into mufti — in his case from his uniform and in hers from the formal suit that she chose for CID stints, so dark and severe it might well have been uniform.

Taking one last look at herself in the cloakroom mirror, rubbing off the red lipstick and replacing it with a softer pink, and all the time wishing that she could do feminine and frilly, she set out. She'd be early. But Mark was already scuttling towards his car, still trying to adjust his jacket round his neck. If she slowed down she'd see him tweak his tie.

Yes. He carefully felt the knot, then undid it and stuffed it in his pocket. Any moment he'd put it back on again.

He did.

So he was as unsure, as uneasy, as she. Heavens, they might be boy and girl out for their first date. She stopped in her tracks. Was this what was happening? Had Mark actually asked her on a date?

But what if he hadn't?

Tiptoeing back to the door, she let it slam loudly as soon as his tie was back in place and walked briskly and unromantically towards him.

CHAPTER SEVEN

'I'm sorry, ladies and gentlemen. I really am. But I really must ask you to show a little consideration! The two visitors per patient guideline isn't there for nothing, you know! A big group like yours can disturb other patients. My friend, just there, is — is dying, you see . . . Thank you. Thank you very much. I hoped you'd understand . . .

'So they're decent people, Elise, despite their tracksuits and trainers and their cans of lager: no argument and they're very much quieter, aren't they? I was afraid there might be trouble — can you imagine my risking doing that in a public place? I'd have been lynched before I got to the end of my first sentence.

'I lied, of course. You're not really my friend, of course, are you? A friend is someone with whom you have some sort of meaningful interaction. You have none with me. A friend is someone with whom you share mutual tastes and interests, and I know nothing of yours.

'I hope you were a literate lady — that you found time to read in whatever life you led. And to listen to music. Did you go to your local theatre and lament the passing of decent weekly rep? I'd hate to think that the lottery was the highlight of your week, or that you shuffled off to Bingo every Thursday. If you had, though, surely your friends would have missed you when you never returned — they'd have reported it to the police. They've had enough time to do so: it's nearly two years since the accident. And I've been to see you pretty well every week. Is it guilt

for what I did? Some sort of atonement? Whatever it is, Elise, I wish you could discuss it with me.

'Thank goodness there seems to be no residual bruising: I truly can't believe I hit you. They might not have let me come again if they'd found out. Worse, they might have had me charged with assault.

'Can you assault someone who is technically dead?'

* * *

'Heavens: look at the time! I'm so sorry — I really must fly.'

CHAPTER EIGHT

In his spot in the still half-empty senior officers' car park, Mark flicked the radio from a wonderfully acerbic John Humphrys interview on Today to an up-beat bit of Vivaldi on Classic FM. He buried his nose in a file, the top page of which he read six times and was still no clearer about, when at last Fran's car came into sight: yes, it was definitely her Saab. He felt his shoulders unbrace, and buried his face in paperwork again: he didn't want to seem to be doing anything as crass as waiting for her, in case she construed it as managerial checking up. In fact, checking up it was, but since it was born of anxiety for her safety, perhaps he could be excused. The number of miles she covered in the worst circumstances every weekend put her at risk, statistically, however good a driver she was, and however safe the car. He felt almost as anxious as when his sons had gone on their first long solo journeys — irritated by their need to prove themselves, furious he couldn't protect them from life, and imagining, every second they passed their ETA, that any moment a stern-faced colleague would present himself on the doorstep with the worst news. But this anxiety was different. He knew that. It masked or augmented, whichever way he looked at it, a dreadful fear that she would be taken from him before — but that part of his sentence he didn't care yet to complete.

Their supper: had it been an old-fashioned first date? He'd felt as tongue-tied as when he'd first taken Tina out, thirty-odd years ago, when the fashion was for sex first and conversation, if necessary, later. But for some reason the young pair had done the best suit and nice frock thing, and had patronised the local Indian, thinking they were as trendy as tomorrow. Whereas his acne'd earlier self had stuttered and stumbled, his present incarnation had had reserves of experience of important meals to call on — even if they'd nearly failed him when it came to the matter of whether or not to wear a tie. Perhaps she'd seen his pantomime: there'd been laughter at the back of her eyes when she'd arrived beside his car punctual to the minute. Perhaps she'd also worried about her appearance. There were two distinct shades of lipstick visible, as if she couldn't make up her mind. And although he couldn't recall exactly what she'd worn, he knew she'd looked stunning. At least, he tried to correct himself, as stunning as an overworked, exhausted woman in her fifties could look.

What had they talked about, what had they eaten? For the life of him, he couldn't remember. He'd been so worried since by her impending trip to Devon he'd lost the pleasures, large and small, he should have cherished. Now she was here, safe and sound, he could recall a not unpleasant restaurant, with quite decent food. He could remember a lot of laughter. If, once or twice, he hadn't caught her face in repose as weary as death, he'd have taken her home there and then, he knew that. And they wouldn't have got much sleep. But to add to Fran's sleep debt would have been the height of irresponsibility, and his job and his marriage had sapped his ability to throw his hat in the air, not caring where it fell.

There'd be other days, other nights: he was almost sure of it. Yes, there'd be something more than the friendly goodnight kiss, which she'd suddenly dabbed on his cheek and he'd chastely returned. And as he saw the inexpressibly weary lines of her face shift upwards into a grin of delight, he was sure. Quite sure. You couldn't feign a smile like that. It warmed the chilly morning. And brought him out of his car in something approaching a leap.

As for her, her movements were slow, and he thought he detected a grimace of pain. Where was the athletic young woman he'd once watched springing about the badminton court like one possessed? Her knees had turned pink with the effort. Soon, he'd ask her to play with him. It'd be good to turn them pink again.

'How are you? How was Devon?'

He put out his hand, like a courtier, to steady her. In fact she rested her whole weight on it, so he steadied her with the other. She was lifting her face for a kiss, he was sure of it, the lips parted, the eyes guiding his, when they heard footsteps and were recalled to the decencies incumbent on two senior officers. So, no long Hollywood embrace, certainly no tipping her elegantly back across the bonnet in an extravagant gesture. Not this time.

As she found her feet, she found her voice: 'I'm fine. And I may have cracked it. The problem, I mean.' She clapped a hand to her mouth. 'I never meant to call *them* a problem.'

'But they are,' he pointed out gently, releasing her slowly.

'To my shame, that's what they've become. The man and woman who begot me, stigmatised as a problem.' She bit her lip on her anger, turning to zap the car. 'What I meant was, I've cracked the problem of them being on their own. I've got someone to sleep in the bungalow during the week.'

'Excellent. Just like that?'

'Not exactly. You see, I don't normally have time to give the place a thorough clean.'

'You—?'

'The poor care workers aren't allowed to touch anywhere their clients don't actually use, so the spare bedroom was pretty grotty.'

'How grotty?'

'Well, they never open windows. Never, ever. Any of them. Windows let in draughts, a bad thing, and let out heat, an even worse thing. So they have a condensation problem.'

'I had an aunt like that. Mould and mildew. Scrubbing with bleach was the only thing to shift them. Not just the window frames, but the walls, too. Is that what you had to do?' He hoped he sounded interested, not furious.

'Well, I couldn't have asked a stranger to sleep in those conditions.'

Which meant that she did.

'And the bedclothes always used to smell musty,' he prompted.

'Tell me about it. I had to waste time washing and drying blankets: they've never believed in duvets, resolute in their belief that nine-tenths of European civilisation must be wrong. And I'm afraid the room still smelt musty, despite all the air spray I've used. Potpourri too.' She straightened her shoulders, as if to deny the effort. 'But the good news is Marie! She works during the day as a care assistant so she knows the job. And she's used to babysitting people who are old or infirm. She's got excellent references and her police check is immaculate.'

'Sounds too good to be true,' he said, smiling. He looked over her shoulder. 'Where's your overnight bag?'

'It stays in the car till I get home. Everything goes straight into the washing machine. There's a complete change of clothes here in my locker.'

'Have you had breakfast yet? If not, we could . . .' He tailed off, suddenly awkward.

'Do you have enough time for me to shower? I want to get rid of the old-people smell.'

There was a distinct mustiness about her, now he came to think about it. But her efficiency — bags for this, bags for that — amazed him afresh. They fell into step.

'So a shower would be welcome,' she prompted him.

'Take as long as you need. My first meeting isn't till nine thirty. And you?'

'Today I go back to first principles. I want a look at our crime scene—'

He stopped, half turning. 'On your own?' He regretted the words and, more particularly the tone, as they left his mouth.

'On my own. I've asked one of the CID lads to check and double check on missing persons and so on. But I've always liked to check crime scenes like that alone. With an open mind. No helpful suggestions from other people. Above all, no phone calls.'

'So you'll be out of reach?' He had to stuff a hand into a pocket to stop him reaching for her, she looked so vulnerable.

'Only while I stand and think. Then I'll switch on the mobile again.'

'You will be careful, won't you? It's near a very dangerous corner. Accident black spot.' For God's sake, he knew she'd passed all the police driving courses going, apart from the one permitting her to drive endangered diplomats and politicians. What was he thinking of, appearing to question her competence? But she hadn't had to take the courses on top of a gruelling weekend's cleaning. She'd probably toiled in the garden, too, and produced those reheatable meals she'd spoken of. She might even, on reflection, feel that being cared about made a nice change. 'I'm sorry,' he said swiftly, all the same, 'I didn't mean to sound . . . but you do look done in.'

For a moment he thought that if he held out his arms she'd fall into them.

But she smiled bravely. 'All the more reason for a shower. The canteen at eight fifteen?'

* * *

Half an hour later they were in the canteen. It was good job there wasn't some sort of test on this conversation either. There hadn't been many silences, and certainly no awkward pauses. Words had drifted backwards and forwards, punctuated by smiles that were more openly shifting from comradely to affectionate. He'd found himself watching the way she spooned her muesli, liking the shape of her hands, even the way she held the spoon. At one point he absently stretched a finger to catch a trickle down her cheek from her shower-wet hair. In a lowlier officer that would have made him the laughing stock of the canteen, subject to sniggers behind cupped hands. At least they were spared overt teasing: chief superintendents were almost certainly above coarse ribbing; ACCs definitely were. Unless the Chief chose to exert a little camaraderie.

* * *

Fran must concentrate. She must. Otherwise she'd go into a daydream about Mark and crash or simply go into a dream and crash. So she kept the heater off and the window down.

As minor roads went, the B2067 wasn't inspiring, although it travelled through lush and well-wooded farming land. Technically it was the most direct route from Tenterden to Hythe, but, snaking round as if made by the proverbial English drunkard, it was much slower than the longer route using the M20 and the A28. Assuming that Tenterden was where you were heading, of course. Or, conversely, Hythe. There was no indication, on file at least, that Elise had business in either. Nor was there any evidence that she had been driving along the road where she'd been assaulted. So had she been attacked elsewhere and dropped where her assailant hoped no one would find her? If so, why hadn't he carried her further from the road? Even from where Fran stood, she could see thickets and overgrown hedges: this was one corner of Kent where they hadn't been obsessed by efficiency and mega-fields.

Turning her back to the wind, she leafed through the notes she'd made on the information in the original file. There were the tracks of a large vehicle parked a hundred yards further down the road towards Hythe, but the driver had never come forward, and there'd been no reason to link Elise with a lorry. If Fran couldn't imagine herself hitching a lift in an HGV, there was no reason to assume a woman of the same generation would, even if her car had thoroughly broken down. She'd stay with her car and use her mobile to call the AA or whatever: other middle-aged women tended to rely on motoring organisations to solve even basic problems like flat tyres.

What if — like so many rural parts of the county — this was a mobile black spot? That was easily tested. No, she had no problem dialling her own home number.

What if Elise hadn't had a mobile?

Come on: this was the twenty-first century. But you couldn't check all the records of all the mobile phone companies, not until you had a full name to go on.

What if you assumed — just for a moment — that she didn't have one, what would she do? Surely, if a kindly — or otherwise — driver stopped, she'd lock herself in her car and simply ask them to phone for help. Wouldn't she?

All the same, Fran wrote, *LORRY???*

She knew that her predecessors on the case had checked and double-checked all the women called Elise on the Hythe area's electoral roll. There were very few, and all were present and correct. The same applied to Tenterden and even — yes, her colleagues had done their best — to Folkestone, New Romney and Ashford.

The wind brought a sudden burst of rain. Poor Elise: this was a lonely enough spot to have lain dying, until some kind stranger had come along to try and save you. Alan Pitt. And all he'd done, according to the notes, was postpone the event. Had he even done that? Had she not died as he'd pumped her chest and breathed air from his own lungs into her? The kiss of life. Or, in this poor woman's case, the kiss of an unconscious life.

Fran huddled back into her car. No bolts from the blue to report to Mark. Should she call with a nil return? It was tempting, just to hear his voice. No. He was an ACC, for God's sake, with a caseload to match his rank. All the same, she checked she'd left her mobile on before she retraced her steps to the A2070, and turned towards Ashford and the William Harvey Hospital.

* * *

As she tapped her registration number into the pay and display machine, she recalled all the times she'd dramatically slewed a police vehicle into a reserved parking slot and dashed into an A and E to gather what she could from a victim of some sort of violence or another. RTAs; binge drinking; domestic abuse: whatever the event, they'd resulted in trauma not just for the person on the stretcher but for the officers dealing with the incident. She'd lost count of the times when, in her early career, she'd lobbied management at national level for emotional support for them. Now counselling was as routine as debriefing. Yes, crime-solving apart, she'd achieved something in her years in the service.

The modern entrance, with its little shops, was nothing like the forbidding echoing entrances she recalled, and she missed the old-fashioned smell of disinfectant, reassuring patients and visitors alike that the fight against infection was being waged with all matron's might.

Fran knew better than to expect long regimented rows of hospital-cornered beds, either, though she was obscurely surprised that Elise should be cared for on an ordinary ward. Wouldn't you expect privacy for her? If not for the dying woman herself, for the sake of those still hoping to recover? Flashing her ID, she introduced herself to the little gaggle at the nurses' station — the new uniforms no longer clearly marked out sisters or staff nurses.

'I'm looking for Elise, your PVS patient,' she said.

'Hang on a mo'.' A weedy young man ran a finger down a chart. An agency nurse? At least the staff back in Exeter had known exactly where her mother was located. Perhaps it was because they'd expected some sort of positive outcome. 'Way down there on your left. Far as you can go. Stop by the fire doors. She's there.' He gestured vaguely, and turned back to the others.

Some eyes turned incuriously at Fran as she walked along the corridor, beds in bays on one side of her. Other patients were involved in animated conversations with their neighbours or with visitors. But as she stopped by the bed marked simply *Elise. Nil by Mouth. Mr Taverner*, she had a sense that she was arousing interest, perhaps because of her height and air of authority. Her outdoor clothes would tell anyone caring enough to work it out that she wasn't another hospital-based neurologist. Nor, of course, was she accompanied by a team of students as likely to be as worried by their debts as by the consultant's testing questions.

Elise. It was a pretty enough name, and some part of Fran expected a sweet-faced doll-like figure to be lying like a child asleep. What she found was a gaunt spectre of a woman, topped by uneven tufts of streaky grey hair, deep scars and cheeks and mouth collapsed. The medical report had mentioned broken teeth. Clearly a set of dentures to fill the gaps would have been inappropriate. Fran's tongue ran round her own mouth, checking on the crowns and bridgework that maintained her own oral elegance.

Tubes went into and presumably came out of the tortured looking body. A conscious patient would have been bullied into physiotherapy to repair damage after surgery. Elise's tendons and muscles were doing whatever they wanted, irrespective of their proper functions, it seemed, with a life of their own, unconnected with reality. They were anchored with splints.

Aware of a presence beside her, Fran remarked sadly, 'A broken puppet pulled by a drunken puppet master.'

'With the drips and drains as badly connected strings,' agreed a man about her own age. He might have been younger: he had compensated for balding by growing a beard Fran would have thought might be unhygienic. His shoulder tags should have told her his rank, which she presumed was senior. What she would have welcomed was a good old-fashioned, navy-blue uniformed ward sister. Instead she had Charge Nurse Mike Penn, according to his name-badge.

'Are you here because you've caught the man who did this to her?'

Fran shook her head. 'Not yet. But I will. I promise you I will.'

'Promise this poor creature, not me. Assault. Rape. Leaves her for dead but doesn't bother to make sure. Bastard. Catch him and string him up, Chief Superintendent Harman.'

So the lad at the nurses' station had been more alert than he'd looked. She could have done without the slightly ironic emphasis on *Chief* however.

'Ms Harman will do,' she said. 'Locking up and throwing away the key is the best I can manage. And to do that I'd need the cooperation of twelve good jurors, not to mention a judge. Have you been nursing her long?'

'Since she came on this ward.' Penn seemed ready to bridle.

Fran gave a placatory nod. 'So it's your responsibility to make sure she's turned and fed and whatever.'

'My responsibility. She's turned to prevent sores, cleaned, powdered. All the palliative care we can offer.'

'I'm sure.' But Fran had lost interest. It was the very first person to have seen Elise that she wanted. Initial impressions — it was those that were vital. 'Poor woman,' she continued, as much for something to say as anything. 'Trapped inside there. Totally at the mercy of strangers. No friends, no visitors—'

'You're wrong there. She does have a friend. A visitor. A middle-aged man. He comes by at least once a week. Sometimes more. Talks to her a bit. Kisses her forehead. Goes.'

'Really!' And why, for goodness' sake, had no one deigned to tell her colleagues about him? 'What does he say?'

A shrug prompted her, but hardly encouraged her to continue, 'Any idea who the man might be?'

Penn shrugged again. 'We can't check up on all the visitors, Ms Harman. Few of my staff are here long enough to get to know their patients, let alone any chance visitors.'

Much as she wanted to throttle him she'd try a gentler approach. But why was the man so firmly on the defensive? 'Of course not. It must be quite a problem, running a busy ward like this with so many agency staff?'

'It plays havoc with our budgets but they're all good nurses.'

She tried again, reminding herself it was easier to question someone on your side. 'But — like my colleagues — so very young!'

'The doctors too. And orchestral musicians.'

That was a surprise. But before Fran could ask about it, Penn's pager beeped and he set off at a brisk walk, Fran in tow. Neither, Fran noticed, said goodbye to the patient. A double step brought them level.

'Is it possible to check Elise's medical file again? I could go through all the official palaver—'

'No need to do that. If you come to the nurses' station I can give you her file — so long as you read it there, of course. She's still an ongoing case so it hasn't been archived.'

The scribbles didn't mean much to Fran. She might have done better to reread the transcript or even the summary in the police file. But she wanted to get a sense of any urgency in the initial treatment from the writing, the punctuation — even the spelling mistakes, if there were any. DOA seemed pretty bleak. But there were all sorts of details of drugs, each initialled. It was the names behind the initials she wanted.

And the name of the solitary and affectionate visitor.

Mike Penn was the obvious source of information, so Fran waited, trying to close her mind to other waits in other hospitals, till he reappeared. She blew a mental kiss in Mark's direction: how long was it since she'd passed half a morning without worrying what might be happening in Devon? She'd always told underlings with problems that worrying never did any good and could well do harm.

Mark had done better then tell. He'd filled her mind with other things. Not least with him, even if he hadn't meant to. Was she just grateful for being cared for? No, the emotion felt stronger than gratitude. Lust? No, there were too many years of simple friendship and now days of kindness for that to be all.

She rubbed her face: if only she weren't so tired all the time. Two years ago, she'd have been winging her way to the next part of the investigation; now all she wanted was a cup of strong coffee. What might do her good was a hairdo — a colour, if she could persuade Suzanne to slot her into the last appointment of the day. Yawning, she summoned the number from the phone's memory.

'No mobiles in hospitals, Chief Superintendent, if you don't mind.'

Penn must simply be making a point. A glance into the ward showed at least five women texting or chattering away. To flare up or not to flare up? Fran compromised with an ironic smile and replaced the mobile in her bag.

'But we might as well make use of modern technology,' she said. 'Would you or one of your colleagues page me the minute he appears?'

'This is a busy hospital, not a dating agency.'

Fran was puzzled. She'd thought they might become allies. If they weren't, she wasn't going to play games. 'In that case, simply ask Elise's visitor his name if he turns up.'

'Against all our rules, Superintendent,' he said flatly. No, there was an edge to it, as if he wanted to be challenged.

She registered the demotion. So the man wanted war. He could have it. 'This is a serious assault investigation, Mr Penn, likely to become a murder inquiry. I could simply post one of my officers here all day every day, but, like yours, my resources are limited. And I fancy six foot two of indisputable police flesh might cause a stir on the ward.' As she got into gear, to her fury she started a flush. A burning, scarlet affair.

Penn watched, with what looked like sour amusement. 'The sooner you get some HRT inside you the better you'll be.'

How dare he! If her face was red, her voice was icy. 'Here's my mobile number. Next time he comes, I want to know.' She flicked her card on to the desk. 'Now, I need to identify some of these people.' As, bridling, Penn hesitated, she added, 'We both want justice for that poor creature. I want to interview the people who treated her on day one. Yes, they'll already have talked to my colleagues till they were blue in the face. But I shall be a new set of ears to hear their responses to what may be a new set of questions. It's worth a try, isn't it?' She managed the smile that had wheedled information out of people more intractable than Penn. Would it work now?

Just about. Penn's face was still sour and grudging as he leaned, stiff-necked, to take a sideways glance. 'JT: Jim Taverner's the consultant neurologist in charge.' He pointed with an index finger with a surprising nicotine stain. 'Those are his registrar, his senior reg, a houseman. That'd be the A and E senior reg, Verity Kilvert — she's still there now, as far as I know. You might catch Taverner in his Outpatients' clinic or on his rounds.'

Any of them might be less grudging than Penn, Fran reasoned. Had she done something to rub up Penn the wrong way? Or was he simply unpleasant by nature? There was no point in pondering it now — the answer would come if Penn called her when the unknown visitor appeared.

CHAPTER NINE

Fran was surprised to find A and E almost calm. To be sure, she'd spent most of her time there either at peak time when it was full of drunks or when there'd been a major incident. A labourer still muddy from a building site was sitting quietly with a blood-soaked rag round a finger. A toddler was neither sitting nor quiet, his dazed looking mother making no apparent effort to stop him strewing the tired magazines on the floor and noisily shaking each unoccupied chair. Fran retrieved a fistful of the magazines, slamming them down on the low table with sufficient force to rouse the labourer, who smiled ironically, but not the mother.

'You could do with a cage for them,' Fran suggested to the receptionist, her usual line — not quite a joke — drawing a smile. 'Which is the sick one, the mother or the child?'

'The child, though you'd never believe it, would you? And if he is ill, he should be at his GP's. But you know how it is,' she sighed. 'How can I help you, Chief Superintendent? You're a bit elevated for a personal visit, aren't you? We usually get lowly constables, maybe a sergeant on a good day.'

Fran returned her grin. 'I needed a day out of the office.'

'So do we all.' She winced as the toddler burst into furious howls. 'But I'd go for a blow on the beach, if I had any choice. Along that new promenade at Hythe, maybe. And I'd treat myself to some goodies at Waitrose.'

However much Fran preferred honesty in all her dealings, she preferred not to join in the game of confessions with the information that she'd have spent it in bed. With or without Mark.

Cue for another flush.

Before she could speak, the receptionist eyed her. 'Black cohosh and red clover,' she said. 'And don't forget your calcium. We see far too many fractured wrists and femurs here.'

Fran nodded. 'I'm here about a patient who passed through A and E. Do you still have a Dr Verity Kilvert working here?'

* * *

Verity Kilvert, apart from looking almost as weary as Fran, clearly wanted to be elsewhere, perching on the extreme edge of a desk tucked behind a curtain in the corner of the treatment room and constantly checking her watch throughout Fran's explanation of why she was there. She was terribly thin. Her wrist was so bony that the watch slopped from side to side. It would have driven Fran mad in ten minutes flat: why hadn't the woman had the bracelet made smaller?

'We do see a lot of patients here in A and E, Superintendent.' She had the remnants of the upper-class drawl that Fran found as appealing as fingernails on a blackboard. Perhaps the thinness was a fashion statement, rather than as a result of overwork: beneath the white coat, her bone and sinew feet sported ballerina pumps Fran could price almost to the pound. Ferragamo. She'd always longed to wear them, but her feet, after years of uniform lace-ups, simply refused to find them comfortable. She shivered: how long before she succumbed to the comfortable flatties with elasticated gussets that had preceded her mother's decline into permanent slippers?

'More patients than you ought, I can see.' Fran jerked her head in the general direction of the noisy toddler. 'But I'd have thought this particular one might stick in your mind. Elise. The PVS case.'

Kilvert nodded.

'I'd like you to tell me about the first time you saw her. You must have been the first of the medical staff to examine her?'

Another nod. 'I thought she was dead. I even wrote "dead on arrival" in her notes. But she wasn't.'

'Or was, depending on your outlook. Could you just describe her?'

'Why?' she demanded, like a petulant child. 'Everything you need's in the file.'

'Not quite everything.' And much she had yet to decipher. 'I want to know what she looked like.'

'I'm a doctor, not an artist!' she flounced.

But the haircut and indeed the face, now Fran came to think of it, were pure Modigliani. 'In my experience, medics are the most observant of human beings, and the most interested. Think, Dr Watson,' she added bracingly and hating herself for doing it. What was wrong with all these medics?

The allusion fell flat. Kilvert was all too obviously wracking her brain for a live colleague. Fran puzzled too: the doctor's surname was strangely familiar, but she could not place the context. Not medical, she was sure of that. Nor police. Verity Kilvert: what a name for the Scrabble board, were proper nouns permitted, of course.

Trying to hide her asperity, and then wondering if she should bother to, Fran prompted her, 'Apart from her terrible injuries, what can you tell me about her?'

The toddler embarked on an ear-splitting tantrum.

'Dr Kilvert, why don't we find somewhere quiet to talk? Even my car's better than this.'

Verity conceded that the staff canteen might be quieter, and would provide a decent fix of caffeine. It seemed to Fran that the young woman was pickling herself from the inside with the stuff but she didn't argue. She too was in need of some and of the sort of buzz that comes with disgusting doughnuts dripping with pink goo. But she was surprised to see them in a canteen frequented by people who should know better.

At last, Kilvert drawing on her drink as smokers inhaled the very last of their fag, Fran began again. 'Elise. Tell me what she was like as a person, not a patient.'

'There was terrible trauma to the head—'

'No,' she insisted patiently. 'As a person. Imagine you were trying to describe her to a man on the bus.'

The young woman shrugged, as if in disbelief at both the elementary concept and the impossibility.

'You mentioned her head injuries. Did you have to cut away hair to deal with them? Think back. What colour was it?' After a moment she prompted, 'Did it go with her eyes?'

'What do you mean?'

'She's got brown eyes, hasn't she? And grey hair? Did she have grey hair then?'

Kilvert grimaced. 'That's funny. She had blonde hair. One of the nurses said it was a sin to cut it all off because it looked as if she'd just spent a lot of money on it.'

Fran scribbled. But if a doctor couldn't remember a patient, how would a hairdresser remember a customer? Answer: if she'd been a regular, very easily. But you couldn't go round asking all the hair salons in Kent if they'd missed a client.

'Mascara. Quite a lot of mascara,' Kilvert declared. 'More than you'd expect on a woman her age.' She looked critically at Fran.

Damn: she still hadn't fixed a hair appointment. 'So she was my age?' An age for dyeing your hair and taking pills, by the sounds of it.

'Late fifties, early sixties — we couldn't say exactly, of course. But the funny thing was, apart from the newly varnished nails, she had really bad hands. The nails were actually quite ugly and coarse, the cuticles all over the place. As if she'd done a lot of manual work. Not dirty. But the skin certainly didn't get a regular dose of cream.' Verity stared at Fran's.

So did Fran, still burning at being thought so much older than she was. She never remembered to wear gardening gloves in Teignmouth, however carefully she gauntleted herself at home. A keen eye could pick out dirt under the dried, cracking cuticles. A manicure was in order while her hair was being coloured. If Suzanne could fit her in, of course, which was increasingly unlikely as the day pressed on without a call to make an appointment.

She chivvied herself back to the present, trying to ignore all the criticism coming her way, but finding it hard to warm to Kilvert. 'Elise's background: a woman who had to work for a living, and not an easy one at that? Or one rich enough to choose to stay at home and indulge a passion for gardening?'

'A working woman tarted up for the day,' Verity summed up, her accent grating again.

Like herself no doubt, Fran fumed. No, she must ignore the pejorative language. She tipped her head encouragingly on one side. A bird hoping for a crumb, Mark had once said, charmingly if without great originality. At the thought of him, she flushed again. Perhaps Verity, now staring into her empty coffee mug as if it were a crystal ball, hadn't noticed.

'Yes, and contact lenses. She wore contact lenses! Now, where's that come from?'

'The coffee, I should imagine. Can I get you another?' She watched temptation flit across the younger woman's face, to be replaced with will power.

'Mineral water, please.'

She said nothing about not wanting a doughnut, so Fran produced two more.

'You really shouldn't be eating crap like this at your age,' Verity observed. 'Whole foods, lots of fish. Phytoestrogens. Boost your Omega oils.'

Damn all these medics and their pertinent advice. 'What about Elise? Would you say she was pre- or post-menopausal?'

Verity pulled a face. 'At her age, post. A bit irrelevant now, anyway. She could hot flush for England and be none the wiser. And X-rays — specific ones — to tell if she had osteoporosis.'

Any moment now she'd suggest that Fran needed them, wouldn't she? Sharply, Fran turned the conversational steering wheel. 'You say she wore mascara. Earrings?'

'No, no jewellery that I recall. You'd be able to check with Admin of course. Or all her property may be with you people. I wouldn't know.'

What was the term she'd once heard? *De haute en bas*? How the nobs spoke to the plebs? Fran had long since earned enough to consider herself classless, but somewhere deep inside a grammar school girl wanted to stick her tongue out. She asked, in the quiet voice she used to alarm her junior officers, 'Did you see the man who tried to resuscitate her?'

'No,' she replied, off-hand. The voice hadn't worked. 'Whoever it was he didn't do a very good job, did he? He'd have done better to save his breath to cool his porridge.'

It was normal for Fran and her colleagues to cover their emotion by using brutal language, either at the crime scene or in the canteen — normal and necessary. The same no doubt applied in hospitals. But it disturbed her to hear callous thoughts spoken in such cultured tones, with a curiously old-fashioned expression to round it off. And if her colleagues spoke like that of the dead, this woman was referring to a living person. Face impassive, Fran merely nodded.

Checking her pad, though she would have been the first to admit that there was precious little jotted there, she said, as if recapping, 'So we have a woman in her fifties, "tarted up" for the day, but unable to conceal her regular manual work. Did you see her clothes? I know they'll have been bagged as evidence and I can check them myself, but did they make any impression on *you*?'

Kilvert raised an eyebrow. 'You're quite good at this, aren't you?'

Patronising bitch. Fran smiled back, encouragingly.

'They were new. And they still had those little plastic threads in, the things that attach the price tags. At least the ones I saw. Blouse and jacket. I only noticed those because she had minute scratches on her neck, as if something had irritated her and she'd kept brushing at it.'

'Blouse and jacket?'

'Yes, as if she'd bought something new for some do she wasn't sure about.'

'Not her favourite Max Mara.'

Kilvert didn't notice the irony. 'Lord, no, Eastex or some such. Brand-new, as I told you. You know, the sort of thing some mums buy for little Jimmy's graduation day.'

'You think that's where she might have been going?'

'How could she? Drat,' she added, quelling her pager, which had chosen that moment to trill. 'RTA — serious head injuries. Have a son, I mean. When she was a virgin until she was raped?'

As an exit line, it would take some beating.

Fran didn't go after her. Let the dead bury the dead. It was Kilvert's job to save the living, and, as Mark had observed, Elise wasn't going anywhere. In any case, she had to deal with the information so casually imparted. Poor Elise. What a way to be initiated into sex — a roadside rape. Did she need to see the gynaecologist who'd treated her? Not, she decided, till she'd rechecked the file, which meant bearding Penn in his lair once more.

* * *

'Private practice? He's left the NHS, just like that?'

Penn shook his head. 'Favours us with his presence one day a week. It just happened to be his day when they asked him to see Elise. And I'm not surprised you can't read his handwriting — not exactly the best calligraphy, is it? And all these abbreviations.'

'Could you interpret?' Fran asked humbly. She didn't wish to wear out her welcome, but Penn was showing his sunny face again, and might add in asides more than Fran could glean from the transcript back at the office.

'Let's see if there's an examination room free. These aren't the sorts of conversation you'd want everyone to overhear. Yes. In here, please, Chief Superintendent.'

'Fran, please. Too many syllables in the title,' she added.

'You know, I've always wanted a few more. Penn. I always prefer to be called Michael, but you know what people are like: Mike it has to be. And you — you've got a nice Christian name too. Only we're supposed to called them first names, aren't we?'

Fran laughed. 'Except mine's my second name. I never could be doing with Belinda. Frances got me too many letters addressed to "Mr Harman". So Fran it became.' She looked at her watch. 'Are you due for a break? I could shout you lunch in your canteen.'

'Senior nurses are paid quite well, thank you.'

God Almighty! What had she said this time?

Penn's pager bleeped. 'You can see I'm busy. But thanks for the offer. Now, unless there's anything else I can help you with, I must be off. Actually, maybe you should talk to Mr Roland-Thomas himself. His real name's Thomas, but he hyphenated his Christian name to it to make it posher.' And he was gone.

Fran used an ironic index finger to push her jaw back up into position.

* * *

She'd hardly settled herself in the car, pondering her next move, when her mobile rang.

'Pa?' It was a good job she hadn't had any lunch: she could have been physically sick.

'You'll have to come down. It's that woman. She's stolen all my money.'

CHAPTER TEN

'I know it's not my usual time, my dear, but I thought it might help if I were to vary the pattern — change the routine. The thing is, most people are tired in the evening, aren't they? I thought perhaps you'd be more receptive during the day. So here I am. I can't stay long, I'm afraid. There's a departmental meeting about restructuring this afternoon. It threatens to be interminable. Well, restructuring is a euphemism for mass-redundancies, of course, so we'll all be wanting to put in our threepenn'orth. The government has this idea that fifty per cent of young people should have a university education. Wonderful. But they don't give us fifty per cent more funding. That's what all this argument about tuition fees and top-up fees is about. Except you wouldn't have heard any of it, would you, apart from what I've told you? When you wake up, what a different world you'll find. Because you really must wake up, Elise. Make an effort. And make it soon. Otherwise it will be too late.

'They're trying to bring in a law to stop parents hitting their children. I never understood why anyone would want to hit anyone. Not until the other day. I still can't believe I did it. But it was frustration, Elise, sheer frustration. I had to get through to you, had to. And nothing I could say or do made any difference. It must be like that with recalcitrant children, mustn't it? Only they're worse in a way because they're noisy, too. You should see them in Sainsbury's when they want sweets. Of course, the management make it worse by displaying confectionary at

such tempting, such accessible heights. But that's nothing new, of course. You must remember that. Like the song, eh?

'Put it another way, Elise. You must remember that. Or something. Anything. And soon. For my sake as much as your own. I can't go through the rest of my life knowing I've reduced you to this. Look at you, face stretched as if you were smiling at something, though I know it's just a random rictus. I think I know.

'Goodbye, my dear. I promise, absolutely promise, I'll be back soon.'

CHAPTER ELEVEN

'But you've only been back in Kent about eight hours!' Mark observed from the far side of his desk, making a huge effort not to explode at the outrageous demand. 'You can't turn tail and go back to Devon now! I don't mean your work: I mean—'

'I know. That's what I told Pa. I haven't even been home yet, as it happens. Which makes this all the more welcome.' Fran gestured with her mug of tea and allowed the chair opposite his to take even more of her weight. 'Thanks.'

'So are you going down?' He was trying to sound casual, but even he could hear the anxiety in his voice.

'No. Big flat no.'

'Thank God for that.'

'I've phoned their care worker, who says Pa sacked the woman I'd got in to sleep over every night on the grounds that she snored. Oh, and he had to make her an early morning cup of tea.'

He let himself laugh with her as he imagined the scene behind the bald summary. 'It sounds a very reasonable response, in fact.' Then he remembered something. 'But what's this about his money?'

Shaking her head, she touched the side of her nose. 'I have power of attorney and pay all the bills. It's only a small town and still has some local shopkeepers, who all deserve sainthoods for their patience. They even deliver without charging, would you believe. So if any money were stolen, it would be peanuts.'

'All the same — stealing from the old is about as low as—'

'Stealing money is Pa's cry for help. He accused my brother-in-law of stealing his treasure last time he and Hazel went to visit — and I don't need my pocket Freud to work that one out. So I think I shall have to go down this weekend for all I was hoping for just one to myself.' He could see the effort it cost not to let herself sigh. She even tried to smile, but her face was too stiff for her smile to be convincing. Stiff with fatigue and disappointment. Yes! He almost came round the desk to clasp her: they'd been talking of going to the coast this weekend, and she'd been looking forward to it. Dare he risk it? Dare he risk a ploy — hell, it was a lie! Did he look as shifty as he felt?

She was waiting.

Clearing his throat and fiddling with the corner of a file, he asked, 'How far from Teignmouth is Salcombe? Because I have a friend who's always on at me to mess about with him on his yacht, and I thought — you know, if the logistics worked out — we could share a car. I'm afraid we might have to head back on Sunday evening — I'm not one for getting up before the crack of dawn.' He'd book in at some hotel near Teignmouth, phone her to tell her his plans had fallen through and at least shoulder some of her burden. With luck he might lure her back to sleep with him in a clean bed in a clean room.

Yes and yes and yes. Her eyes gave her away. So did a tiny tremor as she swallowed a mouthful of tea and said coolly, 'It might mess you around horribly. Every time I'm due to set out for home, they find another little job for me to do.'

'You never know, I might do it for you.' He added quickly, before she could change her mind, 'It's a deal, then?

Split the driving if you like — or you can sleep all the way. So long as you don't expect more than a service area cup of tea,' he added with a severe frown. 'Or snore.'

She laughed. 'I have been known to sing "Ten Green Bottles" very loudly indeed to stay awake.'

She meant it as a joke. But he knew as well as she the dangers of fatigue. Hell, exhaustion, more like. After an obliging smile, he leaned forward, almost senior officer to underling, but not quite, he hoped. 'That's another thing I'm afraid of. Your falling asleep at the wheel. Or taking on board so much caffeine that you don't sleep even when you should. The T-shirt's hanging in my wardrobe. And the sweatshirt, come to think of it.'

She nodded. 'I'm sorry. You've been through this squared. And you lost a lovely woman with years ahead of her. I can't imagine what it was like, seeing her suffer. At least Ian's heart attack was — very swift.'

One day they might be able to talk about their bereavements — this was the first time he recalled her bringing that tutor of hers into the conversation — but not now. He had a point to make. 'There's a difference between wearing yourself out caring for the man or woman you love, and prostrating yourself for your parents — who must be how old?'

'Ninety. Both of them. I told you I was the afterthought. But just because they're old doesn't mean I don't love them, Mark.'

He had to screw honesty out of himself, however much he'd rather not. At last he looked her straight in the eye. 'You come to love people . . . differently . . . when they're chronic invalids, their personalities distorted by pain and suffering. Not less. Differently. All the demands: no matter how reasonable they are to them, they sometimes get to you. And it seems to me your parents are making — on a regular basis — totally unreasonable demands.'

'Perfectly reasonable in their terms,' she snapped back. More gently, reflectively, she continued, 'But you have a point about loving them differently. In a sense, I'm probably in mourning for people who died years ago. When they stopped being the carers and became so utterly dependent on me. Was there a day, a week, a year when I lost them? Or was the change as seamless as it was inexorable?'

He could hardly speak, so tried to bluster, 'Perfectly reasonable! Like your driving two hundred and twenty miles and back every weekend? And twice today! Fran, when you're not so tired, you're going to have to start thinking the unthinkable. Don't flare up. Have another biscuit instead.' He got up to offer her the tin, deliberately changing the mood. 'And tell me how you got on with Elise.'

Perhaps she recognised his fear, or couldn't confront her own. After a sharp blink, she took the biscuit and gave him a terse account of her morning.

'I spent the afternoon looking through some of the evidence bags. Her clothes. And the doctor was right. Everything she had on, right down to her bra, was new. Marks and Spencer bra and slip — they never found her pants. Viyella suit and shirt. Middle-price range. The doctor might have sneered that it wasn't your actual designer gear (I thought hospital doctors were supposed to be underpaid!) but it was the sort of thing I wore to court until I got the last promotion.'

'Any theories?'

'CID tried all the obvious ones first time round.'

'Try the left-brain ones, then.' It was so much easier to talk shop.

'New everything, Mark. Even the soles of her shoes were still shiny,' she recalled. 'It's the sort of fantasy I sometimes have when I have to go down to Devon. That instead of going there I'll take another turning, go to a place I've never been and take on a new identity.'

'I should imagine that the temptation must have been equally great on the return journey, when you had to battle into work and attempt to fit eight days' duties into five working days.'

'That's much easier, thanks to you and this new case.' She bit her lip. 'This is so hard, Mark. I've never shared feelings like these before with anyone in the job.'

'Is it the culture of the stiff upper lip or—'

'That and — something in me. Anyway, now I've confessed I really can't do a runner, can I?' Her tone was far too bright.

He tried to respond in kind. 'Hardly worth trying these days: we could trace you through your credit cards, your mobile phone, the anti-theft tracking device in your car. Not a good time to disappear, Fran.'

'It was for Elise.'

'Whose damn tune I seem to hear wherever I go these days. Famous pianists on Classic FM, tinny music while I wait for my bank to deign to answer my call, even mobile phone tones. Damn Beethoven and his little friend. De dah de dah de *dah* de dum, da di dum,' he sang, infusing a savage irony into the melody. '"Fur Elise".'

'Or in our case, poor Elise.'

They both used the German pronunciation, sounding the final *e*.

His phone rang. As he lifted the handset, he covered it: 'What time are you leaving?' he mouthed.

'Five minutes.'

What a pity. He'd meant to suggest a drink and some pasta at his place. And after that . . . He resigned himself to his phone call, flapping a hand in farewell.

* * *

Having failed to get a hair appointment, at least Fran had talked her way into her GP's surgery. She stared at Dr Jennings in disbelief. 'Let me get this straight,' she told the young woman, who was hardly older than Kilvert. She too was a steady size six, neatly compact rather than bony. She looked as if she had yet to experience the menarche, let alone the menopause, though the receptionist said she'd just returned from her second maternity leave. 'I hot flush for England,' Fran continued. 'I can't sleep; I can't concentrate; there are days I'm not so much depressed as despairing and you say I'm not a candidate for HRT.'

'Surely, Miss Harman, you read the papers. HRT is hardly without side effects. I would suggest that breast cancer is likely to cause you more sleepless nights than a few flushes.'

'Indeed, Dr Jennings, I do read the papers, enough to know that statistically my chances of getting breast cancer are negligibly increased if I take HRT for a short period. Which is all I want it for. To enable myself to do my fairly taxing job as a senior police officer properly until I retire in a few months' time.'

'You're retiring?' Suddenly she appeared interested.

'To look after my elderly parents.'

She was distinctly alert. 'Does either of them have osteoporosis?'

'Pa's shaped like a question mark and Ma's broken both wrists and her pelvis. I'd have thought that a very good reason on its own for me to take oestrogen for a bit.'

'When you're in your sixties, maybe. Meantime, you should take load-bearing exercise at least twenty minutes a day. Every day. There are plenty of excellent calcium supplements. And some people believe that alternative therapies can offer some assistance to your other symptoms, though in my opinion they're little more than placebos. In any case, your symptoms shouldn't last more than a year, two at most.'

A fresh flush burned its way up her chest and neck. 'So you can offer me advice and placebos but nothing else.'

'Correct. I wouldn't want your death on my conscience, Miss Harman. Of course, if you'd had a couple of children and breastfed them for twelve months each, things might be different.'

'What a shame my forward planning wasn't as good as yours,' Fran snapped. 'I have to tell you that I'm far more at risk of having a car crash when I fall asleep at the wheel than of any sort of cancer.'

'In that case,' Jennings said, smiling sweetly and getting to her feet, 'shouldn't you be travelling by train?'

* * *

Mark was there in the car park again at eight the following morning. What a good job Fran had rejected the impulse to return to the duvet and sleep out her sleep. And Mark was surely waiting. He was studying a file, so he couldn't simply by coincidence have arrived a moment before she did. He was definitely waiting. And he had offered her a lift to Devon. So was he waiting for her?

This time it was she who walked to his driver's door, and he who looked up with a grin. Perhaps he'd been there longer than he'd ever admit: it was he who winced and staggered as he unfolded himself. He wasn't old. In her book he was scarcely middle-aged. After all, he was her exact contemporary. But he had given an intimation of his mortality and, when she inevitably sweated, this time it was with fright. This was a friend, someone who might be more than a friend. It was bad enough when her own back seized up but she'd always kid herself with explanations that were probably no more than excuses — the long drive, the heavy gardening, the hours on her feet. But it was worse to see someone else in trouble. To be specific, it was worse to see Mark in trouble.

He quickly righted himself, grabbing the hand she'd extended and clasping it, as she clasped his, a moment longer than necessary. But the sound of an approaching car sprung them apart, and both were ready with charm and dignity to greet the Chief Constable. She effaced herself while the two men strode hierarchically in together. But she wasn't surprised when Mark mouthed over his shoulder, 'Breakfast at eight-thirty?' or that his face lit up as she nodded.

The breakfast conversation, however, was devoted to the Elise case: the Chief was interested in what she was doing and wanted to be brought up to date over his muesli and green tea. Fran eyed his food with interest but not surprise. To have been promoted so far so young meant you had to take care of both body and brain. His muscles told her that some time in the week he found time for regular exercise, too, the sort the doctor had told her to take. Perhaps he balanced reports on the handlebars of his exercise bike.

'Now I've seen the poor woman and spoken to those who treated her on her arrival in A and E,' she said, 'I've gone back to the original paperwork to see if anything sparks any good ideas.'

'And to check for sins of omission and commission,' observed the Chief, earning a dutiful laugh. He peeled an underripe banana to slice on his muesli. 'Good for the heart.'

Fran had better add them to her shopping list.

'I'm not expecting many of either. It's just the fresh eyes syndrome. The other thing I want to do is talk to the man who often visits her. But there's no regular pattern to his visits, and the hospital aren't notably cooperative about letting me know if he turns up.'

'We're perilously short of manpower with the Royal Visit coming up,' the Chief said warningly. 'But if you think he's a threat—'

'A threat? It'd be a moot point if he could kill someone who's brain dead. But I'd certainly like to eliminate him from our enquiries in a fairly low-profile way. Maybe I should take a file or two over and simply sit by Elise. Like a visitor. But even that might put him off.'

'And I'm sure your skills could be put to considerably better use.' The Chief eyed her shrewdly. 'I must confess to finding it very hard to accept that you should be dedicating yourself to a single case, however important that may be. With your management and investigative experience you should be employed on wider projects. I know Mark says this is a special case — and I concede, that it's better to have you sorting out a very tricky situation than taking endless unpaid leave and being no use to us at all — but surely you should be managing others, not acting as common gumshoe.'

Mark compressed his lips till they were white, avoiding Fran's gaze. She guessed the Chief had said as much and more when Mark was cajoling him into this course of action. Anyone would be embarrassed at being caught out in special pleading, she told herself. As for herself, she objected strongly to having all this rehearsed in the staff canteen: the pros and cons of her appointment should surely have been discussed in the privacy of one or other of their offices.

'With respect, sir,' she said, aware as always that the two words always meant the opposite, 'though I'd be happy to have a team at my disposal, it was a large and experienced team that failed to find both Elise's identity and her assailant's first time round. I think finding the first will lead to the second. And at this stage, sniffing round on my own, an unthreatening middle-aged woman, I might just get the breakthrough we need. Then it'll be time to bring in the full panoply of policing skills. Nor will I hesitate to do so. Miss Marple I am not.'

Apparently unaware of the edge in her voice, the bright eyes met hers. 'I can't ever imagine you sitting quietly by the fire entranced by conversations about the church flowers, Fran. Nor, to be honest, can I imagine you arranging the said flowers, though I'm sure you'd do it admirably. No, when Mark told me that looking after your parents was what you had in mind I told him he couldn't be serious. Nor can you, Fran. You're a high-flying career woman. It would be the worst thing in the world for you, and pretty well the worst for your parents.'

'That's not how they see it, sir.' Surely he would realise how he was offending her.

'My son's doing *King Lear* as one of his A Level texts at the moment. There's a bit in there about a child's duty to its parents. Let's see: *You have begot me, bred me, lov'd me; I Return those duties back as are right fit, Obey you, love you and most honour you.* Which sounds as if she ought to be devoting herself entirely to him. But then she adds, *Haply, when I shall wed, That lord whose hand must take my plight shall carry Half my love with him, half my care and duty.*'

Half of her marvelled at his recall and indeed his delivery, not to mention the fact that in his frantic week he still found time to be a good father. The other half seethed at the bland assumption that he could preach like this. Fran shrugged — he might see it as apologetically; Mark, knowing her so much better, would sense the anger and irony. 'The trouble is, sir, I never had a lord to take my hand. A husband and a couple of kids would have been the answer,' she continued ironically. To her parents and her GP alike.

He shook his head. 'As I told my son, the lord's hand in marriage can be a metaphor — remember those from your schooldays, Fran? — for a woman's career. In my experience, you can't go back, ever.'

She felt like a child with her contradiction. 'It wouldn't be going back, sir. It would be to a new town, a new county, a new set of — of occupations,' she concluded.

'Let me offer you Shakespeare again. Who is it that goes to pieces in *Othello* when he loses his job — when his occupation's gone? My own A level this time,' he added with a totally disarming smile. 'Which is why I can't remember the quotation.' Folding the banana skin neatly in the muesli bowl, he drank his tea in one medicinal-looking draught. 'Revolting!'

Neither Fran nor Mark bothered to argue.

'They say it's good for you,' he grimaced, 'mopping up free radicals.'

'I didn't know there were still any at large after this Home Secretary's legislation,' Fran observed.

She enjoyed the Chief's expression until she got as far as the ladies' loo, when yet another flush assailed her.

CHAPTER TWELVE

'I can't stay long today, Elise. I wish I could. I fully intended to, in fact, but that male nurse, the bearded one who blows hot and cold so you don't know where you are with him, he gave me a very funny look as I came in. No, I must be imagining it. Why should anyone look at me? Perhaps he just thought it strange that I should come in before lunch.

'Perhaps, heaven forbid, he fancies me. That's the term my students use. I always thought there might be a touch of the D.H. Lawrence and the latent homosexuality about him. Maybe more than a touch with Michael. Not that he'd experience major difficulties these days, at least in the public arena. I sometimes think our department's run by the Gay Mafia. And then I realise they'd be very unpleasant people whatever their sexual orientation. Take our union representative, now. When I was passed over for promotion I asked him to accompany me to discuss the business with my head of department. Did he back me? Not one iota! It seems he had his eye on the job for himself. What do you think about that? Not very moral? Quite. The pay-off is this. Within a month, a little month; or ere those shoes were old in which he used to pace the corridors of power, he wangled a job in the media and left without notice. Just like that. All those students untaught and untutored, so long as he could get the job he wanted. The media. Isn't it amazing how people have forgotten it's the plural form of the word. I even have students writing about medias, these days, God bless us

all. Criteria; phenomena; bacteria: people get those completely confused. Which reminds me, I hope your nursing staff wash their hands. One hears so much about MRSA these days. I always take the precaution of washing mine, both before and after my visit. Now, I really have a very busy day ahead of me, and I absolutely do not wish to be caught up in protracted conversation with Michael. So I shall love you and leave you, if you'll forgive the cliché. Goodbye, my dear. Remember, it really is essential that you return instanter to your senses.'

CHAPTER THIRTEEN

What had happened to her youth? A more accurate question might be why she had wasted her youth. It tormented her through the morning, despite the pile of information she'd set herself to absorb.

Fran sat at her new desk, in her new chair, chewing the end of a new pencil in a very old gesture. Things might have been different if she had gone to university when she was eighteen, of course. Then in her twenties she could have been building on her degree, developing her career with sensible stratagems, marrying and having a family. But there hadn't been enough money. She'd have had a grant in those days, of course, and would certainly have worked during vacations to keep herself. So why wouldn't there have been enough money? There had been for Hazel, who'd also started an MA but had given up and settled for a teaching qualification. There'd also been plenty of money for Hazel's first wedding, a far from sober affair, quite unlike her second, to Grant. She remembered — she must have been eighteen, waiting for her A Level results — her father eyeing the growing collection of empty Asti bottles on the hotel terrace, sighing with relief and saying he was glad that one daughter wasn't the marrying sort. After all, she wouldn't get far in the police if she went and fell for some man who wouldn't understand shift work.

'You're both good girls and we're proud of you both,' Ma had added, adjusting the brim of her hat and mopping perspiration. Perhaps Ma had been menopausal then, come to think of it. 'And if you can't be pretty, like Hazel, at least you can be dignified in that uniform of yours. Look at her, isn't she a picture?'

And Hazel had been, her colouring brought out by the creamy silk of her wedding gown. The green she'd chosen for her bridesmaids had made them look like candidates for their own funerals, but that was every bride's prerogative. And no, Fran would never have been a belle. If anything, age had improved her. As a singleton, she'd been able to afford the best cosmetics, the best clothes, the best hair care. Her job required her to keep fit, and pleasure and determination had made her a fearsome badminton player, so her figure would have drawn sidelong glances of envy from many women twenty years her junior. She'd once been hoping — in the words of the silver cliché — to grow old disgracefully.

But now she was to look after her parents.

Had their brainwashing that she was not the marrying sort been intentional? Or simply the natural thing to do thirty years ago, an insurance policy for their old age? Leaning her head against the cold window of her office, Fran couldn't be sure she could exonerate them.

She pulled herself up. Perhaps they were simply positively reinforcing what she'd already chosen: straight from A Levels she went into the police, never having time to wear the lovely silly seventies clothes because she was always at work or preparing for the next promotion at work. Her hopes were corroded by the sickening realisation that young women with degrees and none of her experience were readily outpacing her in the promotion race. So she had to abandon the idea of buying her own home to finance herself through university as a mature student. Unlike Fran, who simply had to resign from the force and then reapply, some of her male colleagues, in those dire, pre-equal opportunity days, were seconded to similar courses with their fees paid, and full salaries to support them. But even they reported difficulties at university. Whatever the situation might be now for older people returning to study, in those days anyone over twenty-three was regarded by the bright young things as a cross between a freak and an agony aunt. Her fellow students would as soon have made a pass at a nun as at this weird temporarily ex-guardian of law and order. And no one dared offer her dope.

No boyfriends, then, at university, and none at work. Most of her mates, as bright as she and as underqualified as she, by and large settled for their slower progress but acquired wives, mortgages, cars in the drive and children.

So there was no temptation to be anything except head down every evening in her bedroom at her parents' home. No reason ever to move. Until they pulled the worn carpet from under her feet with the announcement that they'd bought a bungalow down in Teignmouth, having had a very good offer for the house. She hadn't even known it was on the market. And she wasn't to worry, there'd be enough left over for her to have a deposit to put down on a house, when she was ready.

There'd been enough too to buy Hazel a car to console her for her broken marriage. No one could ever say they weren't even-handed.

So her thirties were her rebirth. She became independent at last. She bought her own home, a large, if run-down cottage in a picture postcard village in Kent. Promotions and interesting postings came so fast she was tipped at one time to be the first woman Chief Constable. She was told to apply for a chief superintendent's post in Durham, but that seemed a long way from Devon, where Pa had just had his first heart attack. To compensate, she had a three-year affair with her Ian, an Open University tutor, a kind and generous man who helped her to her doctorate in criminology and died of a heart attack two days after she had received it. So much for walking hand in hand into the sunset with the love of her life.

Not even a child of his to carry. He'd have made a wonderful father, though she was less sure about her own qualifications as a mother. Ruthlessness and impatience with people slower than oneself didn't sit well with looking after children. Or with people entering their second childhood.

And so much for a morning's work, she told herself dourly. It wasn't like her to moon over the past, certainly not like her to lose her concentration so easily. It would be humiliating to have to report back to Mark that while the chief could be both a good father and brilliant at his job, she was simply a resentful daughter, incapable of doing the easy task he'd delegated to her.

Mark.

What she needed was a brisk walk — not least for her poor bones' sake, apparently. She preferred to allude to one of her favourite plays and call it stimulating her phagocytes. A walk, then a visit to Elise. So the walk would involve the car.

Stopping in Ashford to pick up a sandwich, she surveyed the drab main street without pleasure. In the days when she'd been rescuing her cottage, the ironmonger's at the bottom had saved her bacon on more than one occasion, knowing just what she needed when B&Q's customer service stares had been blank. But these days she hardly ever saw the place, beautifully restored, decorated and furnished to the best of her and her interior designer's ability though it might be. As she saw the ranks of estate agents massing in readiness she made one firm promise to herself. She wouldn't sell it. She might rent it out, preferably at an exorbitant rent to city-rich commuters. But of all the things in Kent she could give up, that must stay hers.

She brushed away the vision of Mark and her having Sunday brunch together in the bright kitchen. There was room for his two grown-up sons and their families. It could be idyllic.

Why should he want her anyway, a middle-aged spinster with bulges and grey underwear?

At least she could do something about that. She turned towards Marks and Spencer. But then she thought better of it. No. Apart from the hardware store, Ashford possessed one other specialist shop — a lingerie delight. That was where she'd use her plastic. To meltdown if needs be.

* * *

'Any sightings of our mysterious visitor?' she asked Penn, smiling as if pleased to see him and assured of her welcome in return.

'Someone did say he'd popped in the other day, but he'd gone before I could do anything,' he said, off-hand.

Deep breath time.

'Mr Penn, I know you've more work to do than a single pair of hands could possibly achieve. Believe me, I know how intolerable it is to be asked to add yet another task to your day's list. But this—'

'Come on, Chief Superintendent, you know she's not going anywhere fast.'

Why did everyone have to say that?

Although he was in his later thirties, Penn had produced the 'can't touch me' sneer of a kid wrapped round his tenth can of lager at two in the morning in Maidstone High Street.

She took a step back, to surprise him all the more as she weighed into the attack. 'It's not speed, Michael, it's efficiency. If you can run a ward like this, you must be efficient. And able, and hard-working. So what's your problem with this? I need to talk to this visitor. Whatever I'm doing, I'll drop it the moment he appears. But I don't have radar. I need you to make the call. Or whoever replaces you on the next shift, or the one after that. Do you understand?'

'I suppose.' He turned from her, muttering under resentful breath.

She picked up the words, 'menopausal bitch.' 'If you said what I think you said, I could have you up for a disciplinary before you could say *Women's Ward*. Get me?'

'So it's OK for you plods to be racist and sexist but—'

'I assure you, Mr Penn, in Kent Constabulary, as in every other police area in the country, racism and sexism are stamped on with all the force of official policy. As for ageism, that's not a matter to be proud of either. Now, do you ring me or not?'

* * *

A quick phone call to the hospital's personnel department elicited the fact that Tuesday was Mr Roland-Thomas' day for the private hospital in Canterbury, so she took herself off there, still pondering about Penn's moodiness. He must be hell to work for. My God, what if that was why Mark had pulled her out of her previous work and put her on this, because her colleagues could no longer stomach her occasionally acerbic tongue? But at least it came into its own as she tackled the receptionists guarding Mr Roland-Thomas, his hyphen and his consultant colleagues. Of course all his patients were paying, she smiled dangerously, and entitled to his full attention and their full consultation. Of course they were entitled to be seen promptly. But this was a matter of life and death. Literally. Though she suspected that they might not understand the full force of the words. At least, coupled with her chief superintendent ID, it got her a few minutes of the great man's time. The receptionist shrank behind the desk and pressed appropriate buttons.

To her surprise, the doctor came to the reception area in person, escorting her back to his office and offering her water from a cooler in the corridor just outside. He let her into his room, seating her opposite him in a way that reminded her of Mark. And the two weren't dissimilar. Both in their fifties, well-preserved and well-turned out: they could have swapped tailors. Probably Roland-Thomas would have coveted Mark's full head of still-dark hair: he'd lost most of a gingerish crop. He could certainly have emulated Mark's regular workouts — there was a distinct sag about his midriff.

'Are you saying, Chief Superintendent, that you can't read my elegant fist?' A jocular smile spread across his features as he peered over mandatory half-moon spectacles. She could price those exactly. They were the twins of her last pair, ones her father had sat on last month: chic, elegant, expensive. And insured.

She tapped her notepad in emphasis. 'I'm not saying that at all. After all, I have a verbatim transcript I can refer to at any time. No, it's not your gynaecological expertise I need. It's not the medical technicalities, but your impressions of your patient as a human being, not as a patient. Could you cast your mind back—'

To her fury, she started a flush, one of her deepest ones. As she unbuttoned her jacket, she saw him register it. Let him. It was probably only one amongst a dozen he'd seen that day. To her surprise, however, he jotted on a pad not unlike her own. Touché?

'—to the first moment you saw her? As if you were telling a man in the street? Patient confidentiality apart, of course.'

'Not the injuries?'

'In a few minutes, if we may.'

'I saw a lady of middle years who'd gone to a great deal of trouble with her appearance that even her dreadful injuries couldn't conceal. She reminded me of my mother, Chief Superintendent, dolled up, as my father used to say, to the nines.' He slid into a Welsh accent, then back again. 'Of course, I never saw her dressed. I was more concerned, too, with stemming bleeding from traumatised tissue.'

'Of course. You noted all the internal injuries. This was — and I dare say I've seen nearly as many PMs as you have — a very vicious attack.' Many of them with bodies in far worse condition than the average gynaecologist would come across in a lifetime. 'You speculated that she'd been penetrated with a blunt instrument.'

He made another jotting, looking at her shrewdly. 'She was raped *after* the head injury. Penile penetration was probably difficult. She was probably assaulted by something like a rubber torch, since there were abrasions consistent with — blah, blah, blah.' He waved an elegant hand. 'Anal penetration too. Same instrument.'

'At least she'd have been unconscious while all this was going on.'

'Possibly. Probably,' he conceded. 'According to my neurological colleagues, she might even have been technically dead at the time.'

She nodded. 'So we might be looking for one of those monsters who get their kicks by having sex with the dead. Necrophilia, isn't that what it's called?'

'In that case, wouldn't you have other people with similar penchants on your files?'

'There was no DNA match on file, I'm afraid. But—'

'—that doesn't mean there isn't now!' he said. 'Surely that sort of attack wouldn't be a one-off.'

'I couldn't second you on to my team, could I?' Fran laughed. 'Seriously, this was one of our lines of enquiry, but it's so far proved entirely fruitless. As have all our other lines, to be honest.'

'You know they want to discontinue treatment?'

'That's why we're reopening the case. If she dies — officially — it's a murderer I'm after, Mr Roland-Thomas.'

'I believe if anyone can find him, you will.' He looked half-amused.

'Elise has my solemn promise that if it's humanly possible to bring him to justice, I will. Now, thank you for your time.' She stood, extending a hand. 'Your everyday observation was just as useful as your technical information.'

'Chief Superintendent, may I make another everyday observation? Please sit down, and please don't be offended. You are clearly going through a very awkward time of life. How you tackle it is up to you: there are as many suggestions as there are women with your experiences.'

'I've had at least three suggestions this week,' she agreed. 'All entirely unsolicited. It seems a woman's health enters the public domain when she reaches a certain age.'

'You're lucky it wasn't more. And I'm sorry to have become the fourth with possibly unwelcome advice.'

'If anyone is in a position to offer it I should imagine it would be you,' she conceded.

'In that case, may I suggest — shall we say — a quick fix? Provided there are no contra-indications, I think your GP might prescribe a course of HRT. No?'

'She doesn't approve of it.' She let her anger ooze out.

He responded with an ironic smile. 'Or her practice budget manager doesn't approve of it.'

'Or possibly she's simply too young to have any idea what the menopause is like.' She sank back on to the chair. 'My symptoms include . . . No, you don't need the litany.' Surely to God she couldn't be weeping. Damn and blast, she was.

He leaned forward and pressed his phone console. 'Could you offer coffee, please, Anna, to our next patient. Apologise profusely. I'll be engaged here at least five more minutes.'

Fran dabbed with a tissue she balled and lobbed — accurately — into his waste bin.

'So it *is* a matter of life and death!' Anna's voice tinnily filled the room.

'Very much so,' he said gravely. Flicking the switch, he continued, 'I can't advise you formally when I don't know your entire medical history, and heaven forbid I tout for custom.'

'Would you take me as your patient?' she asked, making her voice as crisp as she could.

He pulled a face. 'Referral by a GP is the usual protocol. Shall I at least take your blood pressure, which is a good indication of whether I can suggest the H word.' Suiting the word to the deed, he nodded approvingly. Then he checked her heart. 'You're remarkably healthy, Superintendent. Tumultuous hormones apart. I'll write to your GP, shall I, if you furnish my receptionist with all her details? Yours too. I can't of course prescribe for you, unless you want a private prescription—'

'I'd pay for it in gold bullion if you were prepared to sign it! I can't express my thanks, Dr Roland-Thomas—'

He interrupted her with a smile that began courtly and ended grim. 'Sufficient if you can nail — I believe that's the term? — the unspeakable animal that so injured poor Elise.'

* * *

Was that really why she'd gone out of her way to see the consultant? Had she ever expected he could tell her anything that Penn or Kilvert hadn't, or that wasn't in Elise's file? Clutching the packet of patches, she almost danced for joy. If that was what pulling rank meant, she would pull every time.

And as she danced, her phone chirruped. It didn't recognise the caller, and for a moment she was hard put to place his voice. 'Michael!'

'He dropped an opened letter. Elise's visitor. Addressed to Dr Alan Pitt. University of Kent. Any use?'

How long had that been lying about on the supposedly clean ward floor? But today she wasn't hygiene monitor. 'I'm on my way now!' she declared. 'And Michael — many thanks.'

If he was about to protest that he didn't deserve them, she didn't hear. Cutting him off short she called back to CID in Maidstone.

'It's only four — he might still be teaching. And if he isn't, I want his home address. Yes. Dead urgent.'

She ran back to her car. It might be rush hour in Canterbury — when wasn't it? — but she'd fight her way through the traffic like Boudicca late for a battle.

CHAPTER FOURTEEN

'You could see from her face what an anti-climax it was, Elise. There was this top policewoman, flourishing her ID card and looking like an avenging fury, right outside my seminar-room door. No, to do her justice, she didn't interrupt the class. In fact, she waited till the corridor was quite clear, and wasn't at all strident. But she radiated power and energy. Such a good-looking woman, too, and so intelligent. She's not just a graduate: it turns out she's got a doctorate in criminology and is a visiting lecturer at a number of universities. Oh, the top ones.

'Very quietly, she asked me if there was a room where we could talk in private. I suggested my office. My office! As if I didn't have to share it with three other people, a room designed for two at the most. That's the price of university expansion, Elise. Anyway, the others were either teaching or had gone home, so we were alone. Alone in that mess of paperwork and books and empty sandwich wrappings: I was so ashamed, I wanted to point out how much tidier my section of the room was than the others'. Maybe I did. Anyway, it wouldn't have mattered if anyone had come in, because instead of an interrogation, we had an interesting discussion.

'She wanted to know why I visited you. That's all. And I told her the truth, that it was because I felt morally responsible for your being in this situation. If I'd done the resuscitation routine better, I might have saved you. If knowing I was inexperienced — heavens, one course of

first aid classes, thirteen years ago! — I'd left well alone, you'd simply have slipped away into oblivion and died. Either option, I told her, would have been better than this living death, as I'm sure you'd agree.

'No, she didn't say a word about suspecting me of wishing to harm you. She was au fait with all the palaver at the time, when they'd taken my DNA and tried to prove it was I who'd inflicted those terrible sexual injuries on you. My God, what a monster, Elise. I'm not a violent man, as I'm sure you'll have realised, and certainly not a man for heroics. But if I knew who had — who had violated you so brutally, so appallingly . . . Yes, I'm still lost for words. Ironic, isn't it, that I, whose business is words, can analyse with aplomb the works of the Marquis de Sade but cannot express my anger or horror at your injuries. I'd always thought, in my quiet bachelor way, that rape was — well, rape. Insertion of the male member into the vagina against the woman's will. In my innocence, I'd always dismissed playground and lavatory jokes as sick fantasy. They wouldn't tell me what that animal used to penetrate you. She did. Detective Chief Superintendent Harman. Frances. Fran. Now why should she abbreviate such a lovely name into such a terse monosyllable?

'She's been to see you, of course. She must have turned heads on the ward, such a tall, elegant woman. Beautifully dressed — she could certainly teach some of my colleagues a trick or two, not to mention those Oxbridge academic women who seem to take a delight in making themselves plain and unattractive. No, Elise, whatever you may have thought, although I'm a bachelor, I'm certainly not gay. I'm still, alas, waiting for the ideal lady. And, to be entirely cynical, as one gets older, the field gets wider. Although I'm not attractive per se, my very rarity value should make me less resistible, if not, I'm afraid, irresistible.

'Perhaps now I'm in the clear, I should ask her out to dinner. It would be nice to see her smile. To make her smile. Her face is very sad in repose, isn't it, as if she's suffered in her life. Well, of course, being a detective you must see things — well, like your own injuries, my dear — that horrify you. And to survive, you must toughen up. I shouldn't think she suffers fools gladly. She has a way of raising one eyebrow that expresses the most exquisite cynicism.

'But she didn't seem cynical about my visiting you. She seemed touched, moved, even as if she couldn't imagine doing it herself. Don't get me wrong. It's just that she sees you as a case rather than a person.

She can't empathise with your situation, for all she sympathises with it. She spent a long time asking me how I found you — that sort of thing. And she does want to talk to me again. She thinks that anything, everything I say might help lead her to your murderer.

'Oh, dear. I'd better explain.

'Now, you may have been wondering why the police should be interested in the case again after all this time. There's talk of a court case to permit the medical staff here to cease treating you. To let your body die. So you see, if your brain, any corner of it, is still alive, you must, must let me know.'

CHAPTER FIFTEEN

Back in the car, Fran buried her face in her hands while the flush washed over her. Why hadn't she thought of that? The simple explanation, that it was Elise's kind rescuer who was visiting her. She must be losing it, losing it completely. How on earth could she tell Mark, let alone the Chief, that she hadn't asked the hospital staff to ask the man simply to identify himself?

Or had she?

Hadn't she asked Penn to find out who he was, the very first time she'd encountered him? He'd said something about a dating agency. That was right. She rooted through her bag for her notebook. Yes, there it was. The summary of their conversation. Thank goodness for all the years of police discipline that made the taking of notes automatic.

This must be what growing old did. It chiselled away at your memory till you could no longer trust it. Then it atrophied altogether, until all you could remember were things from your youth that were much better buried. Like the time she'd put her hair up for the first time and her mother had told her she looked like a scraped earwig. Perhaps she had. But every girl in the class had her hair up that term, and in retrospect she couldn't have looked any worse than some of them. Or she couldn't, if she'd ever put it up again.

Where on earth had that come from?

* * *

She had the whole evening at her cottage at her disposal, once she'd done a quick supermarket shop. The trouble with living her dual life was that she either bought too much or ran out early. One answer would be to batch cook as she did for her parents, but one marathon cooking session a fortnight was more than enough. Ready meals had been the answer till she discovered the salt and additive content: now she indulged herself on Mondays only, when loading the microwave and the washing machine were the only things she could manage. On Tuesdays she used to buy a steak and a bag of salad. But someone in the canteen had come up with the theory that there was more chlorine in the ready-washed salad than in a swimming pool. That seemed a mite exaggerated, but her informant was positive, and one thing her police career had told her was that rumours mostly had a modicum of truth. Now it was steak and do-it-yourself salad, most of which would go to waste. There were weeks when she got round to putting it into a plastic box for her lunch one day, but she usually forgot, and had in any case always prided herself on eating with her colleagues. Gossip, companionship, simply being part of a team: all were important in an organisation like the police.

At least the cottage gleamed, even if it was with someone else's effort. When her parents had become frail she'd not hesitated to take on a cleaner, a woman her own age who'd have made the TV team look rank amateurs. The only guilt she felt was when she cast off her shoes in one direction and slung her jacket and bag in another. G and T time. A double. There. Time to try to relax.

Except the phone light was flashing. Pa? Stomach churning bitter bile, she could scarcely bear to press the ICM button. In fact, the swig of gin was coming back. Now.

She made it to the downstairs loo. She should have mentioned this habit of her stomach's to little Doctor Jennings yesterday, shouldn't she? Only to be told to drink more milk and less gin? Not bloody likely.

Returning with a glass of water and a biscuit even drier than it was supposed to be, she stared at the red light. Time to do the deed.

She couldn't.

Tumbling the carrier bag, steak, salad and all, into the fridge, she staggered upstairs and, stripping her clothes off and leaving them where they fell, she abandoned herself to bed and the embrace of the duvet.

* * *

The answerphone light was still blinking in the morning, the baleful eye of a malign messenger. She dabbed the erase button. She'd phone Pa from work, which would cut short the conversation. Then, knowing it was too late, she dialled 1471. She smacked her face: the number wasn't her parents' after all. It was one she didn't recognise. Flushing like a dull schoolgirl, she called the number, ready to make a foolish apology. All she got was a standard recorded voice, not the owner's, so she was none the wiser. She was damned if she would grovel to a standard recorded BT voice. So she made a note of the number, resolving to try it later.

She should have eaten. What, other than an empty stomach, could she blame for reeling as if she'd been struck in the face when she looked for Mark's car and saw only his space? But she had to pull herself together: a uniform superintendent was waving at her, and she forced her legs to walk in step with him, making her mouth respond to his chatter. She didn't register any of it, too preoccupied with wondering what had happened to Mark and why she should be so very concerned. She'd not bothered to iron the crumpled mess of yesterday's suit, but hung it up to look after itself, found another and driven well over the speed limit so she wouldn't keep him waiting. And now he wasn't there.

Perhaps breakfast would deal with some of the wobbliness. She'd not eaten, after all, since yesterday lunchtime. So she threw her jacket into her office and headed straight to the canteen. It was unusually thin of company, but a solitary meal suited her this morning. A kind enquiry about her health might well have made her cry. Bother the healthy option this morning. She needed comfort food, and what was more comforting than scrambled eggs on fresh toast? Ever since she'd found out who organised the Christmas collection for her and her colleagues, the canteen manageress had been even more particular on the matter of toast.

Fran always emptied her pigeonhole, grateful that in recent days it hadn't heaved and bulged with quite so many directives and policy statements spewed out by the Home Office. This time, apart from agendas and minutes for two of her pet working parties, there was just one internal mail envelope, addressed in familiar writing. Mark's. In the past, envelopes from him had held everything from news of Superintendents' Association meetings to firmly worded unofficial rebukes. The memory of the latter brought the blood rushing again. And unbidden and unwonted tears.

The envelope stared at her from her desk, almost as malevolent as the answerphone had been. Open it? What about checking her emails first?

For heaven's sake!

She tore at the Sellotape to find a handwritten note.

Dear Fran

I hoped you'd ring back last night but you must have been out. I just wanted— something crossed heavily through —to tell you that I've been called away on a damned Working Party deputising for the Chief. But whatever happens our weekend trip stands. Promise. I'll try and call you this evening or tomorrow to fix times, etc.

In greatest haste

Mark

So what, she asked her reflection as she cleaned her teeth in the ladies' loo, should she make of that? Nothing, she told herself. Nothing more than a kind colleague confirming an arrangement. No, not with the word *promise* standing on its own like that. He meant it.

He meant it.

She could stand tall — she seemed to be sagging more and more these days — and plan her day. Which must include tackling her make-up again. The merciless down-lighting made her lids look heavier, almost as if one was drooping over her eye.

But it wasn't her make-up that was at fault. It was her flesh. She gripped the washbasin for support. Surely not. Not tortoise eyes like her mother's. Please God, no. And look at her neck. It wasn't stringy, or anything like it, but she'd never seen the skin look so dry. There, if she tensed her chin, it all looked a bit better. But you couldn't go through life jutting your chin. The sooner she got to her favourite cosmetics counter the better.

Was this why women submitted to Botox? To the surgeon's knife? Not because they didn't want to grow old, but because they didn't want to grow like their mothers?

Pulling herself firmly upright, she produced a bright smile for a couple of women just coming in. They were uniformed sergeants she'd long ago worked with and ready for a gossip: one of them was flashing photos of her daughter's wedding. At last, as detail piled on detail, Fran was more pleased than she cared to admit to have to stride back to her office. She had a day to plan. A woman to identify. A murderer to run to earth.

After doing all they could, her colleagues had rightly put out a call via the TV Crime Watch programme. This morning she watched the video for herself. There was an e-fit of an unattractive square-jawed woman with cropped grey hair. She looked more like a witch to run from than anyone's favourite granny. Or, given the poor woman's circumstances, perhaps great aunt would be a better comparison.

There had been very few calls in response: it wouldn't take long to read through all the transcripts for herself. Anything said to be from Minnie Mouse could be safely discounted, but that was all. The files showed the previous team had been pretty conscientious. They'd made a follow-up call to a man in Scotland thinking it might be his missing sister, but the age was quite wrong, and the colour of the eyes. What about this one from a woman from Hythe who said she's seen a similar blonde woman on the road in question driving a very expensive sports car, very slowly? What about her indeed! Eventually the team had discounted her evidence because she insisted the woman was blonde. Some idiot must have forgotten that when she'd arrived in A and E, before her head was shorn, Elise was just that. Fran was on her feet punching the air even as she checked the woman's details. Ms Sheila Downs. She was a middle-aged teacher, so she probably had an eye for faces. Yes, definitely one for a follow-up visit, this.

It was a good job she hadn't joined the police expecting anything easy. The contact number was unobtainable. A call to BT elicited the news that it had been disconnected when the customer moved house.

'What's the new number?'

'That was in Hythe.'

Yes! 'Was?'

'That's disconnected too, now. And she has no new number.'

At least she talked the Hythe address out of them. To go and doorstep herself or get someone else on to the case? Much as she was tempted to go out on what seemed a fine autumn morning, she thought her time would be better spent talking to Alan Pitt again. In any case, there was young Tom Arkwright, raring to go after his disappointment with his attempts to match DNA from recent crimes.

'I can't understand it, ma'am. All the books say a vicious attack like that's rarely a one-off. You don't suppose he was so overcome with remorse that he's topped himself?'

She beamed. 'Something else for you to check. Any male suicides in the region since the date of the assault. Or — yes — any male deaths. Meanwhile, it's a nice fine day. I want you to trace a possible witness for me. Here's her last address. Sniff round the neighbours, get on to the Post Office, check electoral roles — whatever it takes.'

'Ma'am.' The lad was virtually donning his Superman outfit.

'But you do no more than discover her new address. You don't go and see if she's in. You don't even dream of talking to her yourself. I'm sorry,' she added, with a rueful grin. 'Your time for a great breakthrough will come. But this is my call, Tom.'

'OK, guv'nor. I mean, *yes, ma'am.*'

'You mean, *OK, guv'nor*,' she laughed. 'Be off with you. It's a nice morning. Drive slowly enough to enjoy it. And call me immediately with any news.'

Meanwhile, she addressed herself to her talk to Alan Pitt. Would it be too intimidating to bring him over to police headquarters to question him? It would certainly be more private than that tip he called his office, where each available surface seemed to be covered with photocopies or notes. What terrible working conditions — and, specifically, what a fire hazard. When she'd done guest lectures at universities all over the country, she'd been somewhat feted, and had never realised what conditions might be the lot of the average academic foot soldier.

Talking to him here in this immaculate newly-decorated den might rub salt in, especially as he was hardly to know that the average copper had conditions more like his — with probably even more paperwork. There was a café out at the university, recently refurbished, but she feared it would never reach its aspirations of being a chic watering hole. In any case, it was hardly private enough. She wanted him so relaxed that he remembered things he didn't even know he'd observed.

He roared with laughter when she suggested over the phone that they might find a free seminar room. 'We'd be trampled to death in the rush for anywhere quiet and empty. How about here at my bungalow? Out on the Whitstable road?'

* * *

'What a very pleasant place this is,' Fran said truthfully, looking around in appreciation at the ceiling to floor bookshelves, a good hi-fi and a set of comfortable-looking but not matching chairs. On the walls were what looked like original paintings, not quite representational but not abstract either. Dressed in clean jeans and a plain navy jumper with a shirt underneath, he had the air of having spruced himself up slightly for the occasion. Certainly this time his shoes had been polished. He produced good tea — over the years she'd become a connoisseur of tea — in china cups. The biscuits were homemade. Half of her male colleagues would have decided he was a classic gay. She wasn't so sure. But she wondered why he should have chosen a twenties bungalow on a main road. It didn't seem in keeping with at least her preconceptions of what an academic would choose — a neat, terraced house or a cottage with a sea view. Perhaps he'd inherited it from his parents and simply stuck there. What would happen when both her parents died? Would she stay down in Devon, as she'd thought she would — or was there something in Mark's fears? Should she start regarding it as a temporary upheaval? Would that make it more or less bearable?

'There was a rumour,' Alan began, sitting opposite her on the sofa and crossing his legs, 'that the case was ongoing.' Then he sat forward, as if admitting that his relaxation was feigned. 'It's true, then, that they want to let her die?'

'If she isn't dead already. The part of her that makes her Elise anyway,' Fran agreed. 'Personally in her condition I'd want to die. I can understand people like her who still have powers of communication wishing to choose the moment of their dying, but . . .' She tailed off, shaking her head.

'It's a terrible responsibility — finally ending it.'

'Which is why the medics have to fight the case in court. I have nothing at all to do with that process, as I said yesterday. All I want to do is track down whoever committed what today is grievous bodily harm, aggravated assault, aggravated rape, et cetera, et cetera, and in a few months may well be murder. Which is where you come in.' She smiled, but not reassuringly enough.

Swallowing hard, he asked, 'Should I have my solicitor present?'

'If you want to. But the DNA tests at the time absolutely cleared you, as I thought you'd been told.'

'If the case is being re-opened . . . ?'

'As far as I'm concerned, you're a decent man who did his best in terrible circumstances. If other evidence comes to light, then of course you may need legal representation, but I assure you I'm talking to you as a witness, not a suspect.'

Although by now she practically had his original statement by heart, not to mention transcripts of the increasingly hostile questionings he'd undergone, she asked him to tell his story once more.

'Indulge me,' she said firmly as he protested. 'Talk to me as a simple acquaintance, not someone who's desperate to put you in the frame. You? Correction: *anyone* in the frame. To be honest, I'm as interested in discovering who Elise is as finding her killer.'

'Truly?'

She pondered, focussing on a silver tea caddy. 'That's beautiful, isn't it? I hope you've got it insured,' she said, parenthetically. 'I don't think we shall find the killer till we've found the victim. Do you?'

'You mean it wasn't just a random opportunistic crime?'

She'd decided to be as frank with him as she dared. After all, he was the nearest Elise had to a friend. 'The modus operandi doesn't fit anyone on the file at the time, and no one we've picked up since has confessed to it. Of course, we're checking crimes committed since, too. But let's just say, I have a hunch this guy knew our Elise — in some capacity or other, no matter how slight.'

'*Our Elise* — when neither of us has so much as heard her speak!'

'Don't you feel a proprietary interest in her?'

He dropped his eyes, nodding.

'What do you talk about? The hospital staff say you spend quite long periods at her side.'

'It's to assuage my guilt.' He dropped his eyes to his hands, worrying a wart.

'Your guilt! For not managing to resuscitate her? Heavens, Alan, most people wouldn't even have tried.'

'Or would have left well alone. I'd never done it for real, you see.'

'You tried. You did your best. Which is all any of us can do in this life.' That was a thought to reflect on later. 'Let's go back a few moments before you found her. Tell me about that.'

He bridled. 'You want me to tell you about needing a wee!'

Even that was an interesting choice of vocabulary. 'Even before your bladder needed emptying. Tell me about your drive.'

He rolled his eyes. 'This is going over old ground, Dr Harman.'

'Not with me. Tell me about the place you'd left, the journey, where you were going.'

He flung up his hands. 'Oy vey! Again already!' In his normal voice he said, 'I'd been to a physiotherapist in Hythe. She just happens to be the best one I know, that was why I go all the way down there when there must, as your colleagues were intent on proving, be plenty of other perfectly good ones in Canterbury. Of course it isn't convenient, especially if the weather is inclement. And the B2067 is far from the most direct route to Whitstable, but I wasn't returning to Whitstable that evening. I was going to visit a friend in Woodchurch, as your colleagues established.'

She held up a placatory hand. 'I'm not doubting you or querying what you say in any way. What was the weather like?'

'Cold. Dark. The clocks had just gone back. Threads of mist. It's not a nice road at the best of times. I'd been listening to Classic FM till it got too damned relaxing for words and I switched on to Radio Three.'

'What was on?'

'Some sort of musical news. I switched back to Classic FM. Ironically they were playing "Fur Elise". And no, Dr Harman, I don't think that was why I heard her give that as her name. Her lips moved, the sound came out — poor Elise.'

Poor Elise; 'Fur Elise'. With all those teeth broken or missing it must have been impossible to speak clearly, even had she been conscious of having wanted to. Could what everyone thought was her name really be nothing of the sort? 'This is obviously very upsetting for you—'

'Irritating, not upsetting. I don't see how any of this can possibly help.'

'Neither do I — yet. But it may, Dr Pitt, it may. That's why I think it's important enough to write down.' She flourished her pad and pencil.

'Don't patronise me, woman.' His eyes blazed. 'I'm sorry. If only all this wasn't my fault!' He pulled himself to his feet and started to pace. Pulled, not sprang — it looked as if he'd needed that physiotherapy and might again.

'Please sit down, Alan. And get this idea of fault and blame out of your head. The only one to blame in all this is the man who virtually killed and then raped her. In that order.'

The shock tactic worked. He wheeled round. 'You mean — he . . . a body . . . ?'

She nodded, face as callous as she could make it. 'We're looking for a very unpleasant man, Alan. And one whose back's in better condition than yours. Elise was no lightweight, was she? I can't see you socking her and lugging her out of sight and still being able to bend down to rape her.

OK, let's get back to that evening. Without embellishment, if you please. You drove along a narrow and unpleasant road in difficult conditions. What about other traffic? Please, sit down and reflect. Do you recall any lights coming towards you? Having to move over because someone was driving badly or in a hurry? Was anyone parked?'

He shook his head. 'I even tried hypnotism to help me remember. Nothing. Zilch. Zero. Just the removal lorry, that's all.'

She dredged her memory. Surely it had only been described as a lorry before. Now it was a removal lorry. But now wasn't the time to prod his memory any further. As if to stretch her own back — and why not? The chairs might look expensive, but hers didn't match her spine — she got up and prowled round, pausing by a couple of CDs. They lay on top of a set of neatly labelled drawers; perhaps the mess in his office hadn't been his.

'This was the one they recommended on the radio the other weekend, wasn't it?' She held up a recording of Mozart violin and viola duos.

His face brightened. 'I didn't know you were a musician. What do you play?'

'Only the CD player. What about you?'

'The viola. I used to. But my back . . . I was in constant pain.'

'They have some very good concerts out at the university. With that wonderful string quartet, the ones who play standing up.'

'Ah, the Brodsky. Are you a regular concert-goer?'

'It depends on work. I used to be on the Canterbury Festival Committee, but . . .' There were only so many times you could send apologies. Not that it was work that prevented her going, of course, or being a governor at the village school, or being a trustee of a battered wives' hostel. 'Theatre, too,' she said, trying to make her voice bright. 'For all the Marlowe has such a small stage, I've seen some excellent productions there.'

'Maybe we should . . . when this—' He stopped suddenly, the inviting smile fading.

He'd only been about to suggest they went together, hadn't he? She suppressed a rebuff. But she took it as another indication of his innocence. Would she do better to interpret it as a sign that he considered himself impregnable? She offered a noncommittal nod. 'I suppose you wouldn't remember the name on the removal lorry?'

He pulled a face. 'Actually, I suppose it was more like a horsebox. A bit nearer the ground than an ordinary removal lorry. But I don't recall a name. Sorry. Just that there were some curtains over the front window, not the windscreen, the one over the cab. As if people could sleep in it.'

This time she wandered over to a glass-fronted cabinet full of china. 'Now, I've only ever seen this at antiques fairs.' She didn't add it had such a huge price on its head she'd left it where it was. In any case, it was the wrong period for the cottage.

'Ruskin. Made near Birmingham at the turn of the last century. Are you a collector, Dr Harman?'

'Tunbridge wear.'

She was delighted to see his eyebrows shoot up in recognition. 'I picked up a work-basket on my last outing. I'm desperate for a spectacle case; I saw one once at a fair, but told myself it was too pricey. It wasn't of course.' But her parents, in those days still mobile enough for the occasional day out, had been scandalised by the figures on the ticket, and though she knew she could have haggled for cash, she'd had to leave it. And of course, when she'd phoned the dealer, it had gone. 'Were the curtains open or drawn?'

'They must have been drawn or I wouldn't have noticed, not in the dark. There must have been some light on, mustn't there? So it must have been parked facing me.'

That would fit in with the forensic examination of the scene. Suddenly she was very interested in the lorry.

'When you looked in your mirror, was the tailgate up or down?'

'Up. I think.' He bit his lip. 'Yes, it was just pulling away.'

'Lights?'

'The driver'd not got round to putting them on. Not until I'd driven past. They went on when I checked again in the mirror.'

None of this was recorded in any of his statements: she'd bet her pension on that.

'And then?'

'I stopped to take the phone call from one of my colleagues — we were worried about one of our students. He thought she might be pregnant.'

'By him?'

'Really, Dr Harman! Yes, by him. It happens, Dr Harman, it happens. And before you say anything, it's not always the lecturer's fault, believe me. I don't approve and I never will approve, because it's a misuse of power if the lecturer takes the lead and can result in all sorts of accusations of favouritism anyway. But sometimes — let's just say that the temptation is very strong.'

She let him talk on. This time she had the strongest feeling he was lying, that the pregnancy was his responsibility. But scaring or antagonising him over a matter almost certainly irrelevant wasn't on her agenda. 'So you pulled over to take the call — for which I award you a batch of brownie points, Dr Pitt — and then decided you needed a pee.'

'I'd just finished watering the hedge, as Shakespeare says, when I thought I heard a noise. I thought it was a trapped animal, I suppose. So I went back to the car and turned the headlights full on — I'd left them in parking mode before, just enough to pick my way through to the hedge. Not enough for anyone to see what I was up to. I didn't want to be done for indecent exposure, did I?'

Would that worry the average man? But she wasn't there to concern herself with him. Not this time, at least. 'So it was pretty brave of you to look.'

'I've never thought of myself as brave. No, more likely I'd have called the RSPCA. What else are mobiles for? Except to call the emergency services when you find a dead woman.'

‘Was it they who suggested mouth to mouth?’

‘I don’t know. No. I was already trying. But it didn’t seem to be doing a lot of good so I asked them if I was doing it right. I kept it up until the ambulance arrived. It seemed forever. I’m sure there’ll be a record of how long they took. Another statistic for their league tables.’

He was right. Twelve minutes and forty seconds if her memory was correct. The police had arrived almost simultaneously: what would he make of that?

‘While the paramedics worked on her, I stood and watched and wondered how on earth I’d been able to touch her, let alone do what I’d done. All that blood. The police hustled me away but I could still see. The poor woman, decked out in her best suit and new shoes, and she wouldn’t have looked out of place in the worst and most violent movie. Snuff movies, don’t they call them? I knew that whoever had done all that damage, inflicted what even I could see were horrific injuries was sick, Dr Harman. But not — sex after she was practically dead.’

‘I’ll get you some water.’

Without particular haste — she didn’t really expect him to throw up or faint — she located Habitat tumblers in a cupboard. He’d recently gone for a Shaker look, all the fittings new and clean-lined. Good to work in, she surmised, but not particularly in keeping with the rest of the bungalow.

‘Here.’

‘Thank you.’ He sipped fastidiously. ‘You’ve no idea how hard I’ve tried to bury the memory of all this.’

‘Perhaps now it’s truly in the open you’ll be able to get rid of it. Like lancing a boil.’ Far, by now, from needing to know, she asked, ‘What was she wearing?’ Perhaps his answer might illuminate him as much as Elise.

‘A smart suit. The sort I’ve seen women her age wear to interviews. Very conventional — not the sort to offend with the sharpness of its cut. And I remember looking at her feet. She was still wearing one shoe, a smart patent affair. But not as smart as she’d have us believe. You know those shoes for older ladies, with elastic here and there — that sort. And the heel not very high, but shaped to look as if it was.'

Fran hid her feet as best she could. 'They were brand-new,' she said.

'I've often wondered, what the people at the job interview thought, when she didn't turn up. Though it was a bit late to be on your way to an interview. Perhaps she got the job and they're wondering why she never turned up.'

'What sort of job?'

He shrugged. 'We're getting into the realms of speculation, Dr Harman.'

She didn't jib. She might in other circumstances have used exactly the same words.

'Of course. But you saw her face, her hair, her clothes . . .'

'She'd have been a bit old, come to think of it, for changing jobs. I don't know. What age do you take on a new pub manageress? Or to come down the food chain, a new barmaid?'

'A barmaid!' Only now did she admit to herself how much she'd hoped he'd go against Verity Kilvert's judgement.

'You baulk at the idea? It looked from the poor woman's hands as if she spent most of her life washing up. So I'd promoted her from my original idea that she might be a charlady. Though I don't know why she shouldn't be a cleaning lady. Mine writes romantic novels that don't sell. Very well educated. Oxford. But she doesn't give a damn about her hands. She gardens too. Perhaps Elise did. But I'm not telling you anything new, am I, Dr Harman? I can tell from your face that I'm not. Tell me what you want me to say and I'll say that, if it pleases you!'

Was he flirting with her? He wasn't unattractive, she supposed, but was somehow indefinably not her type. Even if Mark hadn't been on the scene, she wouldn't have felt even a *frisson* of attraction.

'I don't want to be pleased. I just want every smidgen of information you can give.'

'Believe me, that's it. I've thought about it — still think about it, however much I try not to — so often that sometimes I suspect it's not a memory of an event I've conjured up but the memory of a speculation.'

'The removal lorry?' Please God don't let that be a phantom.

He rubbed his face as if trying to keep awake. 'I don't know where that came from. Left brain, they call it, don't they? Actually, according to research, it's actually at the very base of the brain, the primitive part. The part they used for telling stories round the campfire while sabre toothed tigers prowled outside. That primitive.' Suddenly he looked her straight in the eye. 'I wonder if that part of Elise's brain is still alive? And what night terrors she's keeping at bay with her tales?'

CHAPTER SIXTEEN

'I almost asked her out, Elise. Can you imagine that? Asking the most senior police officer I've ever come across out for a date! Why not, you may ask. Well, I'm not in the clear yet, of course, whatever she may say to the contrary. And I'm not the sort of man to wish to ally myself with anyone wearing uniform. Very well, she's plain clothes these days, and very stylishly so: she was wearing a different suit today, in a sort of subdued plum, and if anything it suited her even better than the black one. Trouser suit. She's got the height to wear trousers, legs right up to her armpits as we used to say. She might even look good in an ordinary suit, but I've yet to meet the woman who does. They all look like middle-aged schoolmistresses or shop manageresses up for promotion. I wonder why such ladies prefer the noun with such gender connotations, why they're not simply managers. I don't mean to offend, Elise, not when you were clearly in your best suit when I found you. It was a mistake, I'm afraid. That colour didn't do anything for you at all. Greens and browns: they're your colours. Muted. You should never have considered anything bright: it must have aged you the moment you put it on. The trouble is that as you get older you must wear the colours that like you, not the colours you like.

'Fran — I prefer to think of her as Frances, though I meticulously address her as Dr Harman, and not, as you'll notice, as Chief Superintendent Harman — shares so many of my interests. Music and

china for a start. Theatre. And her turn of phrase, her vocabulary: she's an educated woman, not a country plod. She's good at her job, from what I've seen — well, she must be. You don't see many women of her age so high up in the police force, do you? As soon as she'd gone, I looked her up on the Internet, just on the off-chance, you know? I found her in all sorts of places. Seems she's been on this, that and the other working party. Her name kept on cropping up in murder cases and then stopped — I suppose she got promoted above such mundane tasks as solving crime. So why's she doing it now? It'd be like asking our esteemed Vice Chancellor to come and mark a few first-year exams. There's got to be a reason. I hate not knowing what it is. Maybe it's something to do with her parents — she asked about mine, and I told her they'd left me the bungalow. She said hers were both sick and she spent most weekends with them. I'll have to ask her next time I see her. Oh, yes, I'm sure I've not seen the last of her. And if she doesn't contact me I can always phone and tell her I've remembered something else.

'Goodness me, I wouldn't lie. Not after the way she wormed information out of me today. She's good. Very good. And I know she suspects I had more to do with Naomi's pregnancy than I let on. God, they talk about moments of madness. I wonder why she bothered seducing me, eh, Elise? Not for my looks or for anything I could do for her grade-wise. Not like my prof when I was an undergraduate. The women reckoned he wouldn't put them forward to do an MA or PhD unless he shagged them. I'm sorry if the term shocks you, but it always seemed to me appropriate for mere casual coupling. Things are different these days, at least at universities like ours: we have continuous assessment and standardisation meetings all designed to prevent favouritism. In fact, I've got a meeting later this afternoon likely to go on forever, which is why I came in now.

'Did you ever go to university? And if you did, what did you study? Somehow I've got you down as more the stay-at-home type, cooking Yorkshire pudding for your husband and sons. But you don't wear a ring, do you? I wonder if they removed it when you were in A and E. I ought to remember. Frances would help me. She did today. Or was that Recovered *Memory Syndrome, I wonder — and totally unreliable?'*

CHAPTER SEVENTEEN

Although she naturally had a hands-free mobile phone set-up, Fran always preferred, having helped scrape up the remains of those who'd been more interested in their caller than in traffic conditions, to pull over to take a call.

'Tom?' She tried to sound cool and official, but surely he'd only call if he had something to report.

'Ma'am, I've found her.' Yes! 'The witness, ma'am. The one that was in Hythe. I've found the house and everything. Ms Downs. Only it seems she's a Mrs Adams these days. A bit old to change her name, like.'

The young, God bless them. What on earth would Tom think of her feelings for Mark? That they were nigh on obscene, probably. 'Does everything include a new address and phone number?'

'Everything. She'd left all her details with a neighbour. Do you want me to call her, like?'

She asked, 'What did I say, Tom?' Would she sound stern or merely as if she was trying not to laugh indulgently?

'To leave everything to you, like. But seeing as how you're busy—'

'I've just stopped being busy. I'm just about to leave the A299 and pick up the M2 back towards Maidstone.'

'In that case I should stay on the M2, ma'am, if you want to talk to her yourself. Seems she's up in the Midlands, like. Kenilworth. You know, like the book.'

She was astounded that Tom should have heard of the novel, let alone relate to it. But she'd talk to him about Scott on another occasion. 'Perhaps you'd better give me her phone number. It's a long way to go just on the off-chance.' She wrote it down and read it back. It was something she'd always been meticulous about, ever since a senior officer in one of her teams had arrested a man with the same name as the one they wanted living in Moreton Street, not Moreton Avenue. 'Meanwhile, could you get me a traffic report on the motorways? I might as well take the route with fewest hold-ups.'

Waiting for his return call, she was so anxious to tap in the numbers he'd given her she fluffed a couple. Instead of cursing, she laughed at herself. She'd often done it when she was an active detective, not a pen-pusher — got so worked up and absorbed in the chase that her hands sweated and her fingers trembled. But at last she got the digits in the right order and pressed the call button.

She was rewarded not only by a ringing tone but, before she could even cross her fingers, by a man's voice giving his number. Yes, it was the same as the one Tom had dictated. The male half of what she presumed was the new Adams duo.

'Could I speak to Mrs Adams?'

'Who is it, please?'

Caution, but not a negative: a good sign. She gave her details and explained what it was in connection with. When he didn't reply immediately, she held her breath, just as if she were a child waiting to see which way the Christmas turkey wishbone would break.

'She'll be back in about ten minutes,' he conceded, without apparent enthusiasm. 'But she told your colleagues all she knew, which wasn't, I suppose, all that much and to be honest, they weren't terribly interested.'

'I know they weren't. But I suspect they might have been mistaken. I can't tell, however, till I talk to your wife.'

'What did you say your name was? Your rank, rather?'

She repeated what she'd said before, to be rewarded by a low whistle, not loud enough to hurt the ears.

'They are bringing out the big guns, aren't they?'

'I like to keep my hand in,' she said evenly. 'Now, will she be in for the rest of the day? Because, if it isn't inconvenient, I really should like to talk to her. Face to face,' she added firmly.

* * *

Nigel and Sheila Adams, in their detached modern house, exemplified the very middle of middle England. The *Guardian* lay on the coffee table next to the catalogue of the latest Royal Academy exhibition. In the kitchen was a range of Fair Trade coffees and teas, while there were his and hers Audis parked side by side on the wide drive. They'd welcomed her politely when she arrived at about five-thirty and ensured she was given tea and homemade biscuits and pointed to the loo. He withdrew into a far corner of the room with the crossword, as if making the point that he was not there to interfere but would leap to his wife's protection if necessary.

Fran found it rather touching. She could imagine — and to her chagrin she blushed — Mark doing exactly the same.

'You're reopening the Elise case?' Sheila Adams prompted her.

'Yes. As I told your husband, there are very good reasons.' She paused. The two exchanged a swift and tender smile before he returned to his paper and a thesaurus.

'Which are?' Sheila asked coolly.

'The medics want permission to let her die.'

'The best thing they could do, surely.' After a moment, she added, 'But it would mean that you people would be looking for a murderer, rather than letting the hunt for a rapist go tepid, if not cold.'

'Exactly. Which is why they've asked me to cast a fresh pair of eyes over the evidence. Yours struck me as interesting.'

'Your colleagues clearly thought I'd lost it in a cloud of middle-aged confusion,' Sheila Adams smiled. 'But even oldies keep their eyesight. Some of it.'

'And what did you see? Exactly?'

'What I said in my statement.' There was a hint of challenge, as if she suspected Fran of not doing her homework.

'Your statement will have been filtered by whoever wrote it down, adding as he went his own interpretation, not to mention grammatical slips and spelling errors. What I'd like is for you to tell it all over again in your own words.'

Mrs Adams flung out her hands in a gesture of exasperated surrender. 'I was proceeding in an easterly direction — no? OK. I was driving from Hastings to Hythe, on the A259. Do you know the road? For an A road it's a disgrace, all bends and adverse cambers and straight stretches which are a positive invitation to put your foot down but end in blind right-angle bends. A horror of a road.'

Fran nodded in agreement and encouragement.

'If you get stuck behind a lorry, you resign yourself to staying behind it forever. It's so bad that occasionally I used to go via Tenterden and Ashford, but that road's not a lot better and it's a lot further round. One particular evening, soon after the clocks went back, so it was already dark when I left school—'

'You were a teacher?'

'The head of a failing school, jetted in to sort it out. I didn't. It involved long hell-filled hours and an infinite desire to get home as quickly as I could. So when I saw this brand-new Lotus in front of me, my heart leapt.'

'Brand-new?'

'Well, it had those double letter prefixes to the registration number, and it was showroom clean.'

'Brand-new indeed. Sorry.'

'No problem. Now, where was I? You've induced a senior moment, Chief Superintendent. Yes, I thought it would rocket along, and I could use its tail and brake lights to guide me. But it was far worse than any lorry. Crawl? It was more of a stagger. All over the road, not dipping lights until too late, breaking sharply. A nightmare. Some drunken lout chatting into his mobile, I thought. And then, just before the Brenzett island, she pulled over and parked. Yes, it was a woman. Not on the phone. She looked scared stiff. As terrified as I would if asked to ride a bucking bronco.'

'Age?' Fran hoped she sounded cool; she didn't feel it.

'Late fifties. Blonde hair. And naked fear all over her face. The funny thing is, I'd always secretly fancied a car like that — you know, testosterone on wheels. This one wasn't red, though, which is what I'd have had, but a nice cheerful yellow. A yellow Lotus: imagine that.' She sighed with imagined pleasure.

Over in his corner, her husband snorted quietly. 'Imagine getting in and out with your back.'

'And yours!' Sheila retorted.

'I suppose you wouldn't remember which model?' But Fran knew the answer before she heard it.

'Yes. An Elise.'

* * *

She hadn't punched the air or offered anyone a high five, but Fran must have given away her delight. So much so that she found a bottle of sherry waved before her nose and the offer of supper hanging in the air.

'Go on,' Sheila urged. 'You've got a long drive back. You shouldn't risk it on an empty stomach. And we've got plenty. I always cater for an army. And then Nigel drifts along and cooks a bit more, only better. So long as you like curry, that is? But we're both trying to lose weight so there won't be a sweet, just fruit.'

Fran couldn't imagine anything better, and said so. 'But there's a protocol about fraternising with witnesses in a possible murder case and I can't do what I wouldn't tolerate in one of my team, can I?'

'As a head I used to do things I wouldn't let a junior teacher do, but I suppose that wasn't a matter of life and death. I do understand. When the case is over, perhaps.'

'Yes, please — I'd really like that.' Fran meant it: apart from instantly liking the pair of them, it was good to network, and Sheila was just the sort of woman she'd like to involve on working parties to reduce teenage crime. She said so. 'Unless you're officially retired?'

'Work's fine so long as it doesn't get in the way of pleasure,' Sheila declared. 'All my life I've been beholden to other people. My parents, my teachers, at university. And just when you think you're in charge in the classroom, you realise you're at the very bottom of the pile. I suppose it wasn't so bad when I started, but as government got more and more interventionist — and there are good reasons why they had to, I suppose—'

'Best practice,' Fran nodded.

'Quite. Assuming, of course, that best practice is something the government knows about. Like this latest idea of taking the teachers out of the classroom — which is where they want to be, for God's sake — and letting them mark and prepare while someone else teaches! I daresay it's the same in the police: which is why I find it strange that someone of your rank should be talking to a lowly witness. You should be behind a big desk pushing bits of paper for the Home Secretary.'

Fran smiled her appreciation of the irony. It was tempting to share all her problems: this was a woman with whom she could have shared life stories over a glass of wine. But the motorway called. As she gathered herself together, she asked, 'What pleasure are you pursuing? I'd hate to interrupt anything vital with a murder trial.'

'Any pleasure I fancy.' She shot a sideways glance at her husband that spoke of love and companionship and fun. 'When you're young, Fran — it is OK to call you that? — when you're young, falling in love is as common as breathing. You do it all the time, as often as you can. When you're — let's call it mature! — it's not like that. You feel it's such a rare, precious experience, you mustn't waste a moment.' Fran nodded: she'd had much the same sentiments. 'So far we've watched whales — yes, we watched Wales, too, at the Millennium Stadium! — and swum with dolphins and played tennis as the sun rose over Madeira and flown down the Grand Canyon and drunk champagne at private views and promenaded at the Albert Hall. And that's just this year, since we got married. Nigel works from home — he's an accountant, though you wouldn't think it to look at him, would you? And I do exam marking in a vain effort to maintain A Level standards. But we just want to be together.'

'Children? Parents?' Fran prompted.

'Children, his and hers, are blessedly in Australia and America respectively, so they don't pester and his will provide us with accommodation during the next Ashes tour. Parents. There's the rub. His were in Plymouth, mine in Liverpool. It was OK while there were two of each, if you see what I mean.'

Fran nodded. 'They sort of hold each other up, don't they?' She put her fingertips together, the palms still apart.

'Yes, just like a house of cards!'

Even the same image!

'But when Dad died, and Mum-in-Law got Alzheimer's things got tricky. So we took the bull by the horns and moved them into homes. No, not where they were — what would be the point of that? Here in the Midlands.'

'All together?' Fran risked.

'If only. No, they have quite different needs. Mum's pretty spry, considering, and she likes to potter in the retirement home's garden. Father-in-Law likes to think he's still looking after Mother-in-Law, but he's losing his sight, so they're in a home with far more care. But we can visit both easily. Problem solved.' She dusted off her hands with finality.

'You never thought of looking after them yourselves?' Fran hoped she didn't sound shocked.

Sheila gave her a look that reduced her to the ranks. 'For a start, which ones? Nigel down in Devon, me up there? And when would Nigel and I have got together? Weekends of passion at a motel on the M5, parents' health permitting? And, our lives apart, we wanted the best care for them. Which would not have been administered by a pair of star-crossed middle-aged lovers with backs too bad to lift anything heavier than a gin glass. Fran, being a dutiful child involves getting the best, not being the most self-indulgent.'

'But what if they want just you? My parents — they live in Devon too, as it happens — don't want to give up their home and their independence: they just want me!' Fran stopped short, aware she was giving away far more then she wanted.

'Mum always used to tell me, "I want doesn't get." That applies to anyone, whatever their age.' Before Fran's eyes Sheila metamorphosed into a headmistress, every inch of her. Whether it was her school days' conditioning, or a painful awareness that she had no right to be arguing or, worst of all, a deep fear that Sheila could be right, she dropped her eyes and said nothing. It was either that or explode.

A glance at her watch and a sniff at the kitchen told her it was time to bow herself briskly out. As they all shook hands, wishing out loud that they'd met in other circumstances, Fran applied herself to the problem of getting home.

* * *

Bone-tired, she nevertheless managed to prise herself out of bed and get into the car park at work for eight-fourteen prompt. Mark was already there, working in his car, just as if he were waiting for her. He'd said nothing about seeing her before their trip on Friday. Indeed, he'd implied that he might have problems with it, but nothing, he'd assured her, that was insuperable. Did this mean he'd come in early to break it to her that the weekend was off? She could feel her lip wobbling. What on earth was wrong with her? She waited till she'd assembled her most competent face.

But no matter how bright her smile, something must have betrayed her. His eyes narrowed as he studied her face. 'Another summons to Devon?' She couldn't work out which voice he used — his senior officer or friend concerned to the point of anger.

'Other end of the country. OK, I exaggerate. Warwickshire. A witness in the Elise case.'

'For Christ's sake, woman, when I asked you to take that on, I didn't want you haring round the countryside even more that you were doing already. Couldn't you have sent one of your team?'

'I wanted the pleasure of unearthing a vital piece of evidence myself,' she said coldly. But her lip trembled again.

He hooked an arm round her shoulders. 'A cup of tea in my room before you even think about breakfast,' he said.

Lest this public kindness reduce her to more unwonted and inexplicable lapses into emotion, she asked in her crispest voice, 'How come you're back today? I thought you were supposed to be incarcerated until late tomorrow.'

'We had a mass rebellion. All terribly polite, of course. We said that if they wanted crime to be fought, we should go back to fight it and let the civil servants write the report.'

'That's risky — leaving it in that sort of hands.'

'We thought about that too — come on, Fran, between us we've spent hundreds of years outwitting people most of whom were a great deal more cunning that your average ex-public school civil servant. They're going to write the report. We're going to edit it. And then get them to rewrite it, in line with our modifications. How's about that?'

'As devious and nasty as I should have expected of you. Well done.' They'd reached the door. As they swiped their security cards, she turned to him. 'If I'm due for a bollocking, it couldn't be after some breakfast, could it?'

He stepped back, letting the door close in front of them. 'Bollocking? Who said anything about a bollocking? I just didn't want you sitting in the canteen with tears dripping into your porridge! Though the Scots do say it should be salt, not sugar, don't they?' His words might have sounded bracing but his tone wasn't. It was kind to the point of tender. 'So tell me about this witness.'

CHAPTER EIGHTEEN

'You'll never guess who I saw when I was out in Maidstone this morning. Oh, I'd been researching something in the Springfield reference library. No, nothing important. At least nothing relevant to this conversation.

'Anyway, I saw none other than the great detective. I'd been using the reference library, some books I couldn't get hold of in the university library. Then I slipped into the big Sainsbury's for a few things. And who should be at the cheese counter but Detective Chief Superintendent Frances Harman. All tarted up, too — I hardly recognised her. And she tarts up well, I tell you. The good policewoman was so transformed I hardly recognised her: hair fashionably and indeed boyishly short, coloured by someone who really knows how to do it, and nicely made-up too. Entirely luscious. I asked her, "Are you off for an interview somewhere?" "Indeed I am, Dr Pitt. Only as you can imagine, it's I who will be doing the interviewing." And she turns on her heel and off she goes. I think I'd better wait a bit before I ask her out, don't you? Till she forgets I've caught her on the skive. But I shan't give up — goodness me no. If I can get hold of a couple of tickets for the Brodsky Quartet — believe me, they're like gold dust — I shall certainly invite her. As luck would have it — and believe me, it was entirely coincidental — we fetched up in the same checkout queue. The one for hand baskets only: in her case, cheese and a coffee maker, a couple of mugs, coffee and milk. Some basketful. Some idiot woman had contrived to ignore the sign and

unloaded enough to feed a family for a fortnight. For some reason the checkout girl was in tears. Anyway, we naturally fell into conversation again. It seems she's off to Devon this weekend. She says she's going to see her housebound parents, but I'd like to know what woman makes that sort of effort for her Aged Ps. Takes time off work to make it, too. Though she explained, rather hurriedly, in case I think the entire Kent Constabulary takes time off for beauty therapy, that she's taken time off in lieu. T-O-I-L *Toil, they call it, just as we do, because of the effort involved in getting it. If you're the boss, I should imagine taking it is a damned sight easier. Or would it make it ten times harder? She strikes me as the sort of woman who'd ask — demand! — more of herself than of anyone else. Driven. I wonder by what. By whom. Whatever it is, she's a single and a no doubt single-minded woman: you don't get where she is without a great deal of effort and a great deal of treading on other people's toes. I can see I shall have to think hard about this. But I'll still give a Brodsky concert a try. Now, I simply must fly. Unlike Frances, I've got work to do. I'll see you soon. And Elise, for God's sake make some effort. Please, please make some effort.'*

CHAPTER NINETEEN

Tom Arkwright looked as happy as a well-patted puppy; he might have wagged his tail as he placed a sheaf of papers in front of her, in the exact centre of her quite redundant blotter. (Who on earth had ordered one of those? Surely not Mark!) 'Afternoon, ma'am. There you are. A complete list of all the Lotus dealerships in Sussex and Kent, plus one or two upmarket second-hand dealers. I know you said it was a new Elise, but you never know with those registration letters, and valeting can be ever so good. And I checked these Internet car importers too. And I got details of all the women who'd bought Elises, which is not a lot, of course. Well, not middle-aged ladies. Sorry, ma'am. I didn't mean—'

Fran laughed. 'You're digging your pit deeper and deeper, young Tom. I'd stop before you bury yourself alive. You've done well. What are these?'

'Details of payment — you know, whether the person had their own finance or whether they used the one at the dealership. One lady got bought one as a present, can you imagine that, by a gentleman friend, like.' He shifted his feet.

'How old was the gentleman friend?' she asked, not because she especially wanted to know, but she sensed that Tom didn't want to spell it out.

'Seems he was — well, a toy boy, like. You know, young enough to be her son.'

'Maybe it was her son, Tom. Have you never thought of buying your mum a super car?'

'Maybe when I've paid off my student loan and got a couple more promotions, ma'am. Until then she'll have to put up with lavender bath salts or a bottle of wine.'

'Well, get your promotions quickly, there's a good lad. I'd hate to see her fitting a Zimmer into a Lotus boot! Work like this,' she added, a warm smile replacing her evil grin, 'means her dream car isn't a lifetime away. In the meantime, you could always get her a Burago model — show her what you'd really like to give her. And your dad. How is he, by the way? What did they say when he had his check-up? Yesterday, wasn't it?' By now her face was serious.

'That's right. They think the chemo's done its bit, thank goodness. So it was worth all it put him through. You should have seen him . . . Anyway, now they say he's got every chance, thank God.'

'You get to see him often enough? Bury's a fair distance.'

'Not as often as I'd like. But he won't let me, that's the thing. He says I ought to be building my own life, not sitting like a great garden gnome by his bed.'

'Garden gnome!'

'Family joke. And I'm not at my best with the sick, ma'am. But what I have managed to do is get him tickets for a Man U match — a Christmas present to die for. Shit. Oh, shit.'

She went to his side of her desk, and pulled his head on to her shoulder, letting him cry out his cry. At last, she shoved her tissue box within reach, and bustled off to activate her new percolator. Yes, it appeared to be working. The smell was good, anyway.

'I'm sorry — I — It's just now he's getting better, I can . . . I can't—'

'It's all right. It's all right to cry when you have feelings you can't express any other way. Even at work. And Tom,

I promise you this is just between the two of us. Promise.' She put the mug by one hand, squeezing the other. 'If you do need a counsellor, that's confidential too. And I'll have a word with Personnel: if you want to take them both away — yes, if you're mum's been the carer, she'll need a break too — for a nice weekend, I'll make sure it's all right. Now, why don't you take the rest of the day off?'

He gulped his coffee. 'You know, guv, I'd really rather be working. If it's all the same to you, that is.'

She nodded. And made herself say it out loud. 'I understand perfectly. You know, with my parents . . . But don't kid yourself. Working your socks off is all too often an excuse not to acknowledge and deal with your feelings. Finish your shift, Tom, if you want. But don't dream of working over, not unless it's absolutely vital. Understand?'

'Yes, ma'am.' He swigged the coffee and straightened. Whatever he'd meant to say, it came out as, 'Ma'am — I hope you don't mind my saying, but you look really good, ma'am.'

'Thanks, Tom. I don't mind at all, so long as you'd say the same to your mum when she's made a bit of an effort.'

He bit his lip. 'You know what you were saying about that car . . . Well, how would it be . . . Can you get vouchers for having your hair done and that? Because all this business with dad's taken it out of her, like, and maybe it would perk her up. Unless you think a lady'd be offended.'

'She'll almost certainly say she hasn't got time and it's a waste of money at her age. But I can't think of a nicer present for a woman, especially your mum.' But she could never have given her mother such a self-indulgent present. Not that she hadn't tried. She'd once booked them on to the Orient Express, only to have them refuse to go. Although the trip was only from London to York, they wouldn't make the effort to get to London, even though she drove down to collect them and deliver them. So for years it had been whisky for Pa and silk scarves and Yardley's Lavender for Ma.

'You OK, guv?'

How long had she been away with the fairies? 'Fine! Now push off and sort out some pampering. Shoo!' From the way he looked at her he was worried, but she smiled brightly and waved him to the door.

* * *

Although she'd left most of the working parties she'd been assigned to, she hadn't escaped all the responsibilities associated with them. So she spent a couple of hours editing a report on the policing implications of the mass introduction of ID cards while Tom worked down his list, checking that each woman owner was still alive and well. Having enjoyed the adrenaline burst of successful detection, she'd rather have done it herself, but it would have been pure self-indulgence. As the Chief had pointed out, it was highly irregular for someone of her rank to get anywhere near real crime, let alone get her hands dirty investigating a specific case. So she toiled and sweated over the keyboard while Tom did what both of them would consider more interesting things.

A tap at the door roused her from the intricacies of annexe C(i). Expecting it to be Tom, her invitation to enter was a very informal affair. But the face peering round the door was Mark's.

'Still here?'

'I took TOIL earlier.'

'So I see. Excellent. But there's no need to work overtime just to prove you were entitled to it.'

She straightened. Her back, and more alarmingly, her breastbone cracked noisily. He rolled his eyes. 'I need an osteopath to make my joints do that. Look,' he continued, awkwardly, 'I don't know what clothes you usually take down to Devon—'

'Stuff that would disgrace my cleaning lady!'

'Well, I've just had an email from my yachting mate: he hopes we'll make up a foursome on Saturday evening with him and his wife. Dinner. Nothing OTT — smart casual, he said. OK?'

'But—' Saturday evening was her cooking evening. In the peace and calm after her parents had been put to bed by their care worker. Social services wouldn't let her cancel assistance on the weekends she was down on the grounds that it was better for her parents' routine not to be interrupted. But there was plenty of food in the freezer, and — 'I wouldn't be able to go out too early. But I'd love to come.'

'Good. It'd be better if we were to come to you then: where's a good place to eat?'

She spread her hands, ruefully.

'Sorry: I can't imagine you eat out for pleasure when you're down there. Or that your parents would be able to recommend anywhere. Leave it to me. I'll sort it. Now, get your things together and I'll walk you to your car. No, "but me no buts"!'

'You've been talking to the Chief again — him and his dratted Shakespeare! And Tom — he's actually heard of Walter Scott.' Though she'd completely forgotten to talk to him about it. 'What a literate force we must be.' She saved her document and signed off.

'If only the Home Secretary would give us marks for that when he draws up the league tables: it'd be nice to be top.'

Police gossip got them to their cars. Although a light drizzle was damping everything, neither seemed in any hurry. But despite their apparent ease with each other, Fran felt the same tension that had led up to the kiss that had rounded off their dinner date. Conversation was definitely dwindling. It was like being seventeen again. Two grown people as tongue-tied as teenagers.

She leaned across their briefcases and kissed him, on the cheek, as on their date. If that was what it had been. He responded, with a light peck on the lips.

'Good evening, sir, ma'am!'

They sprung apart as swiftly as if they'd actually been caught *in flagrante*. The latest inspector, all bright-eyed and bushy-tailed. And scoring zilch for perception. They eyed each other ironically.

'By nine tomorrow everyone at headquarters will know we're knee-deep in an affair,' she risked.

'We shall have to oblige them, then,' he said, kissing her generously on the lips. 'But maybe Devon will be a better ambience than the senior car park.'

* * *

This time there were two separate weekend bags, one full of her working clothes, the ones that would smell of old people and damp walls, and a garment carrier that she would hang in the lean-to holding the washing machine and drier until the very last minute. Never quite sure what smart casual might mean in the context of country restaurants, she'd gone for safe with an Aquascutum trouser suit and a silk top. Then she'd panicked. Was black too formal? How about her new Jaeger skirt, cashmere top and pashmina? Diamonds or costume jewellery? Exasperated, she stared at herself in the mirror, arms akimbo. How could a woman who'd been responsible for life and death decisions, who'd controlled enormous budgets, who'd hobnobbed with senior politicians and civil servants without turning a hair, suddenly get the jitters? They were talking supper in Devon, for goodness' sake, not dinner in Islington.

To her chagrin, she nonetheless found herself zipping both outfits in; at least the shoes and bag would do for both. Perfume? What about some perfume? Even if she showered ten minutes before she left the bungalow, she'd still be aware of the mustiness on her skin, in her hair, even if the others weren't. Some perfume would help — that new Christian Dior, for instance. And then a wry grin at herself. For *others* read *Mark*. And don't forget the make-up. Or the new HRT patch. She was due to change that. She stared at it. She'd certainly started to feel better — could such a prosaic, innocent-looking thing be capable of turning a life around?

There was sign of neither Mark nor his car when her taxi — she'd come in by train to save leaving her car over the weekend — dropped her. For a moment her pulse pounded as hard as if she'd been stood up in the middle of a strange city. Mobile phone? No messages. She could switch on the radio and get traffic updates — the A274 could be very bad in rain like this. Or she could sprint to her office to see if there was a message on her voicemail. Why, after all these years of trudging down to Devon and dealing with everything entirely on her own, should she suddenly want an escort and company? Even as she pulled her shoulders straight and retrieved her briefcase, however, his Volvo appeared. His face was set in the grimmest of lines. As he saw her he beamed. Would either, as they walked in to breakfast together, admit to anxiety? She was sure they wouldn't — she would certainly keep mum. But it was just the sort of thing you confessed to your lover over your first glass of bubbly.

* * *

Tom was already at work when she returned after breakfast. ''Morning, guv — cold first thing!'

'Yes, and wet too. Just because you have the weekend in your sights, young Tom, doesn't mean I shan't land you with enough overtime to take you through till Monday.' But her eyes twinkled and he didn't even bother to apologise.

'I may just have enough, actually, guv. These posh car women. I'm only halfway through the list so far, but I've found a couple of individuals who reported having had their vehicles stolen within weeks of purchase.'

'I thought we agreed, Tom, no police-speak. It's bad enough when you sneak it into your reports, but I'm not having you assailing my ears with it at this hour in the morning.'

'Is after lunch OK, then, guv? Anyway, just on the off-chance, I checked to see if they were from the same garage.'

Good lad. 'Well?'

'Nope. Seems it must be a coincidence. Bad luck, but no connection.'

'Dig round for other connections. Including the less obvious ones. Any women you can't trace? Don't forget the garages will have notified DVLA of all the registration details and the drivers should have notified them of new addresses if they've moved. I know, egg-sucking time. But when you want to dash round to get explanations sometimes you forget the obvious. At least I do.' Like worrying so much over Mark this morning. 'Look, I've got a meeting in half an hour — it seems the new Detective Chief Super had already booked the day off so I said I'd cover for him—'

'But how can you take off your very first day?' Tom demanded.

'God knows. Seems very weird to me. Well, starting on a Friday seems weird, but that's Personnel for you. Anyway, we've managed without him this long — we can wait till Monday. Now, if you give me a few names I can get on the blower too.' That way she wouldn't stare at the briefing papers and speculate about Mark and the weekend. She wasn't at all sure that she agreed any longer with Sheila Downs that it was a privilege to fall in love when you were older: falling in love with Mark seemed a dangerous and irritating distraction.

But then, the meeting itself seemed an irritating distraction from the important business of discovering Elise's killer. The chair was a man promoted well above his abilities, who could neither shut up the talkative people with axes to grind nor elicit valuable information from the quieter members. Half way through she'd been tempted simply to elbow him aside. As it was she contented herself with engaging in eye-contact with those she thought it necessary to prompt, and after that the meeting started slowly to get results. Please God that young Tom was moving faster than this. Two cars stolen immediately after they'd been bought. Not from the same garage. But it might have been from the same salesperson. Surreptitious as a teenager seeking an exam answer, she texted Tom to check that, too.

There was no sign of him when, after a canteen sandwich for lunch, she got back to her office. She'd kill him if he'd gone scooting about the countryside in search of information he could have got more easily over the phone. But he came dashing in with such excitement any rebuke died before it reached her lips.

'There's a woman I've found who's not there.'

'Or?' she prompted, trying not to laugh.

'There's this woman on the list and I can't find any trace of her. No change of address, no nothing. So I went to her last known address and they say she moved up north somewhere.'

'And?' She sat down, gesturing him to the chair opposite.

'She was a Miss Marjorie Gray. She lived in St Mary's Bay. Well, I suppose someone has to. But not anymore, not her, anyway.'

'No forwarding address?'

'No nothing. Seems she was a very quiet lady, kept herself to herself. One day she was there. Next she'd left. Someone else moves into her house. Just like that. No goodbyes, no nothing.'

'Age?' She scribbled down the information as if it was a lifeline.

'About sixty, they say. Typical grey-haired spinster-lady. Sorry, ma'am. Though you're not typical, of course.'

'Granted. Spinster — so never married. Lived on her own.'

'Well, only recently. Seems her parents retired down there. Then first one then the other died. And off she goes. Within about three months, they say — they couldn't be more precise.'

'Estate agents?'

His turn to make notes. 'And banks, too, guv — someone will have handled all that money. And a solicitor to do the conveyancing. And her GP and dentist — they'll have needed to send records on somewhere.' The lad sounded as excited as she felt.

It took her a moment to register the phone. Mark!

'Fran — any chance you could pop into my office?'

She gripped the desk — he was going to call off the weekend, wasn't he?

She swallowed lest he heard the disappointment — was there no more intense word to describe her feeling? — in her voice. 'I'm on my way.' Aware that Tom was watching the transformation of her expression, she pulled a schoolgirl face.

'Sounds like trouble,' she said. 'Can you get started while I see what's up?'

* * *

Mark's face was as grim as she'd ever seen it. 'We've got a child abduction. With Henson not here I shall have to take control. I'm so sorry.'

She nodded. There was no argument.

'Is there any chance you could stay and help?' he asked, almost humbly.

'Could you order me to? Please.' Otherwise she had to go down, didn't she?

'I've asked everyone else to give up any spare time this weekend. There are plenty of volunteers. But I've got no one at your level. Not with your experience. A child of ten, Fran. Where do our loyalties lie?'

CHAPTER TWENTY

'She was on television earlier this evening, local and national news, telling everyone that some pervert has kidnapped a child of ten and appealing for her safe return. Frances, of course. Strange — I thought she was dedicating her time to finding the man who'd done this to you. And I thought her weekends were given over to her parents, down in Devon. So why she ups and starts dealing with this, goodness knows.

'There's no doubt the camera lurves her. So many women of her age have either got lovely faces but tubby bodies, or have managed to keep their figures at the expense of their faces. Your face — scars apart — is relatively unlined, isn't it? You carried a fair amount of flesh, though it's hard to remember that now. She's got a few lines, but not as many as you'd expect. Expensive skin care, I suppose. And the camera lights were very cleverly placed to bleach out the worst. Her voice is good, too, of course — and she's managed to avoid the local accent. I wonder where she was born. I don't think she ever said.

'I don't think either of us will be seeing her for a while. The other case will take priority, no doubt about that. Hardly surprising, either. What does it say in the Bible? "Let the dead bury the dead"? And there's no doubt the police will be more interested in locating a child and its potential killer than poking around looking for your assailant, important though they thought that a very few days ago.

'I shan't give up, of course, though I'm tied up with something really important. No, not work, as it happens, though I've so many assignments to mark — when did they stop being called essays? — that I can't see my desk.

'So don't worry, my dear, if I don't see you for a few days. I will come back. I promise.'

CHAPTER TWENTY-ONE

'So you can just get out of here. Swanning round like Lady Muck, just because you're shagging the boss.'

How the hell had the new Detective Chief Superintendent got hold of that? He'd only been in the building half an hour? Fran was so angry she dared say nothing, not until she'd taken another breath and stepped back a pace.

'You wanted out,' Henson continued, 'so you can get out. Get back to your dead case. OK?'

She thought the veins on his forehead would burst, they bulged so fiercely, auguring a stroke or heart attack. And he was how old? Forty-five at most, but a totally unreconstructed officer, complete with beer gut. Where had they dug him out from? In today's police, there were finer, fitter officers ready to leap out of the woodwork when you tapped it. She replied, so quietly that all the interested ears — and there were many — in the incident room had to strain to hear, 'Chief Superintendent, I believe you were unavailable this weekend, when there was an emergency. I can't think of a better reason for me to return to what was my job for some seven years. I suspect Senior Management couldn't, either. I've no idea whether they want me to continue. If they do, I assume — no, listen to me! — if they do, I assume we work in tandem until one of us is given overall command.'

'I'm not working for a superannuated old tart like you.'

'Ageist and sexist, are we, Detective Chief Superintendent Henson? What a pity I'm not black so you could be racist, too. You obviously haven't had the benefit of our in-house training courses.' The observation hung in the air: in her most recent incarnation she'd been in charge of such developments, and everyone in the room had been on at least one course. 'Look, why not get off that high horse of yours and get to work. It's eight-twenty on Monday morning. There's a child out there who's been missing since Friday afternoon. There's a whole new batch of officers to brief. Most of those still here — who've worked without proper breaks over the weekend — are on, so far, unpaid overtime. One of us needs to get authority to pay them. That involves speaking to the Chief — would you like to do it?'

'What are you implying?'

If that was the best the selection board could have come up with, the rest of the candidates must have been awful. She wouldn't have let him past the interview room door. Personnel always said she had a nose for a good candidate. Certainly when they'd appointed against her advice, they'd always come moaning to her that they regretted it. 'If I'm implying anything it's that it's time to stop bickering and get on with today's work. There's a briefing meeting at eight-thirty. I suggest I take that so you'll know exactly where we are. After that it's up to the Chief. Whom you should be talking to now.'

'What about you?'

'Me? I'm going to take a shower. I've been on duty throughout the weekend. When everyone's up to speed, I shall probably go home for a couple of hours' sleep.'

It was a good line on which to turn on her heel and walk out. But she had to stop half a dozen times — to offer advice here, encouragement there. And as she pulled the door, it opened to admit Mark.

'You've not left yet,' he said unnecessarily.

'Briefing and then bed.'

'I'll run you home. Yes, I need a doze and a change of clothes too. We can keep each other awake while I drive. In fact—' he flicked a glance at his watch — 'why not have breakfast at your place or mine? I can't fault the canteen but I just want to crack my own eggs in my own kitchen. As soon as you've completed the briefing. In half an hour, say.'

It made sense. After such sleep deprivation, driving on your own was dangerous. Since she could postpone her shower she could also squeeze in another ten minutes scanning phone calls from the public in response to her appeals. She nodded.

Her briefing was as short but as full as she could make it. Her face was stiff with fatigue, and it required a supreme effort to make the words come out in the right order and at the right speed.

'To sum up, then: Rebecca — it's never shortened to Becky — was walking home from her piano lesson through Ashford's town centre market when she was last seen. At about two o'clock. It was half-term, remember, so the lesson wasn't at its usual time. People saw her swinging her music case as if she was full of the joys of spring. That's it. No sightings after that at all. No contact from a kidnapper. A huge public response but nothing yet worth picking up on.' Then she remembered the way her colleagues had dismissed that sighting of Elise in her bright new car. 'Nothing *apparently* worth picking up on. But we've got a whole new lot of eyes here this morning. I'd like a couple of you — Tom? Enid? — to go through them again. Left brain time: OK?'

Tom offered a none-too surreptitious thumbs up and a wink. At least he'd had some sleep: she'd personally sent him home at ten last night.

'And now, ladies and gentlemen, I'm going to leave you in the most capable hands of the new head of CID, Detective Chief Superintendent Henson.' She hoped she didn't sound ironic. 'I'm going to do what I'm telling you to do — take regular breaks, eat and drink properly. Tired brains don't work as well as fresh ones. And I'm delighted to tell you that DCS Henson has already sorted overtime payments with them upstairs.' She led the spatter of applause, as if she benefited as much as the lower ranks. 'Good morning — I'll see you all later.'

She'd fallen into step with Mark and was about ten yards from the car when her mobile rang. It was a number she didn't recognise, but had a Devon prefix. He caught her as she staggered.

But it wasn't a hospital. It was a woman who sounded as tired as she with the news that not only were her parents fine, they hadn't expected her that weekend.

'What do you mean, they hadn't expected me?' She found she was leaning against Mark's car. 'I wouldn't have put you on red alert if I hadn't intended to go down and then had to let them down! Nothing would have prevented me except—'

'That's what they told Sylvia on Friday, anyway, when she saw them. And they were pretty sure.' Sylvia. All the decent kind women who did the most unrewarding work for less than a pittance seemed to have names like Sylvia. 'I think we need to talk about their future, Ms Harman — have a case conference soon.'

'With what agenda?' She was aware of Mark waiting patiently beside her, trying neither to listen in nor to yawn.

'Their long-term care.'

'I thought I'd made it clear that I was going to move down shortly and become their full-time carer.'

'I suppose that's one option,' the tinny voice said doubtfully. 'Anyway, perhaps we can talk about it when you next come down. We could organise it for — let me see — nine-fifteen on Wednesday.'

'Sorry. You'll have heard on the media about the missing child. I'm assisting the investigation — a vital case—'

'*This* is a very important case, Ms Harman. To us.'

She overrode the criticism, both on the phone and in her own head. '—and unless there's an absolute emergency down there, I can't come down midweek. Ever. And certainly not till we've found this child. I don't know where on earth they got the impression I could.'

'They'll be very disappointed.'

'Why? They always insisted they counted the hours from my leaving on Sunday till my returning on Friday. What's going wrong?'

'Perhaps you didn't make it clear. Or perhaps it's what we need to talk about: their mental health.'

'But I—'

'Have you ever considered the possibility that one or both may be suffering the onset of Alzheimer's, Ms Harman?'

'Alzheimer's?' she repeated stupidly, as if in the first stages herself.

'The carers aren't sure. We need a conference involving your parents' GP and of course yourself. Dr Baker's free on Wednesday, as Sylvia and I are. But now you say you're not.' She sounded personally disappointed.

Wrong-footed, she tried to defend herself. 'It isn't a question of my saying it now — I'm not cancelling on a whim, please believe me. Next weekend's the best I can do. I might just be able to stay over till Monday morning for a very early meeting, but my place is here until this case is over.'

There was no response from the other end.

'Look, I've been literally on my feet for the last sixty hours so if you'll excuse me—'

'We can't just leave it at that, Ms Harman—'

Her voice breaking, she said, 'Then — you have her number — call my sister.' She turned to grimace guiltily at Mark but, leaning against the driver's door, he was literally asleep on his feet. Very gently she retrieved his keys and steered him round to the passenger side.

* * *

Since they were going against the rush hour traffic, it didn't take very long to reach Mark's house in Loose, once an independent village, now more or less a suburb of Maidstone. If she lived there people could call her a loose woman. If Mark had been awake, or if she were surer of where their relationship was going, she could have observed as much. If only she could talk to Mark about Devon. But he was audibly snoring and she had to keep awake herself. She mustn't think about Devon lest she cry. So she thought of variants on the loose theme. Loose cannon. Loose talk. Loose limbed. Loose tooth. Loose box.

She parked without panache in front of his high-fronted, rather forbidding Edwardian house. He awoke on the instant, and got out of the car as stiffly as she did.

She couldn't burden him with the parent problem, not yet. 'Tell me.' She handed him his car keys and then stood aside as he opened the front door, 'What stone did you find Henson under?'

'A Met paving-stone. His references shone. And his interview was outstanding — I was in on it myself. God, all this junk mail.'

'They wanted to get rid of him, then. And probably he was coached for his panel. Any idea why he couldn't come in over the weekend?'

Mark coughed as if embarrassed. 'A wedding.'

'It'd have to be a very close family member for that to wash as an excuse.'

'It was. It was his own.'

'Bloody hell! And there I was ready to rip into him. As it is, I suppose we should commiserate for the poor bugger's missing his honeymoon.'

'We should but we can't. He wanted it kept absolutely confidential.'

'Any idea why? And no, before you ask, not a word, not even a hint of a syllable, will pass my lips.'

'I didn't expect it to,' he said brusquely. He added, dropping his voice as if they could be overheard, 'I gather he's marrying his long-term partner, and there is some urgency. Maybe she's pregnant, maybe she's ill. But not a word.'

'I don't gossip, Mark,' she said, more emphatically than she meant. But someone had: to Henson. She and Mark were lovers, were they? If only. 'Well, the sooner I'm back on the Elise case the happier we'll both be.' She closed the door behind them as he laid his post beside a previous pile on a mahogany table. The house smelt unlived in. Did hers, to a stranger? At least she had strategically placed bowls of pot-pourri to sweeten up the mustiness.

'Breakfast and shower? Shower and breakfast? Which would you prefer first?'

She looked at him; she might have to wake him to give him his breakfast, whereas her brush with Henson and then with the social worker had left her with just enough residual adrenaline to keep her on her feet. 'You shower, I cook. So long as it's no more sophisticated than toast and scrambled eggs. Don't worry — I'll find everything I need.'

He ate in his bathrobe, falling asleep again, head on the arms he'd folded on the table, as soon as she removed the plate. She found a cushion from his sofa to slide under his head. He didn't stir as she lifted him and gently set him down. She smoothed down the ruffled hair, allowing him some dignity.

Time for her own shower then.

* * *

'My God!' She stepped back gasping. What had she done to deserve a blast of icy water? Did Mark always return the thermostat to zero? Little by little she realised he must have set it like that to wake him up enough to eat. Had her thought processes been as slow as that over the weekend? And if so, what vital information had she missed?

She needed sleep as much as Mark did. So she basked in warm water, not caring how deep she drained Kent's reservoirs so long as she was soothed. There was no spare bathrobe. Swathing herself in her towel, she wandered into his bedroom, thinking at first she could simply lie under the duvet as she was. Almost without knowing why that might not be a good idea, she fumbled through his wardrobe and found a tracksuit. There.

* * *

'Fran. Fran. Are you OK?'

In the past she'd been able to wake instantly after a catnap. Now she clawed her way slowly into the realisation that Mark was standing beside her shaking her shoulder. There was a mug of tea on a mat on the bedside table.

'It seems indecent to go straight from breakfast into lunch,' he said. 'Shall we go on to your place first and pick up something on the way back?'

She shook her head: there was no chance of rational thought yet. 'I'm sorry.' She yawned in his face.

He sat on the bed, facing her, easy, relaxed, as if he'd been bringing her tea in bed all their adult lives.

He hadn't. He'd brought his late wife tea like this. As for him and Fran, they'd exchanged no more than the most tentative of kisses. Tina's bed and the middle of an abduction case: this was not the place, nor was it the time for any intimacy at all, whatever her body might say. Why the hell should she be so aroused in the middle of a crisis? How easy it would be to reach for him.

She sat bolt upright. 'Good idea. I could do with some fresh clothes.'

He offered a quizzical look.

'Don't worry. I haven't been stinking the place out in the same things all weekend. I had my Teignmouth bag handy.'

'Including your glad rags for dinner with the Marstons. I'm sorry it all went pear-shaped.' His smile began as rueful, but soon became weary.

She switched on her briskest tones. 'So am I. But I'm even more sorry about the kid. And we ought to get a move on, oughtn't we?' She found her voice sliding to the confessional. 'You know, given a choice between working round the clock twice and dealing with my parents — and now their social workers — I know which I'd choose. And you're to forget I ever said that.' She tried to sound assertive. Perhaps she did.

'You never said a word. When this is all over, Fran, I—' He lifted a hand, to caress her face before kissing her.

Inevitably her phone burst into ironic sound.

'At least it doesn't play "Fur Elise"!' he said resignedly, leaving her to take the call.

It didn't take long for her to join him in the hall, where he was leafing through his mail. Most of it ended in a Sainsbury's carrier, unopened. Recycling, no doubt. He'd retrieved stamps from other envelopes, ordinary British ones.

'Save the Children,' he explained, following her gaze. 'One of Tina's pet charities.'

She nodded, but did not comment. How would he feel if she started to add to his collection? 'That was Tom Arkwright on the phone,' she said. 'Alan Pitt called. Information that simply couldn't wait. And he'll only speak to me personally.'

'Attention seeking?'

'Possibly. But it's like all these things, isn't it? You can't dismiss them just in case. But I asked Tom to call him back and explain that important though the Elise case is, at the moment Rebecca must take priority.'

'Absolutely.' He held the door for her.

Was that why, she wondered, he worked all weekend too? For the first time since the panic had started, she realised that in the normal scheme of things an incident room was by no means the natural habitat for an assistant chief constable.

* * *

Mark seemed happy for her to drive his car to her cottage, so that he could make a series of calls from his mobile. When hers rang again, he held it enquiringly.

'Who's it from?'

'Tom Arkwright.'

'Why don't you take it?' she suggested.

'How would he react to hearing me on your phone?'

How indeed? One officer taking another's calls was not unknown. Did Mark fear that it would lead to gossip, that his name would be inextricably linked to hers? Not that it wasn't. Not after their public kiss. Not when even Henson had managed to pounce on the gossip so soon.

She wouldn't argue with Mark, not now. In any case, maybe a young man like Tom would doubt that any relationship except the professional was possible between two people of such advanced age as his boss and his boss's boss. She pulled into a convenient lay-by and took the mobile, interrupting Tom in mid-message.

'Sorry, Tom.' She was about to explain that she had been driving when she realised that might worry Mark too. 'Problem?'

He must have picked up her hesitation. 'Sorry, guv: did I wake you up?'

'I'm wide awake now,' she said dryly. 'Fire away.'

'It's just this Alan Pitt is acting odd, like. Still says he's got this vital information and still won't give it to anyone but you. Weird or what? And now he's saying he's going away and won't be around for a bit and hopes you won't regret it.'

She rubbed her face with her free hand. 'You know, Tom, I don't like this.'

'Nor me, guv. He must know you're up to your ears in the Rebecca case — if he watches TV or reads the papers, that is.'

She wanted to add the radio into his list of the media but refrained: another generation thing, no doubt. 'What's your take on it?' she asked, interested.

'I thought he might be like a naughty kid in a supermarket — you know, throwing itself around because its mum's got her mind elsewhere. But then, there was something about his voice, guv: something sinister, like, you know?'

'Sinister?'

'Well, I didn't like it myself. So I got on to his mobile company and alerted them. And I want a record of wherever he makes his calls from until further notice.'

'What about the last couple of days?'

'Never thought of that. Guv: we are thinking the same thing, aren't we? Something to do with Rebecca, like?'

'I don't know, Tom. It all seems a bit far-fetched to assume a connection . . . But just on the off-chance, see if he's got any sort of record at all for anything, will you? And run another check on his DNA.'

'It'd be nice to rule out anything dodgy, wouldn't it, guv, even if I am chasing a wild goose.'

'It would indeed. Good work, Tom.' As she cut the call, she smiled at Mark, who had been sitting with his eyes closed and breathing suspiciously deeply, come to think of it. 'You know, when one of these kids has a good idea, it gives me more pleasure than if I'd had it myself.'

'You'd have made a good mother.'

He said it with such emphasis that she was taken aback. 'Good teacher, maybe. But hopeless mother. Unless I'd had an army of back-up. I couldn't have given up the job.'

He gave a short bark of laughter. 'And if you wouldn't have given it up for your kids, why even think about it for your parents?'

CHAPTER TWENTY-TWO

Mark retired to her sofa and promptly fell asleep again while she was dealing with her own mail. Laughing perhaps dourly to herself, she slipped upstairs to change. Before coming back downstairs to load the washing machine, on impulse she popped into her study to check her emails. Most people contacted her at work, of course, but a small and loyal group of friends were prepared to tolerate the delays incumbent on using her personal address. Friends! When was it she'd last had time for a social life? When she hobnobbed with women or indeed men from work, there was a small but perceptible recognition that she had outstripped and thus out earned them. She'd never had too many friends outside the police, apart from a handful she'd met while she was doing her PhD who reminded her that out there was a world without hierarchies. Some of Ian's friends kept in touch, whether for kindness to his memory or because they liked her she was never sure.

Today, spam apart, there were only a couple of messages. The first leapt from the screen with such righteous — perhaps, *self*-righteous — indignation that she knew it came from Hazel, in response to her suggestion to the Aged Ps' social worker. Was it only this morning that she'd made it?

The social worker must have taken her desperate suggestion seriously.

Phone calls from Stornoway were so expensive during the day that Hazel eschewed them. In any case, it seemed to Fran that she much preferred polishing her phrases so that they pierced with maximum pain. Hazel might not be hauling in an indecent salary (was Fran's indecent? She had an idea that she earned every penny), but working she was, and in the name of the Lord. Had Fran never realised the vital role of the minister's wife in the kirk community?

Which century was she living in? And then Fran corrected herself: for the twenty-first century woman, wasn't staying at home the new going out?

So what should she do with the email, of which there was considerably more? Simply delete it? Or she could zing a reply back, pointing out that Hazel was a lady of leisure, those kids of her holy husband well away from the nest now. She had time enough on her hands: let her select a finger and sit and spin!

Hardly.

But perhaps inside that burning ball of her resentment there was a nugget of common sense. Hazel's work from the manse would no doubt bring her into contact with a lot of crotchety old folk, and with social workers whose sensibilities were all atremble. Perhaps it genuinely was lack of finance that had kept her away from Devon for the last five years, and Hazel was too stiff-necked to admit it.

Hi Hazel,

Seems those social workers got the wrong end of the stick when I spoke to them this morning. The truth is, I don't have your experience in dealing with health professionals— an arrant lie, this, given her close contact with social services over many issues during her career.

Could you possibly consider taking a short break from your parish up there and flying down — my treat. It would give Ma and Pa such a thrill to see you, and you'd be able to have a more meaningful dialogue with her care workers than I seem to manage.

I hope I can join you — I'll book into a B and B or sleep on the dining-room floor — but my boss is being a total bastard and has put his foot down: absolutely no leave for anyone in any circumstances until we've solved the present case of child abduction. Golly, do you remember how we all felt when Hamish got himself lost on the moors? This little girl's disappeared from the middle of a town.

How many more buttons might she risk pressing? No, that was enough. Just one reminder:

Just remember, this is my treat. Would Grant be able to come down with you? It sounds as if he could do with a break, and you know how he loves bird-watching out at Dawlish Warren!

Fran XXX

The other message was from Elaine, who, but for Ian's death, would have been her sister-in-law. They'd always got on, and Ian's death had made them even closer, though neither of them referred to him much these days, and when they did, it was never with the lowered voices of the bereaved. It was as if he were simply a given in their relationship. Elaine, a widow who worked for a major pharmaceutical company, had become the best sort of friend: they might not hear from each other from one month's end to another, but when they did, it was if they had spoken only yesterday. But now, Elaine was asking if she could come and stay. Fran read the email again. It was just an overnight stop: Elaine was off to France via Eurostar and needed to stay over and travel from Ashford. No problem. Except the first date was tomorrow. Just what she needed, something extra to worry about. Actually, of course, it was what she needed. A mate. Someone not involved in — in anything. Someone to talk to. About everything. Unless, of course, there was another twenty-four-hour stint. Explaining briefly, she emailed Elaine to welcome her but warn her that there might be an absentee hostess.

She had her own key and the burglar alarm code was still the same.

The machine loaded with her weekend's clothes chugging into action, she headed for the living room. All she could hear was the sound of deep breathing.

She felt-penned a large notice — GONE TO SHOPS. BACK SOONEST — and set off for the village, sucking the fresh air into her lungs to replace the air-conditioned muck that was all she'd had to inhale since Friday. Corner shop though her target was, it was a veritable cornucopia of good things for lunch. They would have the best picnic she could put together in five minutes.

* * *

When she returned, there was no sign of Mark on the sofa, but still the heaviest of breathing. Laying the table in the kitchen for lunch — hardly more than putting the contents of packets on plates — she gave him another five minutes. But they ought to be getting back to work. Putting her head round the living room door, she found him flat on the floor, head on a couple of paperbacks, knees in the air and feet firmly side by side twelve inches apart. His hands lay loosely on his chest.

Should she wake him? He clearly needed his sleep. If so, how?

As she stared down, he opened an eye.

'I was just about to kiss the sleeping prince,' she joked. 'But he might have turned into a frog.' She held out a hand to heave him up, but he shook his head, rolling over and pressing himself up in a continuous and surprisingly fluid movement.

'Alexander Technique,' he explained, accepting just half a glass of wine. 'But you're supposed to be aware of your back lengthening and widening, not deep in the land of nod. Part of my self-preservation campaign. Helps the slumping desk-bound back.'

'I noticed how good you were looking,' she said, passing the salad bowl. 'The gym, too?'

'The in-house one. Twice a week. But I don't enjoy it. Too repetitive. And I hate the music and the TV. Didn't you play badminton once? I don't suppose . . . ?' He held servers full of greenery while he looked at her with shrewd compassion.

'Haven't held a racquet in twelve months.'

'You've been charging down to Devon that long?' His compassion turned to something like anger. 'How long have Personnel known? Did they know when they asked you to pick up the extra responsibility? Fran, Fran — it's a wonder you've not had a stroke or a heart attack or crashed that car of yours.' He replaced the servers, passing the bowl to her. 'If you couldn't complain to Personnel, why on earth didn't you talk to me?' He shook his head sadly, as if hurt she hadn't trusted him.

Why indeed? Because she had been afraid of appearing weak when she had always prided herself on her strength? How many times had Ma boasted, 'Our Fran can open any jar — you should see those wrists of hers! It's that badminton that did it. Always a tomboy, our Fran. Not one for frilly dresses and make-up. No. A tracksuit, that's her natural plumage. With her shoulders, she looks more like a young man, doesn't she?'

Was that why she'd always worn suits tailored more severely than even her uniform? What if she'd worn gentler outlines, kinder colours? Would her life have been very different? She made a swift and silent resolution: if the invitation to meet Mark's friends was renewed, this time she'd wear one of those softly draped dresses so many women of her age wore so successfully. If she had time to buy one, that is.

'Fran?' he prompted.

'I'm sorry. I was trying to work it out. Doesn't make sense, does it?' She passed the flan, then mounted a spirited search in the salad for an olive.

'No. Not even with the prevailing ethos that lunch is for wimps.' He indicated the spread before them with a grin. 'Unless you've been there yourself. I was this far from a breakdown after Tina's death.' He held thumb and forefinger a millimetre apart. 'Fortunately my back was bad — you remember my slipped disc? — which is how I got on to Alexander Technique. The teacher I go to is a very good listener — she actually asks brilliant questions, more like a therapist. I think she saved my life, bless her. She's a lovely woman.' He smiled as if reminiscing about tender shared moments.

A shock so fierce it hurt sliced through her. Was it jealousy? Surely not. After all, she had never had any claims where Mark was concerned. Envy? That was more likely. When had anyone thought of her so generously? Trusting herself only to be curt, she nodded and handed him the flan and the bread. 'Do you want to watch the local news? See what coverage Rebecca's getting?'

To her amazement, he covered the hand with which she reached for the zapper with his. 'Does it matter? We shall know soon enough. Just eat, Fran. And then you have a zizz while I do the dishes.'

'I'm fine,' she insisted brightly. She applied herself to picking at her salad. She could hear nothing but the blood rushing in her ears. She couldn't see for tears.

After a while, he removed his hand.

Why hadn't she turned hers to respond to the pressure? Why couldn't she have turned her hand? Whose response was she afraid of, hers or his? Almost paralysed, she picked on — a radish here, an olive there. An echo of a long-forgotten meal rang in her head. Did she wish to listen or keep it at bay? No, no more painful memories now. Enough had been more than enough.

Mark was holding the bottle over her glass. Speechless, she nodded, and swigged down all he poured. And she'd meant to stay entirely sober. She looked up, foolish finger to guilty mouth.

He said nothing. And she wished she was sober enough to read the expression in his eyes.

* * *

This time he drove. Although she'd been sure she wouldn't sleep when she consented to lie on the floor, Alexander-style, he'd had to shake her awake again. This time he'd brought strong coffee.

As he waited at a halt sign, she listened to her latest phone message. It was from Michael Penn: he'd heard on the grapevine that legal moves to cease feeding Elise would start soon, though she might care to verify it for herself.

'Talk about Scylla and Charybdis,' Mark said. 'Still, that's what people like — like the Chief are there for: to make decisions.'

'The Chief and you,' she corrected him mildly. 'You're my immediate boss, after all.'

'But I'm biased: I like working with you. Like old times, isn't it, this weekend? Sharing the desk, bickering over whose turn it was to use the phone or make the tea? We were a good team. Always.'

'You always gave in when I demanded something,' she agreed, her sleep having apparently freed something up. 'Which is what a good boss does.'

'You certainly never did as you were told,' he said, his voice amused.

'You rarely told me to do anything. You were a wonderful sounding board, though. Is that the right term? It was great to bounce ideas off you at the end of the day. And not about budgets and policy documents and responses to crazy Home Office directives. Real issues. Is that why you emerged from your ivory tower this weekend to help in the incident room?'

There was a tiny hesitation. 'More or less. I'm not at the cutting edge of detection any more, Fran, and that's a fact. But I thought just manning a phone would help. A missing child . . .'

'It was certainly good for morale. Everyone appreciated it. Me especially,' she added, 'since my position was tenuous, to say the least.'

'What a load of balls! And if you don't believe me, ask the team. It won't have done Henson's first week any good, that's the trouble. In any case, I could hardly have swanned down to Devon to mess round in a boat, could I? But it was you who pulled everything together, Fran.'

'Nope. I just facilitated. We've got a well-oiled system now—'

'Thanks to you!'

'—and everyone just knew what they had to do. Pity it didn't work. God, that poor child. Mark, do you mind if I make a call?'

He shrugged: she could go ahead.

But the call she made was to do with Elise. 'Tom: any calls on Alan Pitt's mobile?'

'Haven't checked recently, ma'am. It was the next thing on my list, like. Well, next thing but five.'

'No problem.' Or was there? 'Tell you what, get a general call out for his car. Locate and — yes, intercept. If Dr Pitt wants to play games with me, I'll play games with him. OK? And Tom, have you had a lunch break? No, I thought not. Well, take one. Now. Before you do anything else. That's an order. And take half a dozen others with you.' She cut the call, turning to Mark. 'Only it's Henson that should have said that, isn't it? Shit!'

He shrugged. 'I'd no idea you still thought Pitt was in the frame.' He must have been as tired as she still was, despite the caffeine: he was driving like a Sunday crawler. All he needed was a cloth cap.

'His DNA cleared him. But his refusal to talk to anyone but me really rattled Tom — it's as if he's taken it personally.'

'Not very professional!'

'Oh, it's not a vendetta. But I think he's half on to something — something neither of us knows about yet.'

'Something you feel in your bunion?'

'Exactly. Anyway, we shall see. Did I tell you what I did this morning? While you were asleep? I got my sister on to my parents' case — I think.' She explained.

'So you won't need a lift there this weekend?'

She heard what she was sure was disappointment in his voice. Her heart lifted in response. And sank again. How could she possibly embark on a love affair that might last only the couple of months it would take to work out her notice and move down to Teignmouth? 'Depends on the Rebecca case, doesn't it?' She added, more positively despite herself, 'Whenever you offer a lift, be sure I shall accept it.'

'Good.'

'Tell you what, why don't we go and have a look at Ashford, just in case.'

It wasn't in case of anything, as they both knew. But Fran always liked to check and recheck a possible scene of crime. Mark, silent, seemed content to walk almost in her wake as they explored the parts of the main street and its offshoots where the market was held. Every lamp-post carried a poster with Rebecca's face on it.

'There'll be a reconstruction on Friday,' she told him. 'I've asked the heads of all the local schools to release their pupils for the relevant period, in case any of them were round here. And we've got one of Rebecca's cousins to retrace what we know of her steps.'

'You've done well,' he said, but absently.

She chose to address his words, not the distance. 'Not well enough! I feel a total failure, Mark: Elise, Rebecca, my parents — can't sort any of them.'

'You will.' He slowed to a halt and looked around. 'Funny little town, isn't it? Unlovely.'

'But quite old. I remember reading up on it when I thought I might live here—'

'With Ian? Would you have sold your lovely cottage and moved *here*?'

'It was all so long ago I can't remember if we'd got round to discussing where we'd live.' If only she could have framed the words he deserved to hear — that just as he would have died for Tina, but now needed to live for himself, so she too had moved on from Ian. As it was, she sounded brusque, dismissive, even to her own ears. What had happened to her? Only a week ago she'd bought new undies from the very shop they were standing outside so she wouldn't be embarrassed when they slept together. Nothing like the wonderful fuchsia set currently dominating the window, more was the pity.

Could a senior officer, burdened by two major enquiries, really take two more minutes out to slip in and buy them? Why ever not?

But first her mobile and then his chimed in. And, answering the calls, they turned as one and returned to the car. At last, when they were sitting soberly side by side, eyes on the road, she managed something. 'This business of my parents — and Hazel — is really knocking me about. Things I want to do, things I want to say: nothing comes out right. I'm sorry.'

Safely strapped in, he did what she'd hoped he'd do. He released the wheel and squeezed her hand. This time she managed to return the squeeze. Yes. Perhaps it would be all right.

CHAPTER TWENTY-THREE

The Chief looked embarrassed as he sat down on the far side of his desk, but said nothing as he gestured Fran into a chair. She folded her hands in her lap, waiting. She had a fair idea of what was coming: the terse note on her desk telling her to go straight to his office had been a good indication. Henson had no doubt thrown his toys out of his pram and demanded her removal from the case.

After the initial surge of fury, she realised she'd be very grateful if he had. She owed it to the child to drive through every possible aspect of the investigation in as short as possible a time in the hope she might still be alive: if that meant graciously handing over the case to a younger, more energetic officer, so be it. Equally she wanted to obtain justice for Elise, and now time was getting short for that.

'Tell me about the Rebecca case,' the Chief said suddenly.

Why? Surely Henson had updated him? Or, more likely, Mark? 'We've obtained every inch of CCTV footage we can. We've virtually torn apart the family computer. She doesn't possess a mobile phone—'

'No mobile!'

'A pleasantly old-fashioned family: she has to use the family TV and computer, and she's learning classical piano.

As decent and normal a kid as you'd wish to find, according to her teachers, likely to romp through her 11plus. Wants to be a doctor and work for *Médecins sans Frontières*. Friends' computers and mobiles — zilch so far. No threats, no stalkers, no nothing. It's as if someone lifted a manhole and pulled her down. My God. I never checked for roadworks!' Borrowing a ballpoint from his desk-tidy, she wrote on the palm of her hand.

He laughed dryly. 'I was under the impression that you were supposed to be running the investigation, not doing everything yourself.'

'It took me many years to learn to delegate, then a few more to remember to. It's taken me two days to forget. I think it was working solo on the Elise case — solo but for DC Arkwright. He's a very bright officer.'

'What sort of progress are you making there?' Ignoring her plug for the young man, he leaned back, shielding his eyes from the westering sun.

What had happened to his interest in the missing schoolgirl? Maybe he'd come back to it. She reached to adjust the blinds. 'Very slow. But we've had some significant breaks recently. I'm fairly sure the victim's not actually called Elise, but that her car was. Several other brand-new Lotuses were stolen soon after they were bought, but not from the same dealer. We were just tracing the actual salesman when this case blew up and it was all hands on deck.'

'Do you want to stick with this or get back to Elise?'

There was a choice? 'The situation in Devon hasn't improved, sir.'

'My son was telling me that one regime — the Romans? — used to tie people they didn't like to two horses, which were driven in opposite directions. Very painful. And of course, lethal. The result would be two dead half bodies, quite useless.'

Fran responded, 'That sums up the situation of a lot of women like me, I should imagine. It could be even worse: I could have children to worry about.' Or a lover.

'I believe there's a government initiative to allow carers such as yourself time off work: let's hope it works better than some of their other initiatives. In the meantime, what would you prefer to do?'

'Judgement of Solomon time: it's a decision only you and Mark can make, sir. With considerable input from Chief Superintendent Henson. I am, in all honesty, doing a high-profile part of his job, a situation he must find very difficult. I would. For all one says he's new in post and has got to get up to speed with all departmental issues, in his position I'd want to be involved in a case with, one hopes, a very good outcome.'

'Would you be his second in command? Bring him up to speed on both the theoretical and the immediate case?'

'No.' The monosyllable was intended to be flat. 'And I wouldn't want him to be second to me, either. The team will work well without my input, sir. As you just pointed out, I'm an administrator, these days, not a flatfoot. I'm best at sorting out resources and acting as facilitator. I'm sure Chief Superintendent Henson can do both at least as well as I. And if I return to Elise, there'll be no divided loyalties amongst the team. No playground taking sides, which, much as it's to be deplored, is inevitable.'

He raised an eyebrow. 'Funnily enough, I've already intercepted a little delegation heading for Mark. I thought it would put him in an invidious position if he had to deal with it. It seems the teams want you to stay.'

'I hope you gave them short shrift.' Since when had the police been a democratic organisation, she added under her breath.

He nodded, as if agreeing to her unspoken sentiment too. 'I'd heard you were a good officer, Fran: and you are. I just wish there was something we could do to keep you here — a half-time consultancy, perhaps.'

Her heart leapt. But she shook her head. 'My parents' health isn't going to improve, sir. I shall get less reliable, not more. All that commuting when under pressure—' She gave an expressive shrug.

'Why not bring them to a retirement home up here?' he asked.

'There is one: they'd have to agree. And people their age like things very much their way.'

'Would you be paying for their accommodation? In that case, Fran, you're entitled to call the tune.'

All this nice, clear-cut advice! She shook her head. 'I suspect that doesn't apply to one's parents. Now, sir, I ought to be going back to check on those roadworks. And then I'll return to the Elise case, taking Tom Arkwright with me, if that's all right by you.'

He laughed. 'I think it's for the best. Obviously, Henson'll have first call if things really get tricky. You're looking very much better,' he added, as she got to her feet, 'if I may say so.'

Perhaps she was. There was her new hairstyle for one thing, which suited her far better than any she'd had recently. As for her debilitating flushes, either she'd been too busy to notice them or they'd started to subside. That was one good thing to come out of the Elise case, at least. Even if the Chief had wrong-footed her over Tom. At the door, she paused. 'May I ask you something, sir? In absolute confidence?'

'Go ahead.'

'Tell me — why did you think it would be invidious for Mark to deal with that deputation?'

'Good God, Fran — how could the man possibly deal with it? When you and he are . . .' He gave an expressive gesture. 'I thought it was common knowledge.'

'Sir.' She turned smartly and left the room.

* * *

'My office. Now,' Fran muttered as she passed Tom's desk. Deputation indeed. And what might his part be in it? She sat ostentatiously the far side of the desk and folded her arms. 'Well, young man?' She could sound a termagant when she wanted to.

Snapping to sudden and rigid attention, he fixed a spot on the wall an inch above her head. 'Ma'am?'

At least she could award him points for picking up nuances, admittedly not so subtle in the present instance.

'This deputation to the Chief: what do you know about it?'

'It wasn't to the Chief, ma'am: it was to the ACC — Mr Turner.'

'And what part did you have in its organisation?'

'None at all, ma'am. On the contrary, if anyone had asked me—' He stopped abruptly.

'If anyone had asked you — what would you have said?' She kept her face stern, least she betray herself by laughing.

'Sooner we could get back on the Elise case the better. I don't mind being a small fish, ma'am, because I shall make sure I get bigger, but it's better being a small fish in your pond than in Henson's. If you see what I mean.'

'I take it you haven't yet said that to Chief Superintendent Henson.'

'Not on your life, ma'am. It'd be letting you down, like, wouldn't it?'

Would it? She couldn't see how.

'Being insubordinate, when you've always stressed the need for appropriate use of management structures, ma'am,' he continued. 'But please don't ask me to tell you who it was, ma'am, because that would be inappropriate betrayal of a confidence.'

'It would indeed,' she said. 'Plus it was a damned silly trick, and I wouldn't wish to know which of my colleagues had been stupid enough to get involved. OK, Tom. Take the weight off your feet and update me.' As she unfolded her arms she noticed her message to herself. 'No! Not yet!' She held up the hand like a traffic policeman's. 'Before we do anything else, go and check the CCTV footage of the Rebecca case and see if you can see any of those striped — or otherwise — tents they sometime erect over holes in the road. I think BT use them for a start.'

His face fell. 'I thought we were back on the Elise case. Now that you're back in your own room, like.'

'We will be soon. But truly the hunt for Rebecca is urgent enough to transcend office politics — go and do as I say. I'll phone Dr Alan bloody Pitt and leave a message he won't like.'

Was that the best policy? Although she'd have liked to blaze at him with a broadside, she wondered if a more emollient approach might produce better results. So, when, as expected, she was asked to leave a message, she was almost silky — but not enough to arouse his suspicions, she hoped. 'Dr Pitt. This is Fran Harman here. I'm sorry I've been unavailable — the current case has been placing demands on us which sometimes make us appear discourteous to people wishing to reach us. But I now have some news for you and would be grateful if you would call me as soon as you receive this. Just in case you don't have it handy, this is my number.' There. She'd been half-tempted to give him her mobile number, but had decided against. He was the sort of person who could have stalking proclivities. Was another visit to his bungalow in order? A surprise one this time? Or was he simply winding her up and wasting her time?

She compromised. As soon as Tom had checked on road works in Ashford High Street, she'd get him to check on Pitts' calls and the intercept request. Meanwhile, it wouldn't do any harm to sit and remind herself where they'd got so far and plot their next moves.

* * *

When Tom hadn't returned almost an hour later, she decided it was time to go in search of him. He'd probably got deeply involved in his searches for the workman's tent and lost track of time. In any case, though she was no longer directly involved in the search for the child, she couldn't pretend she wasn't, like everyone else, deeply concerned. But her mobile rang. Elaine!

'Are you OK, Fran?'

'Why shouldn't I be?'

'Because I said I was coming to stay tonight, and you said I'd be welcome tomorrow.'

'Ah. That's what happens when you do your emails with your eyes closed. You're just as welcome tonight. In fact, things have changed here so I may be back at a civilised hour. You still like Chinese? Great — our usual menu for two? Excellent. See you about eight.' So she'd better make sure she left work by seven-thirty. At least she could phone ahead for the meal . . .

* * *

There was no sign of Tom in the incident room, so he wasn't whiling his time away with a good gossip. Hating herself for looking like a nagging mother, she wandered apparently casually down to the room where all the video equipment was kept, to find it empty, all the equipment switched off.

She wouldn't demean herself by standing outside the gents' loo hollering, nor by hunting him in the canteen. She didn't need to. Staggering under a tea tray the size of a coffin lid, he emerged from the lift, followed by one of the computer inputters, a girl of no more than eighteen, carrying a smaller tray on which she could see plates of biscuits. Top marks to someone for thinking of the workers, bottom marks for turning Tom into the minion. Following at a discreet distance, she heard a male voice bellowing from the far side of the room. Though she didn't pick up every word, the gist was enough. Tom had taken far too long to do the bidding of the owner of the voice.

A quiet word was evidently called for. Apart from the fact that she believed that Tom was her deputy, no longer a member of the larger enquiry team, it was a wicked waste of resources to send a constable as bright as he on such a menial errand. If she could identify the owner of the voice, she would tell him so, though not in front of his peers. Ritual humiliation had never been part of her arsenal.

A stringy man she didn't recognise seemed to be the source of the problem. His presence in a room where she thought she had at very least a nodding acquaintance with everyone was disconcerting enough. That he should be senior enough to be giving orders was more of a problem. There was no sign of Henson, but no reason for there to be. As she and the Chief had agreed, officers at their level should be thinking about policy and direction, not dealing with everyday minutiae.

Her instinct was to jump down the stranger's throat, and emerge, kicking, at the far end. But just as she'd tempered her response to Pitt, so she felt it advisable to employ her diplomatic skills. Waiting by the door till Tom had finished his waiter's duties, she caught his eye and beckoned him over, drawing him outside before she spoke.

'Who's that weaselly little guy who thinks you're silver service?'

'Someone from the Murder Investigation Team.'

'MIT! You mean they've found—?' If Rebecca's body had been located, and she hadn't been told, then diplomatic was the last thing she'd be.

'The Chief Superintendent thought it would be better if we work in tandem, ma'am. You can see how optimistic *he* is,' he added miserably.

It made sense, though it wasn't good for the CID team's morale, driven as they were into efforts like hers by the hope that they might find the child alive.

She nodded noncommittally. 'What's his name? And rank?'

'He's another new kid on the block. Friend of the new super's from the Met. DCI Patton.'

'Any relation to the general?' But Tom looked completely blank, so she continued, 'Did you have any joy with the CCTV footage?'

He shook his head, indignant. 'They said they'd checked and double-checked and that I might as well make myself useful. That's how I ended up as tea-boy.'

'Did you give any hint that I might not be best pleased to lose one of my best officers to such a lowly task? An excellent detective who happens to be my only detective?'

His mouth tightened in a grim smile. 'As to that, ma'am, it seems I'm not any more. Henson says I'm still part of his team.'

'As a tea-wallah. Great. Get on with whatever Patton wants you to do for the time being, Tom. I'll sort things out — if you still want to be my little fish?' She smiled affectionately. He responded.

* * *

She and Henson did exchange smiles, largely because Mark was leaning on the back of one of the chairs in Henson's office, gripping the back till his knuckles whitened. Perhaps Henson's comment about her being a superannuated old whore had reached Mark's ears. Though, she conceded, there might have been other complaints. She nodded respectfully to Mark, as if thanking him for tacit permission to interrupt them.

'Carl, there may have been a misunderstanding. I believe young Tom Arkwright's off the Rebecca case unless things really hot up. He's back with me, on—'

'Then you believe wrong, Ms Harman. I need all the officers I can get and now you've decided to slope off—' To her amazement, and possibly that of both men, she laid a warning hand on Mark's arm. What the hell was she doing? A word from him could have sorted everything. She removed it quickly.

'Mr Henson, choose your words more carefully. We're all tired—'

'Even those of you who took the morning off?'

'Even those of us who took the morning off,' she smiled. Let him dig his own pit and hop into it. 'So let us not waste our limited resources on having a row. As I'm sure the ACC here will confirm, the Chief Constable has told me to return to the Elise case. I agreed, provided that DC Arkwright could continue to assist me whenever I need him. So I'd like him to stop being general factotum to the MIT DCI and return to the tasks I've asked him to do.'

‘Including looking at the CCTV tapes for the umpteenth time?’

She raised the hand, the ballpoint scrawl still visible. ‘Exactly so. So what I’d like is for him to be asked to do just that, to look for what I asked him to look for and then return to the Elise case, unless, of course, he can be truly useful in your investigation. Thanks.’ She nodded to both men and withdrew.

By the time she’d returned to her office, having gone via the loo, there was a cup of coffee waiting for her, sitting on a scrawl from Tom: *Checking video. T.*

CHAPTER TWENTY-FOUR

'Let me get this straight,' Elaine said, waving her chopsticks in surprisingly elegant emphasis. 'You really like this man who happens to be your boss, he's an old friend of yours, you fancy him like mad, he's single — OK, a widower, and you say falling in love is inconvenient. What planet are you on, Fran?'

'This one, more's the pity. I have to go down to Teignmouth as soon as I work out my notice. And I go down there practically every weekend as it is. How can I possibly make space in my life for falling in love?'

'Won't wash. You made space for Ian, in the middle of your PhD, in the middle of a huge case here.'

Fran dropped her gaze, and then lifted her eyes again. 'There was a future in that. We planned to live the rest of our lives together.'

'Are you saying you should only love someone as a long-term investment? Not a lot of romance there, Fran. Hey, looks as if we'd better open that other bottle.'

'If I have another drop I shall be asleep with my head in all these little plastic trays — neat, aren't they? You can wash them, fill them with your own food for the freezer and microwave them.'

Chopsticks now suspended over a choice king prawn, Elaine regarded her with pained exasperation. 'You weren't always like this, Fran. What's gone wrong?' She put them down and opened more wine regardless.

'I was always like this. It's just that it shows more now I'm middle-aged. I can't eat late at night, drink as much, stay awake as long. Where's all the fun?'

'With this Mark, by the sound of it. What does the poor man say about being dumped before he's even started?'

'He hasn't been dumped. We just haven't quite . . . He was going to give me a lift to Devon last weekend only this missing child case blew up and we both stayed to help.'

'A lift? Doesn't sound very romantic.'

'Nothing about Devon is very romantic. Not the part I go to anyway. But we were due to go out to dinner with some friends of his. Hence the hairdo.' She tugged at it.

'Which he has seen. And remarked on?'

'Briefly. Well, we worked right across the weekend with hardly a break.' But he could have said something more. Other people had. When she had bumped into him at the supermarket even that loathsome Pitt had said it with his eyes. 'Any more?' She looked in something like despair at the food congealing in all those microwavable plastic dishes.

For answer, Elaine got to her feet and shot off, returning with the kitchen bin, into which she swept everything, chopsticks and all.

'Hang on — I told you, I wash and recycle—'

'Bugger recycling! For God's sake, Fran, how many little plastic boxes do you need?'

'A lot. For my parents' meals.' She explained.

Elaine snorted, but made no effort to retrieve the boxes, instead grabbing the bin and disappearing. 'Let me get this straight too,' Elaine said, as she returned. 'You work your socks off here and then every weekend you drive some two hundred-odd miles to Devon where you slave full-time and then drive two hundred-odd miles home — or, if I know you, straight into work, where for five more days you toil before setting off to Devon.'

Fran nodded. That summed it up, didn't it?

'No wonder you've no time for this Mark character. So he decides to make a bit of time with you — well, they get big jams on that route — by offering you a lift. And back?'

'He didn't suggest I thumb a lift. Actually, he's been extraordinarily kind these last few weeks. Patient, tolerant. We've had dinner—'

'A good snog afterwards?'

'You're incorrigible! But today, when I had a stand-up row with another officer, one who, incidentally, referred to me as a "superannuated old whore", presumably because everyone except Mark and I seems to think we're an item—'

'Hang on. Did this bastard say that in front of Mark? I'm losing the thread. I must have had too much wine.' Elaine inspected the bottle and poured another glass each.

'No.' She meant to answer Elaine's question, not decline the wine, though she should have done. She got up to fetch mineral water but before she could leave the room Elaine continued her cross-examination.

'In front of anyone else?'

'A roomful of interested ears. So—'

'And has he been had up for a disciplinary? Fran, why ever not? You really aren't yourself, are you? Anyway, this row later in front of him — did Mark take your part?'

'No. I actually put my hand on his arm to stop him. It was my row and I didn't want him chipping in.'

'He's your senior officer, Fran: he's entitled to chip in.'

'Well, he didn't. Afterwards, I rather expected him to summon me to his office or come round to mine. Or phone. Or something. Even though I wanted to be here to welcome you — Elaine, this sounds awful — I hung round doing my filing and checking my emails for ages, just in case he made contact. But he didn't.'

Elaine pulled a face. 'On the other hand,' she added, 'if he's senior to you he must be a very big wig — mightn't he just have been busy? Why don't you phone him?' She tossed over the handset. 'Go on, phone him — while I go and have a pee. Heavens, is that the time? I've got to get up at the crack of dawn to get that train!'

'What shall I say?'

'Well, you could tell him you're both being bloody fools pussy-footing around, but I don't suppose you will. Listen, Fran. Life isn't a dress rehearsal, so far as I know. So what if you and this guy have only a few weeks together? If it doesn't work out then a few weeks is quite long enough. If it does, then you'll just have to find some way round the Devon problem. OK?'

Fran let the handset fall into her lap. She retrieved it and replaced it on the phone, which she switched to answer-phone mode. Kitchen next: she had to lay breakfast things for Elaine.

'Now what are you up to?' Elaine stood, hands on hips, in the doorway.

'Breakfast things.'

'I thought you always ate at work? And I shall be having a champagne breakfast on the train, thanks very much.'

Fran nodded. Switching on the dishwasher, she asked idly, 'What are you doing in France this time? Selling a load of anti-ageing pills?'

'Better — doing the shops, buying more than I can afford, eating at the best restaurants.'

'I wish I could come with you.'

'Next time maybe. This time I'm doing what you should be doing: I'm meeting my lover.'

* * *

Had Elise ever had a lover, if not, of course, in the physical sense? A gentleman friend, then? Awoken early despite Elaine's efforts to be quiet, Fran arrived at work when the night shift were still keeping the search for Rebecca ticking over.

To her amusement, the whiteboards continually updated with developments now bore the words *Roadworks? Workmen's shelters?* Where had they got that from, eh?

The gloom of the early morning was clearing to reveal a bright sunny day. She might just be magnanimous in victory and lend Tom Arkwright to the other team, and make herself scarce, doing the basic gumshoeing she'd started to enjoy again. Elise, aka Miss Marjorie Gray, had lived in St Mary's Bay. Why not give herself a trip to the seaside? She could doorstep the neighbours as well as Tom, better, probably, given the likely age of the people she wanted to talk to. She might even find a nice seafront café for breakfast. When had she last seen the sea? It seemed it was possible to spend an infinite number of weekends in Teignmouth, English Riviera resort par excellence, without even seeing it, and certainly without feeling the spray in your face.

In the absence of any communication from Mark — she had checked both her pigeonhole and, less hopefully, her desk, she resolved to set out at once. St Mary's Bay wouldn't compete with Paris and a lover, but it would have to do.

Would the rest of her life consist of things that would have to do?

Leaving a note for Tom, confirming he was to report to Henson, but not for Mark, she straightened, pulling her shoulders back and looking as bright as she could. She would stride through the outer office as briskly as if she were meeting the Home Secretary himself.

With luck, she could vacate her car park space before Mark arrived.

Or would it be even better luck to come face to face with him? To be forced to do what Elaine had advised — confront the issue face on.

There was another way he might have communicated. She switched on her computer and scrolled through her incoming emails. Nothing.

But that didn't mean she couldn't send him one. What would it say? For a start, that she was leaving the building and might be away till lunch or longer. At her level there was no need to give an account of herself, not in any formal sense, but she had always instilled in those she trained that being off on a job was no excuse for keeping management in the dark about their movements. Why not add something else? A simple invitation for supper would do. A repeat of last night's meal, without the references to little plastic boxes — though Mark, with his recycling tendencies, would probably thoroughly approve.

There. It was done and sent. Not so very hard. The hard part would be waiting for his response. It was a good job she had St Mary's Bay to occupy her thoughts.

* * *

Miss Gray had lived in a cul-de-sac of bungalows in a pseudo-Spanish mode, all with names like *Hacienda* or *Casita*. There was, if not a forest, then a plantation of For Sale signs, about half with Sold tacked across them. She rang the bell — the chime was incredibly protracted — of Buena Vista, Miss Gray's former home. No one responded. She applied her eye then, on impulse, her nose to the letterbox. There was nothing to see, but the smell of old people seeped unmistakably back. She recoiled as if from the stench of decomposition itself.

The houses to either side of Miss Gray's bungalow still had their curtains drawn. Perhaps knowing there was nowhere in the immediate area that opened its respectable doors for breakfast before ten encouraged oversleeping. Fran's stomach rolled plaintively for the canteen meal she'd ignored. So where were the signs of life? At last a Passat shot into the close, swinging stylishly on to the drive of the house opposite Buena Vista, missing the For Sale sign by inches, and parking with precision two inches from the garage door. From it emerged a middle-aged, track-suited couple, she opening the front door while he dug in the boot for a multi-racquet tennis bag. This house had no name in curly wrought iron letters affixed to the wall. A distinctly *sub fusc* sign by the For

Sale sign conceded the house was *Hermosa*. Fran found herself liking the couple before she'd even met them.

They didn't, however, respond to her ring immediately. After a few moments' interval, she applied her thumb again, and the door was answered by a man possibly in his later fifties, maybe early sixties, wearing a bathrobe.

She flashed her ID. 'Chief Superintendent Fran Harman. Kent CID. May I have a very few minutes of your time? I'm making enquiries about one of your neighbours.'

'I was just about to have a shower.'

It sounded as if the woman was already doing so.

'I could wait,' she said mildly.

He nodded her in, and led the way to the living room, a room decorated in a spare modern style that Fran warmed to immediately.

'If you really don't mind, Chief Superintendent, I'll go and change.'

'Take your time, Mr — er? If you want to shower first, that's fine by me,' she said expansively, surprising even herself.

'Drayton. Neil Drayton. My wife Julie will be with you in a moment. I'm afraid we don't have long. We're meeting some friends in London for lunch, then a gallery. Can't miss the train.'

'Don't worry — I'll be as quick as I can.' She sat on the sofa and looked round: prints, china, a lovely piece of coloured glass — the Draytons had the knack of home-making.

Mrs Drayton appeared, her white, cropped hair still wet. 'Time for tea or coffee, Chief Superintendent? We usually have coffee but—'

'Coffee's fine, thanks.' Fran got up and followed her hostess into a kitchen labouring under the impression that it was in some mythical prairie farmhouse, all dark wood and curlicues. 'As I told your husband, I really need some information about one of your neighbours, one who may have left the area about two years ago.'

Mrs Drayton pulled a face. 'We've not been here much longer. There's a very brisk turnover rate in Death Valley.'

'Death Valley?'

'This close. Look at the For Sale signs. Deaths, all of them. Except ours. Retirement's one thing, but hanging round for the undertaker's quite another. That's why we're leaving. We thought we'd fit in, but we don't. Moral: when you reach retirement age, settle with a load of youngsters — much more fun. Well, not the very young: they need babysitting. But people in their forties and fifties — people your age, still active and interesting. And whatever you do, don't even think of retiring to a seaside resort. In the summer you can't park and in the winter you don't want to. Sea views! Have you ever watched the sea in the winter? It makes you suicidal.' She made instant coffee in mugs, and, apparently as an afterthought, tipped Waitrose biscuits on to a plate. The hands were those of a much older woman than Fran had expected from the face and figure. So how old was her hostess?

'Where are you moving to? Somewhere nearer your children?'

'Why on earth would we want to do that?' Mrs Drayton seemed genuinely astonished. 'We're going to try out Exeter. That's supposed to be vibrant and full of life. We're only renting, so if we don't like it we can move to Birmingham. Or Nottingham. Or wherever.'

Mr Drayton, hair also still wet, bounded into the living room a moment after their return, depositing himself on the sofa and stretching long legs. His age? The fashions in the photos of them on top of the TV suggested they must have been in their seventies. No, surely not. Did people still play tennis at that age? Without the photos she'd have put them in their mid-sixties. Somewhere they'd found a fount of protracted, if not eternal, youth.

She produced the old e-fit of Elise. Miss Marjorie Gray.

'Imagine her with dark hair — greying, at least. Could she possibly have been a neighbour?'

'Not that nice quiet woman, what was her name?' her husband joined in.

'You do know her, then?'

'Well, it's not a very good likeness, if it *is* her. Mind you, we hardly saw her.'

'She kept herself to herself, you mean?'

'She did, but that wasn't what I meant, is it, Julie? I meant we're hardly ever here to see her. We've just got back from the Galapagos Islands, Superintendent. Hey, are you sure you're a chief superintendent? On TV it's always a couple of detectives, usually a DCI and a constable or sergeant.'

She held up her ID again. 'We rarely do more than flash them, I'm afraid. And I'm afraid the TV's wrong — it's usually one constable, two at most, that you get, but this is a one-off case and I just fancied keeping my hand in.'

'Better than being behind a desk on a day like this,' he agreed, nodding out of the window.

'Assuming it might be Miss Gray, do you have any idea what happened to her?'

'There was talk that she sold up and moved away as soon as her parents died. There was a rumour,' Mrs Drayton added, leaning closer, 'that she sold the house for cash for far less than its asking price. And she tried to throw carpets and furniture and curtains in as well.'

'Really? Now why should she want to do that?' Fran wondered aloud.

'A clean break, she said. She was making a clean break and going back up north,' Mr Drayton supplied.

'You've no idea where up north?'

He shook his head. 'There's a lot of it, isn't there? So if you were trying to trace her . . .'

'In fact,' Mrs Drayton said, 'I have an idea that the purchasers demanded she completely empty the house. The smell,' she added delicately. 'A bit musty. You know how it is.'

Mrs Drayton looked discreetly at her watch; Mr Drayton was far more open. 'Our train, Superintendent. We can only stay another five minutes.'

'You've been more than helpful as it is,' Fran said swiftly. 'I suppose you wouldn't recall which estate agent dealt with the property?'

'A local one. Burgoynes, I think. Or Butterfield. You see so many signs, Chief Superintendent.'

'So I see. Now, I'll leave you to enjoy what I hope is a wonderful day. But — before I do — perhaps I could ask you one more favour? No, it's not urgent. Could you possibly identify the person we think this is?' She tapped the e-fit.

'A body!' Both recoiled. 'If it's our duty,' he conceded.

'Not a body at all,' Fran said reassuringly. She added, more honestly, 'Actually, it may be even more upsetting.'

CHAPTER TWENTY-FIVE

Waving her energetic hosts goodbye, Fran tried another couple of Elise's possible neighbours, now, according to their curtains, ready to tackle the world. One old lady, apparently as sane as Fran when she invited her in and offered her tea, declared with total conviction that Elise was the Prime Minister, and if only she could remember her name she wouldn't have to go into a home, would she? The other neighbour, a man so old his skin was reptilian, laboured under the impression that Fran was there to check his colostomy bag.

Her notes recorded that for identification purposes, the Draytons were the best bet. They did not record her dry cough as she wrote the words.

The morning sun was warm, despite an increasingly searching wind. Why not leave the car where it was and go and look at the sea? Because she was supposed to be working, that was why — just as she was in Teignmouth.

So why did she turn the car not towards Hythe, but to New Romney and thence Dungeness? How long was it since she'd seen the moonscape of shingle, dominated by the nuclear power-station, that monolithic testament to industrial brutalism somehow far more in keeping with its surroundings than the brightly-coloured eccentric little houses and bungalows that seemed to sprout at random? And certainly more appropriate than the jolly little railway station. No, today there was no narrow-gauge train to catch back to the mythical somewhere she and Mark had once spoken of.

Mark? There was no reply yet to her supper invitation.

Her suit and elegant shoes were ludicrously inadequate to deal with the wind here, the sun failing in its battle against lowering clouds. Even her lungs had trouble, the air being forced in and sucked out according to whether she was facing the sea or bracing her back to it. On impulse she turned into the wind, and yelled at the top of her voice, '*Blow, blow, ye hurricanoes! Blow!*' No doubt the Chief would be able to identify the play. She couldn't. But she could identify with whoever was battling against irresistible elements.

Was there anywhere like this she could seek refuge when she was down in Devon? How could she tell, when for as many years as she could remember Devon had been Teignmouth, and one very small corner of it at that?

A refuge! A place as bleak and arid as this? A symbol of her life, more like.

* * *

She'd come so far south and west she decided not to head back to Maidstone via the Hythe junction of the M20, but to pick up one of the roads Sheila Adams had so despised, the A259. From it she could pick up a much faster road north to Ashford, and thus the motorway. On impulse, however, she pulled into Ashford itself, parking behind the police station, where she was always sure of a decent cup of tea in the canteen, and often some friendly company, especially in the CID office. She ought to enquire about what the uniform inspector's son, her godson, and his fiancée had on their wedding list. She could also get warm: even the Saab's heater hadn't been able to penetrate the Dungeness permafrost.

But she wasn't sure whether it was the wind at Dungeness that had so chilled her. Was it not the way the Draytons had calmly dismissed any notion that they might wish to be near their children in their old age? It had always been assumed that her parents wanted her to look after them, but that might have been the family equivalent of custom and practice. Ever since their move down, her mother had insisted that Fran would have the place when they no longer needed it, to quote her euphemism. They had even signed it over to Hazel and herself, in a conscious attempt to compel social services to pay for their accommodation should one or both of them ever be forced into residential care. Fran had vociferously opposed the idea: she was in no need of any money, and rather thought it was her civic duty to stump up whatever was needed. But Hazel had overruled her — she was as poor as a kirk mouse, she said, drawing a laugh from her parents and even the solicitor, and if anything happened to Fran then she certainly couldn't do anything to help. In vain Fran had pointed out it wasn't a matter of helping: it was simply that her parents would have to sell what was in no respect a family home, with none of the sentimental attachments that that might imply, and use the money to support themselves. Hazel and her parents were on precisely the same wavelength, and when Pa had reached ostentatiously for his heart-pills, clearly unable to deal with any stress, she'd simply buttoned her lip. After that it had been all too easy to be drawn into her mother's ghoulish plans for changing the place to suit her, when all she'd ever want to do was scream that she wanted none of it, ever.

An irate tap on the window brought her back to Ashford. But the frown on the face at the window turned to a smile when the woman offended by her apparently illicit parking recognised her. DCI Jill Tanner, a slightly younger contemporary, pulled open the car door and welcomed her with literally open arms: 'We've had a breakthrough! That new chief superintendent of yours — no one likes him but he's had a real brainwave!'

'Nothing to do with workmen's striped shelters, I suppose?' Fran eased out of the car and returned the hug.

Tanner's face fell — then lit up. 'Don't tell me — he's one of those bastards that insists all his underlings' ideas are his own!'

'We've all tried it on, haven't we, Jill? I know I did, until someone older and wiser told me it was more important to win hearts than score points. But it's plain daft at his level: everyone knows we're only administrators and policy-makers. Let the kid who had the idea get the praise, that's what I say.' She grinned. 'He deserves it.'

'Ah! Another of your protégés. Come along in — you're frozen. Where have you been?'

'Better just put my parking pass on the windscreen . . . Now, tell me about these workmen's huts, and where the Great Panjandrum has got now he's discovered them on the CCTV tape.'

Jill stopped dead. 'One of your protégés my arse, Fran — it was your idea!'

'You don't need to have bright ideas when you're as close to retirement as I am.'

They swiped their access passes. 'But you're going to teach at Canterbury Uni aren't you?' Jill asked. 'Senior lecturer in Criminology, we heard. The job's got your name on it.'

'Has it indeed?' Fran could drop her voice once they were both inside. 'Well, I certainly didn't put it there.'

'I told everyone it was rubbish — you'd do better to have a part-time secondment, wouldn't you?' Jill led the way through to the CID office.

Fran's welcome wasn't guaranteed today, however, since the squad would harbour a lurking resentment that the big boys at HQ had muscled in on their abduction case. But there was a general waving of hands.

'The idea is that someone pre-planned the whole abduction,' Jill said. 'Apparently Forensics have found a McDonald's drinks cup with traces of some new date-rape drug, not Rohypnol, something sexier, in a bin near the market. And one of the CCTV frames shows a workman's shelter that isn't there fifty minutes later. Your mates are busy checking with McDonald's about who Rebecca might have met there — apparently her parents regard it with total abhorrence, so Rebecca wouldn't ever have let on she went there.'

'So someone laced her drink, lurked outside in this shelter thing till she tottered by, grabbed her and kept her there till he could pop her in a van — plenty of those on market day — and drive off. There's forward planning for you,' Fran concluded.

'Hmm. I wonder how soon the Great Panjandrum will work that out entirely off his own bat,' Jill said.

'I'd better get on the phone and let him have the idea now,' Fran said.

* * *

Although he demurred at first, Tom was delighted to learn that he'd had another idea, and promised to get on to it straight away. He also supplied her with a list of Lotus showrooms: while she was in the area, she reasoned, she might as well do a bit of doorstepping on the local dealers. 'And guv, the ACC's been looking for you. Dead urgent, he said. You'd better get on the blower to him now.'

'Thanks, Tom. Now, go and float that brilliant idea to the powers that be. Thanks for sharing it with me first!' she laughed.

If her voice was steady, her hand certainly wasn't. Why had Mark left a message like that and not simply phoned her? A glance at her mobile showed her she'd let the batteries run down. Should she use an office phone here? No, she certainly wouldn't risk the sort of conversation she might have with Mark with all these ears cocked: if rumour had settled her future occupation so finally, it had probably already decided what she'd wear on her wedding day. Why not, with the Chief Constable setting the pace?

She accepted water from the cooler, had a word with everyone she knew, and melted away as swiftly as she could. After all, they all had work to do.

At least Ashford wasn't a mobile black spot like so many parts of East Kent. And at least the phone jack was in the glove-box where it was supposed to be.

Mark responded first ring, his voice flooded with either pleasure or relief: it was hard to tell. But then he became apologetic. 'Fran: I'm so sorry — I'm going to have to turn down your invitation for this evening.'

She was just framing her mouth to announce brightly that it was short notice and she quite understood when she realised he was still speaking.

'But I wonder if you'd be very kind and help me out. The Chief's had to drop out of some charity speaking engagement — his wife's gone down with some bug — and he's asked me to take his place. His wife was included in the invitation, you see, so I could really use an escort. It won't be quite the meal we planned for Saturday, more rubber chicken than haute cuisine, but—' He was gabbling like a teenager trying for his first date. At least, the sort of teenager she'd been. No doubt the young did things differently these days. Fewer words, more grunts, perhaps.

Think Elaine! 'I'd love to. Give me the details.'

She scribbled them down, doing mental calculations as he spoke. Black tie, so that meant long skirt. A hotel way out in the sticks, so one of them had better stay sober.

But he was saying something she hadn't expected.

'I was wondering if you'd like me to book accommodation? I'm sure expenses would stand it.'

Her turn to say something he hadn't expected. And perhaps she hadn't either. 'I'm sure they would — especially if it was only one room.'

He sounded deeply offended. 'And have it all round the office before we'd even switched off the light!'

'Oh, Mark,' she said, 'don't you think it isn't already?'

'I beg your pardon?'

Was he feigning his anger? Or was he winding her up?

'Just ask the Chief,' she said, adding as lightly as she could, despite her thumping pulses, 'Now, what time is one of us picking the other up? We have to get there, after all, whatever the rooming arrangements.'

Still uncertain of his mood and feelings, she agreed that she should collect him. Then she cut the call abruptly. She might have a car showroom to visit, but she also had a set of fuchsia underwear to buy.

* * *

'No records at all?' she repeated, her voice hard with disbelief. 'You must have some idea of which salesman sold your cars. After all, don't they survive on commission?'

The middle-aged manager opposite her, Stuart Timms according to his name-tag, smiled deprecatingly, as if granting her the right to her anger. 'Since we took over the dealership, yes. We have details of all our transactions, down to the smallest washer for the largest car on computer. And the details are also held centrally, so up at headquarters they know exactly how many small washers the biggest car uses. But that's now. Our predecessors were less efficient.'

'Presumably you inherited staff records?'

'Only for those employees we kept on. Which was not all. You're welcome to those. I'll be happy to get them printed off. Fortunately, unlike our predecessors, we've dispensed with quill pens.'

He smiled and disappeared.

Fran was amused, despite herself. Where had such an articulate man sprung from? His suit was less sharp than she'd expected, too. Despite the merchandise glossily displayed on the forecourt and indeed in the showroom itself, he was no conventional second-hand car salesman. In fact, he was extremely attractive for a man of his age, which was almost certainly the same as hers and Mark's.

If she allowed herself to think of Mark, and his response, opaque at best, to her suggestion, she would lose focus again. So how could she while away the time until Mr Timms' return? Looking at the cars was one way. Would she ever again be tempted to buy such an excess of gleaming automobile? What had driven Elise — or possibly Marjorie Gray — to it? She flinched at her own inadvertent pun. But why buy such a car if you can't drive it? As for herself, she seriously doubted her ability to get in, and certainly out, with anything approaching dignity, unless they had a model for the middle-aged which came with an optional winch.

'Go on, try it,' Timms suggested, coming up so quietly she jumped.

'Not my style.'

'You never know what your style is till you try,' he urged.

'I know what my job is,' she countered. 'Looking at the paperwork you've been kind enough to find me.' She flicked through them. 'I don't suppose you inherited an employee who's your folk memory, did you? Someone who knew everything about everyone past and present, the sort who knows more than the person himself?'

'You're talking about our Harry. The cleaner. Camp as a row of pink tents but so clued up I sometimes think he reads the contents of our waste bins for pleasure.'

'Get a shredder. But Harry might be useful. What time does he work?'

'Five till eight. If we're short, he'll stop back to do some mild valeting. But no, he won't be in till tomorrow, I'm afraid.'

So much for a lie-in after tonight's function. Maybe the separate room idea wasn't such a bad one. If she was to have glorious sex with Mark, she didn't want it inhibited by an alarm call. She smiled. 'Where's the employees' door? And will he come if I ring?'

'I'll be here myself to make sure you're admitted promptly.'

'That won't be necessary.'

'Not necessary, but a courtesy.' Less unctuously he added, 'So long as you time your arrival somewhat nearer eight than five.'

'I think I can promise that. Thank you, Mr Timms. I'll see you tomorrow then.'

'You will indeed. And I'll have an Elise ready for you to test drive.'

* * *

Had detective work always been so frustrating? Had the person you needed to see never been there, the vital paperwork always incomplete? Fran was due half an hour on the phone, chasing up paperwork from all the available dealers that way. Email or fax — it was up to them, so long as she didn't have to hang around waiting any longer. As for test-driving an Elise — well, it was a long time since her sports car days, and though they'd no doubt come on a long way since then, she must simply put it out of her mind.

If only she didn't feel so weak. What was the matter with her? She couldn't be sickening for something, could she?

Hunger, more like: no breakfast and no elevenses. And she'd been so anxious to speak to Mark she'd slipped away from Ashford nick with no more than a cup of water. It had better be a very early canteen lunch.

* * *

And now it was time to chase Alan Pitt. He seemed to have gone entirely to ground. He'd made no phone calls, not unless he'd bought himself a prepayment phone, and, more worryingly, made no withdrawals from his bank. There was no credit card use, either. But his statements showed he could simply be living off his fat, as it were — he'd made large cash withdrawals the previous week, and especially after he'd seen her in Sainsbury's. Drat the man and his stupid games.

She called Michael Penn, to confirm the case had top priority again, and that she planned to take a couple to see 'Elise' who might be able at last to identify her. 'I suppose our friend Dr Pitt hasn't been to see her recently?'

'Not since last week. I don't know whether I did wrong, Chief Superintendent, but I did tell him about the court case coming up. He didn't seem upset or anything. He just went and sat by her as usual, and then gave her his little kiss and marched off. No backward glance or anything dramatic. But then, why should he? I mean, the courts'll take forever, won't they? He can sit and have his cosy little chats, well, monologues, really, for many a month yet.'

'But he hasn't come back since—?'

'Friday or Saturday. Oh, after you were on TV. Imagine, me talking to a star of TV and radio!'

Was he being winsome or sarcastic? She wouldn't respond to either. 'Well, I suppose it's not a very long gap.'

'No, not really. Tell you what, I'll give you a bell if he turns up, shall I? As before?'

'Michael,' she said, registering the change of tone, 'I'd be more than grateful. It really makes our job so much easier when people like you are on our side.' Was that laid on a little too thick?

'I only wish I could help with this other business, Fran,' he responded, all matey. What had brought him back on to her side? Surely he couldn't really have been won over by her five minutes of fame? 'Have you had lots of calls?'

'We've been inundated, I'm glad to say. I don't know how the poor child's parents are coping, I truly don't. I can't even imagine how their family support officer copes, come to think of it.'

'Any "clues"?'

It was always like this — people wanting the inside knowledge. 'Don't worry, Michael: we're getting there,' she said positively, if obliquely.

'I'm sure you are — the only question is, are you getting there fast enough?'

CHAPTER TWENTY-SIX

Michael's was a good question, one she wished she could have answered. Popping her head round her office door, she caught Tom's eye, and gestured him in.

In an almost conspiratorial voice, she asked, 'What's the latest?'

'They're still waiting for the results of DNA tests on the McDonald's beaker. The straw should provide rich pickings, like. But they've also got to sort out any other DNA samples, including those from the McDonald's team member who served her.'

'If someone remembers serving her, surely they remember whoever she sat with — after all, if someone got close enough to doctor it . . .'

'Busy time, they say. Everyone sharing tables. And the CCTV's not helpful.'

'That's an odd thing about CCTV. You drop a bus ticket — not that you would! — and your mug'll be there, fair and square. Someone doses a child's drink and all you get is a foggy silhouette. Tom, I'm sorry: I interrupted!'

'So you did, guv,' he said equably. 'I was saying if they did manage to isolate her abductor's DNA, they'd still have to match it with DNA on the national register.'

'Not to mention finding the owner and his whereabouts. I suppose he's not made any demands for a ransom or anything?'

'Not that I know of. Any news of Elise, by the way?'

'Plenty.'

His eyes rounded at the thought of test-driving the Lotus: 'But why not take him up on his offer, guv? I'd give my teeth . . .'

'I used to drive a Merc sports once,' she recalled wistfully. 'Pale blue convertible. But that was then, Tom, and this is now. At my age I want comfort and luggage and safety, as well as pzazz. But the lines, the colour, the sheer glamour — yes, it's a super young person's car.' So why had Elise bought it? 'It's a pity you're so valuable to Henson: you could go in my place.'

'I could anyway if it's so early—'

'So you could!' And save her the problem of an early morning after what she hoped would be a late night. 'But the object of the exercise is really to talk to the cleaner, who might know the names and current whereabouts of the staff the current dealership let go. Apparently, although it trades under the same name and sells the same cars, it's now got new owners. Don't ask me how it works, because I don't really understand. And I'm not looking for just any old employees, I'm looking for those who went on to other Lotus dealerships, remember. To lead us to a car-theft scam. So don't lose focus when you whiz round Ashford's lovely dual carriageways in a very pretty car. I'll phone Stuart Timms and tell him you'll be there about seven forty-five, shall I? On the other hand,' she said regretfully, 'you really ought to clear it with your DCI — just in case there's a panic.'

'It's only spitting distance from where I live, guv. I'll leave my mobile on — come on, who's to know?'

'But who's to get found out if anything goes wrong? You and me! Clear it, Tom — or would you prefer me to?' His face gave the answer. 'OK. I'll have a very quick word with Henson. But you'll owe me — right?'

* * *

Her motto had always been that coincidences happened to those who made them, so she would contrive to meet Henson while he was talking to someone in front of whom he couldn't possibly deny her request. Mark, as ACC (Crime) would have done nicely, had it not been for the ambiguous ending to their phone conversation. The Chief Constable would have been even better, but it was clear from the cluster of sleek cars in the visitors' spaces that Important People were in the building, and that he was their natural target.

She saw Mark's amongst the suits and uniforms striding towards the main meetings room. No chance of a private word to resolve the ambiguity of their phone call, then. But at least she could smile and flap a hand to him to re-establish that they were friends. He hesitated a moment, but, grinning like a schoolboy, took half a step back and stopped beside her.

'You were right about the rumours,' he said, his face by now straight as a clergyman's at a graveside but his eyes less under control. 'The Chief's the main source, too. As a matter of fact, he's just suggested we take over the room he and Mrs Chief had been allocated.'

'It'd be a serious matter to disobey orders,' she said, shaking her head solemnly. 'It might be a terrible threat to your career.'

'It might indeed.'

The pause was one of the most glowing she'd ever known. At last she had to break it.

'Meanwhile, Mark — I need a big favour. I want to borrow Tom for half an hour's work tomorrow. An hour at most. It's for the Elise case. And he'd do it much better than I. Man to man car talk. You know the sort of thing: salesmen thinking woman use gear-leavers for their handbags,' she lied.

'Of course. Tell Henson you've cleared it with me. Funny, he's shaking down well, despite the rocky start — he's making real progress.'

'Mmm,' Fran murmured non-committally.

He stared intently at her face. 'It's you and Tom making the progress, isn't it? You're feeding Tom ideas!'

She blushed. A blush, she noticed, not a flush. 'There's more than one way to skin a cat, Mark. But just so Henson continues to think he's wonderful, I shall make myself scarce this afternoon. Alan Pitt, the man in the Elise case, has taken it into his head to go walkabout just when they've started to move with the court case to end her treatment. And just when we think we've ID'd her, too.'

'You've got that far! Well done!' His face lit up with pleasure. He glanced at his watch. 'Hell! No time for an update now—'

'We'll sort it. And Rebecca, too. But while we've plenty of time in the Elise case, the courts notwithstanding, we don't have that luxury in hers. Go on, go to your meeting, Mark. Your carriage will call for you at seven.' To the amazement and shock of both of them, she reached up and dotted a kiss on his lips. And swirled away like a girl at a dance.

Or, she admitted to herself, like a girl of her generation at the sort of dance that involved layers of frothy petticoats under taffeta skirts.

She thought back to herself as a girl just in her teens, her stiletto heels and American tan stockings, thinking she was the Belle of the Ball. It would have been nice to wear the lipstick she'd bought from Boots or somewhere — Outdoor Girl, in a very pale pink Ma had stigmatised as common. The hair she'd tried to grow for a French plait — the scraped earwig look Ma had derided — was held back by an Alice band, surely no longer fashionable by then. With her long slender limbs and size eight figure, she'd thought of herself as gawky at thirteen, but photographs of herself at the time told another story. Perhaps it was because she was the second child that there were so few photos of her in the family albums. The enlarged snapshot on the mantelpiece, alongside the studio portrait of Fran on her graduation day, showed her at her passing out parade almost comically severe. The dancing girl marched away, blue serge replacing the flirting petticoats.

Tonight? She had no time now to get the sort of dress she'd promised herself, so she'd be elegantly tailored in a female equivalent of a man's dinner suit. But at least, she told herself, she could sport fuchsia underwear.

* * *

If Alan Pitt had indeed gone away for a long spell, he'd wisely left no signs, like drawn curtains, to attract intruders. His front gates were shut, but he was the sort of man who might well open and close them each day as he drove out of the garage. This had a metal roller gate, so there was no way to tell if it was occupied. No bottles cluttered his steps, but who these days didn't buy supermarket milk if they were at work all day? Post? She tried peering through the letter-box, but her view was blocked by what looked like a sheet of green baize, so she couldn't see if letters had accumulated. She made a note to check with Royal Mail or whatever they called themselves these days to see if he had asked for his post to be retained.

Now for the neighbours. Her poking around had aroused depressingly little interest: she'd have preferred a Neighbourhood Watch representative to come yelling at her. Which neighbour should she try first? The one opposite was the far side of the busy A291, so it was unlikely that anyone would take a close interest. Left or right? As she mentally tossed up, the decision was made as a people-carrier pulled into the drive of the one on the left, a much-extended bungalow with a loft conversion. It disgorged three loud, school-uniformed children, the middle one of whom was about Rebecca's age. The mother, in a voice that seemed to Fran to be deliberately projected, told the girls to change quickly so they wouldn't be late for their musical appreciation lesson.

Keeping her face impassive, Fran approached, ID in hand, and introduced herself. 'I'm just wondering, Mrs—?'

'Haywood. Natalie Harwood.'

'I was wondering, Mrs Harwood, if you had any idea what time Dr Pitt might be back.'

'Is he in some sort of trouble?' Clearly the woman felt some sort of gesture was called for, a metaphorical gathering of her chickens about her, but the children had already done as they were told.

'Not at all. He's been extraordinarily helpful in dealing with a woman with memory loss, and I wanted to update him.'

'One of his students?'

Now why should she ask that? 'An accident victim. Do you know what time he usually gets home?'

'I'm usually out ferrying the children somewhere: music here, dance there — you know how it is.'

Fran's smile indicated duplicitously that she could not only guess but sympathised with Mrs Harwood's tough life. 'Actually,' she said, 'he did say last time we spoke that he might have to go away for a couple of days. I suppose you wouldn't have any ideas?'

Mrs Harwood was clearly under far too much pressure to take any notice of Pitt's social life. Accepting Fran's card with some reluctance, at last she said, 'Maybe old Mrs Wallace?' She gestured to the unextended bungalow the far side of Pitt's.

Old? Mrs Wallace might have been about sixty, but these days — and especially not in Fran's book — surely no one of that age was considered old. Thin and with iron grey hair, she might have looked older than a woman resorting to hair colour, but she clearly had every one of her faculties, inspecting Fran's ID before inviting her in. Moreover, Pitt trusted her enough to ask her to keep his spare key.

'Some conference, up north somewhere, he told my husband. I thought it was a funny time of year for a conference, right at the start of the most difficult term, but perhaps I'm out of date in such matters.'

It would be so easy to indulge them both by asking about Mrs Wallace's past. The books lining even the small entrance hall were a sufficient clue. 'You've no idea where or how long?'

'He was in a great rush. I did ask, but it was like talking to the wind.'

'And what day was that?'

For the first time the woman looked less than sure of herself. 'Hell, these senior moments! The trouble is, Superintendent, that you lose track of the days . . .' She screwed up her face in an effort to remember.

My God: imagine losing your marbles so young. Fran bit her lip in distress.

'Let me think: Wednesday I was in Cambridge. Thursday was the London Library . . . So it must have been Friday. I'm sorry, Superintendent. I'm absolutely wrapped up in a research project and—'

She could resist no longer. 'What are you researching, Mrs Wallace? Or is it Professor?'

The older woman chuckled. 'It used to be. When I was teaching in Sheffield I got myself bogged down in a research project that was far too big for someone with a teaching commitment. A big, Casaubon-like project.'

'Casaubon?'

'A character in *Middlemarch*, Superintendent.'

Fran grinned. 'Ah! One of my retirement books! I have a list, Ms Wallace, of books I ought to have read years ago. That's about number five. I wish I could discuss the rest of them with you—'

'But you really only wanted to talk about Dr Pitt. A strange man. Lives, as far as I can tell, an entirely blameless life, yet he seems to attract suspicion simply by breathing, does he not?'

'I wasn't aware of any suspicion.' Fran meant it as a statement, but willy-nilly it turned itself into a question.

'There were one or two rumours, Superintendent. In the past we attended several conferences, having interests in much the same period. Indiscretions of the groping-the-waitress sort. It always seemed to me that, living a curiously cloistered existence, as soon as he found himself in a distinctly uncloistered environment he used to let himself out on the razzle whenever he got the chance.'

'Why should his existence be cloistered?'

'A self-imposed punishment, I fancy. Was there not a whisper of a student pregnancy?'

Was there indeed? 'But Professor: you were at different universities — how on earth would you hear such a rumour?'

'Because one of my colleagues received the blame for the affair. That's why he left Kent and came up north, where it might be supposed we take a more bracing view of such goings-on. Unfortunately he is no longer with us. A premature death, but I don't think we can blame Dr Pitt for causing it. He was caught in a train crash. Some woman stalled her car on a level crossing. The train was partially derailed.'

'You liked him?'

'More than Pitt, yes. Who worries me.'

'Why did you choose to live next to a man you had reason to dislike?'

'Coincidence. I hope Hardy's on your retirement list, too. I came down here because my husband's job brought us. He's on a year's secondment — he may be an academic like myself, but his knowledge of biochemicals is useful to a pharmaceutical company down here. So for twelve months we're strangers in a strange land. But we can't wait to get back, Superintendent. And that's nothing to do with Dr Pitt. We miss our friends too much. And I would prefer a neighbour other than Pitt, to be honest.'

'Because of what he did to your colleague? Or because he's a bad neighbour?'

'As a neighbour he's impeccable. On refuse day he puts out all the items carefully sorted for recycling; never plays loud music; maintains his dull little garden. What more could you want?'

'A positively nice neighbour?'

'Perhaps he is. All the same . . .'

Fran surprised herself: 'How do you rate his research?'

'It's in a different field from mine, of course, so I'm scarcely qualified to comment.' She smiled, as other people smiled when they spoke of children or a favourite sporting moment. 'Mine's concerned with the rise and fall of the epistolary novel — novels written in the form of letters, like *Clarissa*, which ought to be another on your retirement list. He's got this curious obsession with a novelist he actually professes to loathe, DH Lawrence. I can't make him out.'

Fran shook her head. 'Neither can I. But he left neither forwarding address, nor any indication when he would return?'

'Ah! To hear the neither/nor construction used correctly — and in dialogue such as this, too! You are, Chief Superintendent, a natural reader of the great English novel!'

* * *

'And so I might be,' Fran told Mark, 'but it doesn't get us any further forward with either case.'

It was so good to hear her laugh, and to laugh with her. 'I'm not clear why you're pursuing this Pitt character with such vigour, Fran,' he said tentatively, though even as a passenger in her car he might have been entitled to ask in an official voice.

'Neither am I, not a hundred per cent. You'd expect me to be throwing my weight into the Rebecca investigation—'

'Except, in the interests of preserving the peace you want to steer clear: I can quite see that.'

'Or to be pounding on every Lotus dealer's door demanding information — though I've done that by phone already: there should be a pile of faxes waiting for me tomorrow morning. But I've done something I've hardly ever done. I've arranged for my calls at work to be rerouted to my mobile. And I've got a round-the-clock trace put on any calls coming in.'

'In case Pitt calls again.' It wasn't a question. He knew her too well.

'Yes. I'm getting obsessed with him.'

'You're getting suspicious of him,' he corrected gently. 'Turn left here. I believe,' he coughed ironically, 'that there's valet parking. And they deliver our baggage to our room. Pukka do's, the Chief goes to.'

'He does indeed.' She handed over the car to the uniformed flunkey and walked up the broad steps of the elegant country house turned hotel, side by side with him. She'd scrubbed up wonderfully well: there wouldn't be a better turned out or more attractive woman at the function. Something had brought back the spring in her step and had straightened her back.

He had wondered how she would dress tonight. Whenever he'd seen her at similar functions, she'd worn an evening version of her usual severe suits, and had never looked less than queenly. In this dress she looked almost sculptured: she didn't need the flowing outfits some women wore, presumably to hide their expanded waists. He sucked his own stomach in. What if she thought him too old, inadequate as a lover? It had been so long, and then with Tina. Married sex was altogether easier, more predictable, safer.

God, he wanted Fran now. Now.

How would she feel? Was she a slow seduction woman or did she enjoy urgency?

'Tell you what,' she said out of the corner of her mouth, 'let's not mention Alan Pitt for the rest of the evening.'

'What a good idea,' he agreed, tucking his hand possessively under her elbow.

CHAPTER TWENTY-SEVEN

Mark, preparing to make the keynote speech, had retired to the cloakroom for a post-dinner spruce. Fran did the female equivalent, wanting no criticism to come his way because the dish of supposedly upmarket pheasant (it had in fact proved almost impenetrable) had eroded her lipstick. She took the opportunity to check for phone messages. There were none, neither directly to her nor redirected from HQ. So far so good. Why then did she feel so uneasy? It was the sort of feeling she had when one parent or the other was ill. She checked her watch — it was too late to call Devon now, her parents' bedtime being nearer eight than ten. Then, of course, one or other would wake to use the commode in the night, and both would complain of insomnia. In vain she'd tried to persuade them that going to bed later would ensure a better night's sleep. Pa insisted that he wanted to get a few hours in before Ma's tooth-grinding woke him, hard to comprehend since she wore dentures, and Ma demanding the chance to beat her husband's snoring, entirely credible because his stertorous breathing could fill the entire bungalow. She stared at the phone — was it really too late?

By then she was alone in the cloakroom. All the other women were returning to the hall. It was Mark's big moment, and she was letting him down! Had she had a skirt, she would have hitched it up and run; as it was, she lengthened her long stride and arrived by his side possibly before she was missed. Now all she had to do was smile and applaud like a good little woman, which was very easy. Mark was a good speaker, trenchant, witty and — mercifully — brief. Much as she deplored as uncritical sycophancy the transatlantic habit of rising to one's feet to applaud even an after-dinner speech, she led the ovation for Mark. And why not? He was her boss, her friend and — as from about ten minutes after their checking in — her lover.

It was hard to reverse that order the following morning as they walked through the car park. They had celebrated their coming together well but not at all wisely, and, with hardly any sleep, would have to get through the day on adrenaline and duty.

After their usual decorous canteen breakfast — Mark was still inexplicably desperate to give as little away about their relationship as possible, and had eschewed the hotel meal on the grounds that they'd arrive at work suspiciously late — Fran smiled at her reflection in the ladies' loo mirror. It felt wonderfully like love, and why not?

Any moment now a thousand and one reasons would come crowding in. But she wouldn't let them. She'd breeze through everything the rest of the day brought, even though the first was an encounter with Henson, who might even have been hovering outside the ladies' door, he was so eager to make his point.

'I hear you've got young Arkwright racketing around the countryside doing your donkey-work again. I thought we'd agreed—'

'I think you'll find I cleared it with the ACC. And DC Arkwright should be in by nine or very soon after.'

'Has it escaped your notice that a child is still missing and that every member of the team is expected to pull his weight?'

'Not at all. How's your trawl through the utility companies going? Your search for the workman's shelter?'

Afflicted with selective deafness, he turned on his heel and stalked off.

At least the car dealers had been more cooperative. She had a pile of faxes and plentiful emails to work her way through, and took a strange pleasure in sorting out which employees had passed from one to another. But none of them worked for dealerships whose customers had had their newly-purchased cars stolen. At this point, it dawned on her that some time in the last week she'd started to re-invent the wheel. The Car Theft Unit might well have their suspicions. Unless the boss was another Henson, they would be happy to exchange information with her, especially if they could claim glory in a possible collar. As soon as Tom returned, she'd send him off to pool ideas. She glanced at her watch: he must really be enjoying his test drive to be so very late. Meanwhile, it was time for another attack on Alan Pitt's phone. Today's message was even more terse. 'Please get in touch with me immediately when you get this message.'

There was one way she could flush him out, perhaps. By using Elise herself. Poor Marjorie (or whoever she was), to have your name, your very identity, lost the moment you lost your life. What would it be like to wake up now and find everyone calling you by another name? Would you prefer it to your own? Would it make you a new woman?

Which was another point: somewhere Elise had had a life. She'd sold one house: she must have bought another. She must have a load of furniture somewhere. What had happened to that? And what had happened to all the things that would identify her? Her handbag? It would have held her driving licence, if not her passport: people wanting a new identity would give a lot for evidence of one these days. Was another Marjorie Gray wandering the streets of some city 'up north' who had no right to the name?

Where the hell was Tom? She needed legs, now — at least a set of fingers to dial phone numbers. There was no argument: she'd have to ask for more help, even when her colleagues could least spare it. She'd better talk to Mark, and though a phone call would have usually sufficed, today it had to be face to face.

If it could have been mouth to mouth, body to body, she might have enjoyed it even more. But apart from a wonderful locked-door kiss, the door swiftly unlocked and Mark retiring to his official side of the desk, they presented to the Chief, surging in unannounced, no more than two senior officers sitting discussing a tricky case.

'Tell the media Elise is regaining consciousness!' he repeated, staring at Fran as if she had two heads. He took a chair and pulled it to her side of the desk.

'I have to flush Alan Pitt out somehow,' she said. 'I don't know why, but thirty-odd years in the job tell me I have to. I'd stake my pension on it.'

'It's very risky. When people find it's untrue—'

'With due respect, sir,' Mark interrupted, 'who the hell will care? She's lain there like the dead for nigh on two years. People will think, "Oh, jolly good: there's hope for me if I bang my head!" and that'll be that.'

'So you'd trust Fran's call on this?'

'Absolutely. Which reminds me, sir, how's your wife?'

Fran didn't so much as blink, though she'd have given much to understand the logic behind his change of conversational gear. The Chief didn't appear even to notice it.

'Still quite poorly. Seems she's reacting badly to some pills the doctor gave her. Everything go off well last night?'

'Very well indeed,' they said together, as one.

'Mark's speech was all you would have wanted, sir,' Fran added, aiming for factual and probably achieving coy and knowing. 'Meanwhile, what I really need is a couple of officers.' She explained her fears about Elise's documents. 'At the very least, apart from her very expensive car, her assailant's probably got his hands on her bank balance, which, given the price of property down there, is certainly worth having.'

'And maybe . . . In these days of terrorism, we can't be too sure when it comes to identity theft. Henson isn't going to be happy — we still haven't found that child, you know. And not a word from her kidnapper. Murderer now, more like, given the time-lapse.'

A knock at the door heralded Carl Henson, clearly put out to see both the Chief and Fran in Mark's room, and then further irritated by the realisation that to reach the only free chairs he would have to scramble over their legs. For a moment it seemed that he would, but he settled for standing up, perhaps aware that it made him look like a naughty schoolboy, especially as he showed no inclination at all to open the conversation.

As if to prompt him the Chief asked, 'How's the Rebecca case going, Carl?'

'Slowly, thank you, sir. But we have had a little breakthrough. It seems a workman's shelter was temporarily removed from where it ought to be, placed at the edge of the market, a pretty pathetic affair by all accounts, and then moved back. Now, it could be a prank, of course, but it could be altogether more serious.'

Fran held her breath: would he acknowledge his debt?

'Chief Superintendent Harman holds the latter theory, I believe, so we've chosen to go with it.'

They smiled at each other, a good professional smile that softened neither's eyes.

'But there are other crimes, Carl. And Fran's rooting round in what we thought was a dying, if not a dead, case that has turned up all sort of leads. There may even be a terrorist link,' the Chief added portentously. 'So with great reluctance, she needs a couple of constables. That lad Arkwright's up to speed on the case. I'm sure you can you spare him. And perhaps Uniform can come up with someone bright enough to work on their own initiative,' he added, as if thinking aloud.

'She's welcome to Arkwright, and that's a fact,' Henson snapped. 'Look at the time, and there's no sign of him yet.'

'Ten-twenty? He should have been back here by nine,' Fran agreed, tutting in irritation. 'Well, he won't be any loss to your team, will he?'

'I'll send him to you with a flea in his ear,' Henson said.

'That's OK. I'll insert any fleas myself, thanks.'

Henson's mobile spared him having to respond. He bowed himself out.

'Thanks, guv,' Fran smiled. 'And the announcement about Elise?'

'Will it distract attention from Rebecca?' Mark frowned.

'It shouldn't. Only one person will be interested — Alan Pitt. Unless,' she added thoughtfully, 'it flushes out the assailant as well. It's a risk I hadn't thought of.'

The Chief pondered. 'We certainly can't offer round-the-clock protection, and if I know the hospital they can't either.'

'What if we don't make a media announcement?' Mark put in. 'What if Fran fixed it with the hospital authorities that that's the official story but simply notified Alan Pitt? A selective lie.'

The others nodded. 'On the other hand, flushing out the assailant is the object of everything Fran's been doing for the last weeks,' the Chief said. 'Let me think about it. Fran — get on to the hospital authorities, so they all sing from the same hymn sheet. We'll need their permission whichever line we go for. Now, Mark, what I really came to see you about was our response to the latest HO directive.' He looked expectantly at Fran, who took the hint with alacrity.

Tom was glued to the computer in the outer office as she returned, but, catching her eye, grabbed his notepad and scuttled after her, looking as hangdog as if Henson had fulfilled his promise.

A big grin was transforming his face when he observed hers. 'I'm truly sorry, gu— ma'am,' he said, pulling himself swiftly to an approximation of attention. 'But I was on to something and I thought if I pursued it I'd save you a lot of time. And your phone was switched to voicemail,' he added, nodding to it.

'And my mobile?'

He blushed to the tips of his ears. 'I thought perhaps you wouldn't want to be disturbed, like. You know.'

'I suppose a call when I was in with the Chief might have been a tad irritating, but you should have tried, Tom. OK, sit yourself down and tell me what you've found. And make it snappy, because I want you to go and talk to Car Theft.'

'Again? Because that's where I've been, ma'am. Can't think why I didn't go and chafe the fat with them before. Now, they've just picked up a team stealing four-by-fours to order — mind you, I'd give the bloody things away, all their pollution and consumption, plus the ladies on the school run can't park them—'

'OK, Tom — cut to the chase. I'm halfway to forgiving you, but if you don't spill the beans soon, I'll return you to Henson for the duration.'

'Ma'am. Now, it seems they had a spate of thefts of high-powered sports cars a couple of years back, like. Porsches, Audis, Lotuses. All very efficient, usually from the owner's drive, which you'd have thought a bit risky. But, d'you know, guv, there's one gang specialises in stealing the wheels from cars on driveways. Alloy, of course. So the owner gets up and find his whatever it is sitting on four piles of bricks.'

Fran coughed. 'Lotuses?'

'Sorry, guv: I do like my cars, you know. Anyway, like I was saying, all these posh cars vanished. Hundreds and thousands of pounds' worth from driveways in Kent and Sussex. And then the thefts stopped. Just like that.' He clicked his fingers. 'And the last one was reported stolen two days before Elise had her accident. How's that for a coincidence?'

'How indeed? All the car thefts or just the Lotuses?'

'All. Oh, I don't mean nationwide, nothing like that. Just those down here.'

'Quite.' She interrupted what she feared would be another long explanation. 'Tell you what, see if Interpol have reported similar spates anywhere else.'

He looked puzzled.

'You don't think . . . Elise, like . . . I mean, it's such a coincidence!'

'You think that Elise was at the heart of an international gang of car thieves so that when she was hospitalised, the crime stopped? Elise? A woman older than me?'

'Well, women's lib and all that, ma'am.' His face fell as he conceded, 'Actually, there have been more thefts recently, with a similar MO.'

'You mean removal from front drives?' If only she'd had more sleep and less passion. No: just more sleep after the passion.

'No, with removal vans. Actually, those horseboxes where people can sleep in the cab.'

She rubbed her face. 'Let me get this straight. A team of car thieves used to operate by stealing expensive cars and shoving them in horseboxes to get them away. They stopped doing it at the time of Elise's accident, and were inactive for a while, but now they've resumed their activities.'

'That's what I said, guv.' Tom looked genuinely pained.

'Any theories why they might have stopped suddenly and then been resumed?'

'Well, seeing as how she was hurt so badly, ma'am, you don't suppose someone might have had a fit of conscience, like? Either that,' he added, more prosaically, 'or they made so much loot they could afford to have a break.'

'Quite. And have our colleagues got any theories?'

'They said to leave the information with them. They mentioned Interpol, too, come to think of it.'

'Well, that saves you a job. Did you get anything about any Lotus dealership employees?'

'Just the one. Everyone else went down-market, like. But there's a bloke called Kevin Gregory who moved to a dealership near Canterbury. So when we did the test drive that's where I went. Canterbury. Seems he arrived with references you'd have written for yourself, like, but after a couple of months they let him go. A waste of space, they said.'

'Find him. Today. But you've done well, Tom. Especially the bit about horseboxes.'

'Of course — the guy that found Elise saw a horsebox nearby. Parked without lights. Right?'

'Right! So we may just be beginning to see light at the end of the tunnel.'

'Tell you what, guv — bet it's a train's headlights!'

Perhaps it was. But for the rest of the morning Fran chose to see it otherwise. Although the promised uniformed constable didn't materialise, she had immediate success herself with her phone calls to estate agents. The chipper Draytons had been entirely correct in thinking that Burgoynes had been the estate agents responsible for selling Elise's bungalow. In the all too predictable sing-song that estate agents' receptionists favour, the young woman at the other end confirmed that they had her solicitor's details, and would be happy to fax them on receipt of a faxed request with an official heading. Not quite idly, Fran asked, 'Is there anyone in the office who might remember Ms Gray?'

'It was Miss Gray,' the young woman's voice corrected her. 'And I remember her well. We used to call her the Invisible Woman, because she merged with the wallpaper. But — it was really strange. She could be so stubborn.'

'In what way?'

'Well, we kept telling her it was easier to sell a property that looked like a home, if you know what I mean. Furniture and flowers. But she stripped it. All of it. I used to see her staggering along to Oxfam or whatever with these huge bags. Day after day, she'd pass my office. Books, pictures — you could see the patches on the walls where she'd taken them down — china, glass.'

'It was her own idea? There was a rumour that the purchasers wanted the house stripped.'

'Hers. She removed everything. One day I stopped her and said, "Don't forget to leave enough mugs for the removal men," and she looked at me ever so odd, and said, "There won't be any removal men".'

'No removal men!' Fran slipped her voice into gossip mode, but in truth she was intrigued. It was as if Elise was systematically getting rid of her old life in the most literal way. Not to mention starting another one: the hair, the make-up, the clothes so new the price tags had scratched her skin. Surely the change of identity couldn't be to escape the consequences of criminal acts?

'I know: it's really weird, isn't it? And she took a far lower offer than we'd hoped for because she said — yes, really! — she wanted to make a quick getaway.'

'You've been more than helpful,' Fran told her, promising a fax within the next few minutes and eliciting a promise of an immediate response.

Her next call was to the Draytons themselves. To her surprise they were in, though just about to dash off for their French class. She reminded them that they'd been prepared to help her.

'We were wondering what could be worse than identifying a dead body!' Mrs Drayton giggled nervously.

'I think you might find identifying a live one even worse,' Fran said quietly. 'She's not a pretty sight, Mrs Drayton.' She explained.

'You mean she's not just like some grown-up Sleeping Beauty!'

'Alas, no. Now, would you like me to arrange for a car to collect you?'

'And have every single curtain in the close twitched to within an inch of its life? No thanks, Superintendent — we'll get there under our own steam. Some time this afternoon? Would three suit?'

Photocopies came through to the central CID office, not to individual desks. In the past, anything for her had always been brought to her hot from the printer, but now everyone was involved in the higher profile, and indeed, more urgent case. It was time to stretch her legs and get a drink; she'd collect her fax and empty her pigeonhole at the same time.

The fax was waiting for her: now she had the name of Elise's solicitor and details of her bank account — a phone and Internet one. She also had an armful of what she hoped was largely redundant post, most of which she might as well deposit in the recycling box or put for shredding straight away. But there was a note that interested her. Computer-printed, it said, 'Ask Sergeant Simpson about last evening's phone call.'

Intrigued, she collected a tumbler of water and looked for Simpson. She wouldn't be in for another three or four hours yet, not if she was on the evening shift. But she didn't take her desk home with her, and Fran leafed through the scrawls that she supposed passed for notes in Simpson's case. Almost at the top of the pile was a name she recognised: Professor Wallace.

Seizing it, she marched into her office and dialled the Wallaces' number. She wouldn't drop Simpson in it, not with a member of the public, but this afternoon she would suffer.

Apologising profusely, she explained that she had been completely tied up.

'All I can say is that I hope you enjoyed yourself!' Mrs Wallace cackled. Her voice soon serious, she continued, 'And it wasn't necessarily you we needed to speak to, since it — well, perhaps I'm overreacting, Superintendent. All we wanted to say was that a couple of weeks back young Dr Pitt had a long over-the-garden-wall talk with Jeremy about drugs, Rohypnol for one. Which we found curious for a bachelor without need for it. He told some long cock-and-bull story about one of his students believing she'd been a date-rape victim.'

'Your husband doesn't believe the tale?' It shouldn't be impossible for her to check, of course, assuming the girl had ever reported it.

'Let us say that what interests him in retrospect is that Alan returned several times to the question of whether it was worth this mythical girl reporting it to the police, given the absence of traces in her blood stream.'

'Mrs Wallace — exactly why does this conversation worry you and your husband?'

'Let us just say that the intensity of his enquiries unnerved my husband.'

'I'm very grateful indeed for the information. You've no idea how helpful it may prove.'

Rohypnol. Why should Pitt want to know about Rohypnol? The obvious way to find out was to ask him. Which got her back to square one.

CHAPTER TWENTY-EIGHT

'We're off to the Outlet afterwards,' Mrs Drayton announced, with a little girl swing of the hips, as Fran met her and her husband in the William Harvey Hospital foyer. 'Shop till we drop time. Not proper day clothes — though Neil here gets some real bargains in shirts. And if he ever wore a suit, I'm sure he'd get it there. But you need to be a size eight teeny-bopper to get the best out of the Outlet formal clothes-wise. Sports goods, though, even specialist stuff: you can get real bargains. The trouble is, like I say, there's not a lot of everyday clothes for women our age, I'm afraid, Chief Superintendent.'

Fran nodded as if interested, declining to engage with the idea that she and Julie Drayton were in anything like the same age range. What she did register, with some alarm, was the woman's nervous anxiety, which grew in loquacity as they made their way to Elise's ward. Fran had left a phone message for Michael Penn, warning him, and requesting a short conversation with him afterwards. He flapped what appeared to be an idle hand as she approached, but fell quietly into step behind the little procession as she led the Draytons to Elise's bed.

Halfway, however, she stopped and addressed the Draytons firmly, Penn nodding agreement behind their backs. 'You do realise this is not going to be very pleasant? If you have any doubts, any doubts at all, please tell me and we won't go ahead.' She exerted, however, every ounce of willpower at her disposal to make them agree.

Jabbering about civic duty, a point she couldn't dispute, they insisted. So they continued, Penn still hovering in the rear. Then, as if a conjuror, he stepped forward to pull the curtains back from round Elise's bed. Fran couldn't understand why they'd been closed in the first place, since their normal state was open, but she allowed him his moment of drama. As the Draytons peered at the figure before them, Penn's moment became protracted as Julie lost control and scream after scream echoed round the ward. Before Fran knew it, he had grabbed Julie and whisked her away, leaving an ashen Neil to whisper, 'Yes, that's Marjorie. Oh, God.'

There was a paper kidney bowl on the bedside locker. Well done Michael, Fran observed, as Neil made use of it. She sat him down, turning the chair so he could no longer see the cause of his distress. As if from nowhere, Penn was back again, ushering them both out and waving to a nurse who looked about ten to get rid of the evidence.

Fran found herself in a room so blandly decorated and furnished it must be the place where doctors gave relatives bad news. A homely-looking young woman was already sitting with an arm round Julie, pressing tissues and tea on her.

Penn was hovering outside the door.

Fran smiled and joined him. 'Thank you: all this is brilliant. Even the sick-bowl.'

'I pride myself on my stage-management,' he said.

'Rightly. Well done. Now, I need to consult you about something — do you have a minute to spare?'

* * *

'The only problem as I see it,' Penn said, leaning back from his desk, 'is the one you anticipate: security. So I wouldn't truly be happy to invite her murderer in without one of your people here undercover. But Alan Pitt — he's been here often enough, hasn't he? He did slap her about a bit once, in an effort to bring her round, silly man. He didn't think I'd noticed, but there's not much I miss, believe me, Chief — Fran!'

'I believe you, Michael, don't worry. Which is why I asked *you* about publicity, not some leather-seated chief exec — though I suppose I ought to have a word with him too.'

'If you can find him, Fran, you're a better man than I, Gungadin, as my old dad would have said. Mind you, if you flashed your rank at him, and bullied a bit, he'd almost certainly play ball. Or get your secretary to talk to his: that sort of ploy often works. Jim Taverner, the consultant, will be doing rounds in a couple of hours' time — I'll deal with him, if you like.'

'You're being more than kind,' she said, smiling and getting to her feet.

He looked her quizzically up and down. 'That hair's very chic: you've got the bones to wear it too. No wonder our Dr Pitt's got the hots for you.'

'I beg your pardon!' She didn't know whether to laugh or be outraged. Chatting her up in Sainsbury's was one thing, telling third parties quite another.

'He still talks to Elise all the time as if she could hear and understand. Admirable but suggests something a bit wonky up here if you ask me. Anyway, I happened to be passing when he came — what? end of last week it'd be — when he was telling her he might be asking you out. How about that?'

'How about that indeed!' she repeated grimly, adding, as if it were truly news to her, 'Thanks for the info, Michael. It could be very useful. Meanwhile, I'd best check on the Draytons and be on my way. We still have to run Elise's murderer to ground — sorry?'

'Elise. You called her Elise. But really she's Marjorie—'

'Gray. Marjorie Gray.'

'I'd better get her notes changed. But Elise is so much more romantic, isn't it? As if she had a life — oh, I don't know . . . Gunrunning between East and West Germany, before the Wall came down. Or the mistress of a spy — provided you could find a straight one!'

'Whereas Marjorie . . . ?' she prompted, amused but touched.

'Too John Betjeman for words! Hollyhocks, dear. And blowsy roses. And flat shoes with elastic sides. Not to mention her poor surname. Oh, Fran — promise me you'll find something about her that wasn't grey.'

* * *

'Sergeant Simpson: my office, please.' Fran was shaken enough by the Draytons' reactions to Elise to be even sharper than she intended. After all, everyone was under extreme pressure and it was easy enough to forget to pass on a message. Easy, and forgivable. Except, of course, when you were supposed to be following every lead possible in tracking Rebecca's abductor, and this news about Rohypnol might just have a bearing. As yet, she couldn't think how and why, but none of her day's activities had quite convinced her that there was nothing in it. She'd phoned Mark and asked if he could call a small case conference involving the main CID people, Carl Henson included, and herself. He'd agreed readily enough, despite an air of surprise, whispered a couple of entirely private suggestions and confirmed they'd enjoy each other's company that evening. Since the meeting would take place in five minutes, there was a time limit on the bollocking she intended to give to the hapless Simpson, a woman in her later twenties who reminded her vaguely of herself at that age. As penance, she got her to check on possible date rapes on university students.

Which reminded her, where the hell was the uniformed constable supposedly at her disposal?

It was a question she put personally — there was no justification for this apart from the delight of seeing the expression on his face as she popped her head round his door — to Mark. He got on the phone almost immediately, eliciting the information, which he condemned fluently, that the officer allocated to the case had had to go home sick and there was no one else, every free officer having been commandeered for the Rebecca case.

Mark tore his hair, and spoke so quietly that Fran would, in his interlocutor's position, have been as afraid as the irritating Simpson.

Fran expected them to enter the conference room separately, but to her surprise and delight Mark gestured her in before him in an almost possessive gesture.

Henson wasn't as sensitive to the nuances of body-language as some of his colleagues. 'Search Pitt's house? Why the fuck would you want to do that?'

'Copper's nose,' Fran replied as if self-deprecating, but gratified by the murmurs of agreement from some of the older officers. 'There's something about the man I don't trust. I find his remorse over Elise unnatural. I don't like his sudden interest in Rohypnol or, presumably, its derivatives. I don't like the fact his disappearance coincides with Rebecca's. He doesn't return my calls — he's not used his mobile at all, in fact, or his bank account. Although there's a stop and search request out to all forces, there's been not a single sighting of him or his car.'

'Just some weird academic, Dr Harman.'

She ignored the not very subtle insult. 'Weird enough possibly to invent a conference on something in the generic north: I've not been able to check the existence of one yet, but it's unlikely at this point in the academic year, I'd have thought. There's only one way to flush him out, I think — to tell him that Elise is showing signs of returning to consciousness.'

'And the hospital—?' Mark prompted.

'No problem, so long as we contact him specifically, not the press. But of course, we may have to do just that if my message to his mobile doesn't work. In that case, we'd have to provide a presence, which would be hard enough in the current circumstances. Now, I'd like to see if Pitt's DNA matches that on the McDonald's beaker. It'll be on record because at one time he was a possible suspect in the Elise assault.'

'No one else's does, so it's worth a try,' someone chipped in.

Mark nodded his go-ahead.

'Meanwhile, I really would like to search his house. The next-door neighbour holds the key. We can do it with or without a search warrant,' she added dryly. 'So long as I can think of some excuse. Yes, I do believe I left my gloves behind when I interviewed him there.'

'Get a warrant, for Christ's sake,' Mark groaned, making show of tearing his hair. 'You're not some maverick newcomer, Fran!'

The mood lightened. If the ACC could tell off his bird, it was all right to chip in too.

'What exactly would you hope to get out of this Pitt's place?' Henson demanded, just as if, in fact, she were some maverick newcomer.

'His computer, for a start. It's possible to buy Rohypnol over the Net, and since he's an academic, not a medical doctor that should raise questions in itself. And I'd like to see what else he's been up to.'

'Well, he can't have been communicating with young Rebecca, that's for sure. Her family PC is as clean as the proverbial. And her friends'.'

'All of them? Internet cafés?' she asked.

'Not at her age, surely.'

'Worth double-checking,' Mark said, pre-empting any argument. 'Now,' he continued, looking at his watch, 'remembering what I've said all about overlong hours, I'd suggest one last trawl of incoming information before you head for home. Thank you, ladies and gentlemen.'

'Except,' said Fran wistfully, falling into step with him as they left, 'I wouldn't mind sorting out the warrant and checking Alan Pitt's house this evening.'

'Arrange for a warrant by all means. And fix a small team to come with you tomorrow. But as for this evening,

Detective Chief Superintendent Harman, we have our own private meeting securely booked. I'll see you in half an hour.'

* * *

Simpson had done better than check police records: she'd also contacted the university medical centre and counselling service to see if any date-rape allegations had been made in the last month. None had been recorded.

'So it looks as if you're on to something,' she said, leaning comfortably against Fran's door-jamb. 'I really am sorry, guv — about earlier.'

'Was it policy?' Fran asked directly. 'A request from above to put anything to do with me at the bottom of your in-tray.'

'Not a direct order,' Simpson said carefully. 'But I was wrong, guv, and there it is. I suppose I couldn't volunteer to help search Pitt's house tomorrow, could I? We all need role-models,' she added awkwardly.

And mentors, Fran thought. It would be good to promote yet another young woman's career, nudging her into this team, recommending a move to that. She'd done it so many times, watching with delight as her protégés and protégées had climbed steadily up the promotional ladder, sometimes, as in the case of a deputy chief constable in one force and a commissioner in the Met, outstripping her.

But she wouldn't be here to see Anna Simpson move up. She'd be down in Devon worrying about Zimmers and incontinence pads.

* * *

After a stop off at Mark's house for him to check his post and repack his overnight bag, they fetched up at Fran's. The plan was that they should have an intimate, romantic dinner with whatever she had in her fridge and freezer and then relax in the most appropriate way. In actuality, a trail of clothing indicated the haste with which they changed their minds.

'There was a film once called *Woman in a Dressing-Gown,*' Mark observed, setting the kitchen table somewhat later. 'As if wearing a dressing-gown were the height of decadence.'

'Or should it be the depth? Yes, starring Laurence Harvey, as I recall. Terribly risqué.' She passed him plates. 'And you know, there is something wonderfully sensual, the two of us swanning round wearing nothing but a layer of silky fabric.' She ran her hand down his chest suggestively.

* * *

Hazel's email brought her down to earth with something of a bang. She'd considered Bel's offer and she and Grant would fly down this weekend, a pastor from another kirk being willing to take over Grant's Sabbath duties. She would be obliged if Fran would meet her at Exeter airport.

Take a weekend out? Fran didn't even know what day of the week it was, let alone feel capable of planning ahead. All she knew was that Friday was reconstruction day, and she expected — indeed, prayed — that the switchboard, staffed with every officer with eyes and ears, including herself and Mark and possibly the Chief Constable, for all she knew, would be jammed with helpful calls. So suddenly there was another imperative: Rebecca must be found one way or another before Friday evening.

Hazel

We're still working flat out on the child abduction case — all leave cancelled. So I can't guarantee meeting you. I'll pay for a taxi too, don't worry. If I were you I'd put the bedclothes through the tumble-drier before you make up the beds.

CU soon

Fran XXX

She made a swift call to her bank to send extra funds through to Hazel's account before going in search of Mark.

He was evidently very pleased to see her.

CHAPTER TWENTY-NINE

'There's something terribly erotic,' Mark reflected, 'or maybe perverted, in watching your lover sitting stark naked in bed, while she phones another man who fancies her. And don't forget to conceal your number!'

'Already have.' She pouted a kiss but applied herself to the phone. 'Alan: I've got some wonderful news about Elise!' she cooed, enthusiastic as if she actually fancied him. 'Please, please call me straight away!'

He watched her: she always tilted her head when she spoke on the phone. Long ago, he'd told her she looked like a bird after a worm. OK, the image was clichéd, but she did. Wagging her head to show there was no response, she replaced the handset.

'Not surprising,' he commiserated, 'given that most sensible people would be in bed or the shower at this time.' He looked at the radio alarm, its services not required this morning: six thirty-seven.

She replaced the handset and looked the still sweating Mark in the eye. 'Which means you'd better have first shower, while I scratch together some breakfast. Unless you'd really prefer the canteen?'

'They might object if we make love on the canteen floor,' he said.

* * *

While he tidied her kitchen, she tried Alan Pitt once more. Still no response.

She sat down at the table, scratching her head. 'Do you think he might cut out the middleman, as it were, and head straight for the hospital?'

'You know the man better than most: what do you think?'

'One more phone call, then. Whatever did we do without them?'

Her face was a picture when he got not into his own car but into hers. 'Are you off your head? ACCs don't get their hands dirty on real cases. They sit behind big desks and make decisions.'

'Of course they do,' he agreed. 'As do chief superintendents. But if you want a bit of real policing, how do you think I feel?'

* * *

Mrs Wallace said much the same thing when Fran collected the bungalow key. Returning to the doorstep, she began, 'I know that some of my erstwhile colleagues rhapsodise about the Golden Age of Crime Fiction, Chief Superintendent, but this is so much more exciting. All these people looking serious and pulling on gloves. It looks as though you're about to perform surgery.'

'That's not a bad analogy,' Mark smiled. 'We shall be delving into every nook and cranny as delicately but as ruthlessly as a surgeon.'

'You're not expecting' — Mrs Wallace indicated the silent troupe of white-clad officers at the bottom of the driveway — 'a body, are you?'

'I sincerely hope not,' Fran replied. 'But we always take care not to contaminate anything. The worst-case scenario is that we need it as unequivocal evidence; the best is that Dr Pitt will come home from his conference and want to sleep in a decent tidy house tonight.'

'Conference! Well, I must confess to doing my own bit for law and order — please note the capitals! — Ms Harman. I got on the phone and then searched the Internet too. I have to report, ma'am,' she continued, pulling herself into a parody of a junior officer reporting to a senior, 'that I could find no academic course relevant to the interests of Dr Pitt. I think he was telling a whopper!' she said, grinning like a child at her vocabulary. 'Bathos,' she concluded in her own voice.

'I'm very grateful,' Fran said. 'I truly haven't had time, nor the staff, to be honest. The hunt for Rebecca's taken all our resources.'

'Are you telling me that this is not part of the search for Rebecca? You certainly have plenty of resources now.' Her eyes twinkled.

'What you've just told me entirely justifies them. Thank you, Mrs Wallace. I can't tell you not to peer round your curtains, but I can ask you not to put yourself at risk should there be any — action.'

By no stretch of the imagination could she see any promise in Mrs Wallace's expression.

They entered the house quietly, then, with none of the affront of breaking down the door. And when Fran stepped inside, calling out, routinely, 'Police! This is the police!' she did so without conviction. She raised a warning hand, and stopped on the mat, using her senses as she'd told generations of young officers. Sight: there was a pile of mail, pushed aside by the door. But there were also a couple of opened envelopes on the side table. There was no sound, except her breathing and Mark's, standing at her shoulder. She would touch nothing she didn't have to, even though she was gloved. Smell: no, to her huge relief there was no sickly sweet stench of death. But — she turned to Mark and made exaggerated grimaces to suggest he sniff too — there was a smell of occupation. She compared it with her hall, and more particularly Mark's, after a period when it had been left.

She stepped back outside, half-closing the door, and looked enquiringly at Mark. 'The place has been occupied until very recently,' she murmured, so quietly he had to bend his head to hear.

'You mean — he's still in there?' he mouthed back.

Shrugging, she gestured for reinforcements round the back and by the garage door.

Everyone moved quietly, as she'd insisted in her briefing. The officers she waved into the house moved as if they were playing a children's game.

'Cooee! Hello, there! Superintendent Harper, is it?'

Fran wheeled. It was Natalie Harwood, waving vigorously from her drive. Hoping her anger wasn't too apparent, Fran strode across, pinning a smile across her face.

'If it's Dr Pitt you're after, you won't find him today,' Mrs Harwood said. 'No, he was off ever so early.'

'Off — today?' Fran swallowed bile. 'I wish you'd let me know he was back, Mrs Harwood.'

'Well, I couldn't since I didn't know he was here till he left,' Mrs Harwood replied, with some tenuous logic. 'And I was going to call later, but I had to get the girls off early — they've gone to London to—'

'What time did you see him?'

'Oh, let me see . . . It must have been about half-past six. Yes, because I was just telling the girls if they didn't hurry they'd miss—'

'Which way did he go, Mrs Harwood?'

'How do you mean?'

'Towards Whitstable or towards Canterbury?'

The woman stared as if Fran had just started speaking Chinese.

'Did he turn left or right?' Fran was ready to scream.

'Oh, left. Whitstable. I think. I don't know.'

'He could be picking up Thanet Way and the M2,' Fran shouted to the nearest PCs. 'The reg is on file. Get a call out now. Stop but approach with caution!' She turned back to Mrs Harwood. 'Was he carrying anything?'

'How should I know? He got the car out, locked the garage from the inside, came out of the front door and drove off.'

Fran got back to the house to find Mark rigid with anger, addressing an inspector she didn't know who presumably didn't know her or Mark either. 'I don't want a full-scale forensic examination,' Mark was saying, 'not if it's going to take five hours. I want the swiftest gathering of evidence you can manage. And I want to know where he could have kept Rebecca.'

'But current Home Office procedure dictates—'

'Let me make it clear, Inspector, I don't give a flying fuck about Home Office procedure. I want that child found, and I want to know where he was keeping her. Fran — was his car big enough to carry a child?'

'Yes: an M-registered Passat. Overshoes, please.' She snapped her fingers at the hapless inspector, and scanned the rooms quickly from the hall. 'The loft? Look, there's an access panel. Get up there, now! Oh, for God's sake, there's a pole there.' Aside to Mark, she said, 'It's identical to one at my parents' place. And there's a knack. The steps should be concealed inside — yes, there we are.'

She stopped halfway up, her head and shoulders only in the roof space. 'Good God, there's a tent up here! And an Elsan. That's where we need meticulous forensics,' she declared, coming down. 'He was too bright to keep her down here. OK, get moving. And,' she added to the young man carrying away Pitt's computer, 'I want every single word, every full-stop off that hard disk. Faster than you know how,' she added with a grin.

He grinned back as he left.

'No deadline?' Mark queried.

'No need. I've worked with him before.'

* * *

It was with a feeling almost approaching anti-climax that Mark and Fran returned to Maidstone. They had done all they could, and more than they should. Now it was the responsibility of their colleagues to piece together the picture and locate Alan Pitt.

As Fran locked her car, Mark asked, for perhaps the fifth time, 'So where the hell could he be taking her?'

'If I know him, somewhere so ordinary, so prosaic, we could kick ourselves . . .' She stopped abruptly. 'Mark, I'm going to Ashford. I've just got this feeling. He does care about Elise, you know.'

He checked his watch. 'I've got a damned meeting,' he said, disappointed as a child deprived of Christmas. 'But I really don't want you to go alone. And everyone else is busy . . . No, Fran, it won't do, will it? I've got a whole constabulary to run. You grab young Tom or whoever and tell me all about it later.' He reached for her hand, drawing her towards him and kissing her. 'You will take care, sweetheart, won't you?'

* * *

They were halfway to Ashford, Tom driving, when her radio crackled into life. A voice far unlike the usual almost bored tones of the control room rang out, 'They've found her! She's alive!'

There was no need to ask who. Fran was almost crying with relief when she replied, 'Details?'

'Outside her school, ma'am. Just like that. Ready to go in with the rest of them, it seems. Only of course, she didn't have her uniform or anything.'

'I suppose no one saw her arrive?'

'School run time, ma'am? A thousand witnesses and none. Chief Superintendent Henson's on his way now, ma'am.'

'In that case they won't need me. I'll carry on where I was heading — the William Harvey, in Ashford.'

Tom looked reproachfully at her. 'Wouldn't you rather be where the action is, ma'am?'

'Too right I would. But it's not my party, Tom. I've got to visit the sick. And you can come too.' He brightened like a puppy promised walkies. 'Actually, you may not want to see Elise. She's not a pretty sight.' She explained the effect on the Draytons.

'Why are you going then, guv?'

'Copper's hunch. If you ever get one, act on it. Now, I'm going to phone the ACC to get the details. No interrupting, but I promise to pass them on to you afterwards. OK?'

'The ACC who's—?' He broke off.

'Who's my bloke. That's right. Well,' she added, skittishly, 'there's no point in phoning the other one.'

Tom might make of their conversation what he would, but in effect all Mark did was confirm the original news, adding that Rebecca had been reunited with her parents and despatched also to the William Harvey. 'She's confused, that's all — no complaints of injury.'

'No abuse?'

'None that she reports. Of course, there'll be a thorough medical examination when she's deemed up to it. But she's alive. I'll stand us champagne tonight, my love.'

'You're on!'

CHAPTER THIRTY

'I'm sorry it's been so long, Elise. Well, not so very long, not really. Though it seems like a lifetime. I've done something really stupid, Elise. Really stupid. Some people will think it was bad, wicked even. But really it was stupid. And I think I've just done something even more stupid. Yes, coming here to see you. Frances said you were getting better, but you're not, are you? You're just the same. She tricked me. So she must know . . .

'I just wanted to do what I can't do to you. Watch someone sleep, really deeply, so deeply they're almost unconscious, and then wake them up. That's all. I never meant any harm, any more than I meant to harm you. And actually, I did a lot less. They've got these clever drugs, you see, that knock you out and you come round not remembering anything. They actually use them for pain relief for minor operations, I gather. So I got hold of some through the Internet and tried them out. And they worked. But it all got out of hand. God help me, I don't know why I did it. Everyone must have been wild with worry. And all those police officers. Frances herself. Now perhaps she'll take me seriously. But I won't be able to take her to the Brodsky concert, I can see that. She'll be much too angry. Tell you what, I'll give her the tickets: perhaps she'll find someone else to go with.

'I got hold of a little tent for her, so she'd keep warm. No, not Frances. Rebecca. The little girl I drugged and took home. And a little

portable loo. I didn't want her seeing the house in case she could identify it later, despite what they said about the drugs taking away your memory. We played games: I taught her draughts and chess — don't they teach these children anything these days? Scrabble, Monopoly — while she was awake, I kept her thoroughly amused. Well fed, too, even if it was frozen meals I reheated in the microwave. I swear, I swear — and the doctors will be able to confirm this — that I never harmed her. She's still virgo intacta. I like younger girls, Elise, but not prepubescent children, God help me! I'm not — what will they call me in prison? A nonce! No, I'm not a nonce. Not that that will save me! Though I sensed a trap, I came anyway. I wanted to say goodbye, because I can see they won't let me come again, not for a while. I just hope they'll let me see you once more if they ever stop treating you. Or, of course, if you ever come round. But you won't, will you? Not like little Rebecca.

'That Michael Penn — he's looking very hard in this direction. I think he means to come over if I stay with you much longer. Now, I shan't be back, maybe never, and so I want you to remember this, my dear: I wouldn't have had this happen for the world. Not for all the world.'

CHAPTER THIRTY-ONE

Fran watched his quiet, touching little farewell, and hardened her heart.

Tom stepped over to make the arrest as soon as he left the ward — she'd decided it should be his collar, not hers. Not quite shrugging with resignation, Pitt held out his hands as if expecting to be cuffed.

'Why did you do it, Alan?' she asked him, trying to keep her voice calm, despite all her instincts to yell and scream at him. 'We heard what you told Elise, but that doesn't explain everything, surely?'

'I don't know. I really don't know.' He started to weep. 'I really have been so stupid, haven't I? Making Rebecca better didn't help Elise, did it?'

'I doubt if anything will,' Fran said gently.

'You heard what I said about Rebecca? I didn't touch her, Frances. I swear I couldn't have treated my own child better.'

'Not that that's saying a lot, these days,' Tom muttered furiously.

Hushing him swiftly, she set them in motion down the corridor. 'Her name isn't Elise, really, you know. It's Marjorie. Marjorie Gray.' She paused for a response, but he gave none. 'I shall drive you back to Maidstone, Alan, but after that you'll be talking to a different set of police officers. And I'm afraid they'll be more determined to find answers than I am. Do you have a solicitor?'

He shook his head. 'Only the sort that makes your Will. I need something a bit more serious now, don't I?'

'There'll be one on call at Maidstone,' she said. Would it be unprofessional to recommend a top-class one, who might well not be on the roster? She'd ask Mark what he thought. And then caught herself up short: why should she need to discuss a matter like that with her lover? She never had in the past.

Leaving Tom to walk him to the car, she phoned Mark, surprised that she'd not told anyone the news. And surprised that it didn't feel like good news. The truth was almost self-evident, surely: Alan was mad, not bad.

'You've what?' Mark's voice leapt out at her.

'Arrested Alan Pitt for the abduction of Rebecca Court. I put my phone under Elise's pillow and picked up everything he said on Tom's phone. It won't do as evidence, but it was enough to permit an arrest.'

'He's confessed to you?'

'To Elise, in fact. And then he admitted to us that being able to wake Rebecca at will wouldn't bring Elise round. Which reminds me, remind them to get blood and urine tests done on the poor kid now. These rape drugs are almost untraceable after a few hours, aren't they?'

'I'll get on to it straight away. Fran — are you all right?'

'I ought to be ecstatic, oughtn't I? But I just feel sad, Mark — very sad.'

'I'll have to see what I can do about that, won't I? Fran, this is truly the most wonderful news! Very, very well done. I'm so proud of you.'

By the time she caught up with them, she did indeed feel better. But, as she updated Alan on all her discoveries about Elise, she realised her main emotion was a profound sense of anti-climax, and a realisation that her own case, finding Elise's murderer, was still far from over.

As the tears rolled down Pitt's face, she did one more thing: she called the best criminal lawyer she knew and arranged for his presence at HQ.

* * *

'How does it feel to have saved a child's life?' Mark asked as they walked into the canteen for lunch.

Before she could reply, she was almost flattened by a barrage of noise as the entire canteen burst into applause: she might have tried to take a back seat in the case, but the police rumour machine knew exactly who had done what. Forgetting the queue, she walked straight over to Carl Henson, and opening her arms, forced him to give her a footballer's hug.

'This was a team effort and don't you forget it!' she muttered, as she smiled broadly.

'But—'

'I don't want any credit. Too old.'

'I noticed you got Tom Arkwright to do the honours,' he said, slightly mollified.

'And the paperwork,' she grinned. 'That should keep him off the streets a bit.'

By now Mark had caught up with them, and there were further handshakes all round.

'But we could have done without Brian Shelley as his solicitor,' Henson shot at her.

'I don't think Pitt could. He's a total mess, isn't he? What does the Medical Examining Officer say?'

'The words "nutty as a fruit cake" entered his diagnosis somewhere,' Henson conceded. 'The bloody scrote keeps asking for you to interview him.'

She shook her head firmly. 'Carl, he's not a scrote. He's a sick man.' She raised her voice. 'Tell him I'm too busy hunting Elise's killer: that should shut him up.' She added ruminatively, 'What he never said was how he came to put his plan into operation — I wouldn't mind eavesdropping on that part of his interview.'

'I'll see what I can do,' he said shortly. Then, perhaps remembering who was standing right by Fran, he added, 'Won't he smell a rat if we move to a different interview room? The one with the two-way mirror?'

'He can sniff all he wants, and so can Shelley,' Mark said. 'But he's accused of a most serious crime and can't yet expect to be treated as a patient, not a criminal. Anyway, lunch: I've got a most exciting meeting to go to. I don't think.'

'And I've got a criminal to run to earth,' Fran capped him.

* * *

Once the adrenaline had subsided, Fran's legs would hardly carry her. She sat at her desk, surveying the list of things Tom had already done for the Elise enquiry and wondering, as helplessly as a rookie detective, where on earth to start next.

The phone broke her reverie.

'Fran? You haven't forgotten about tomorrow, have you?'

Did she know anyone with a Scottish accent? It dawned on her so slowly she could almost hear the electrical pulses in her brain that this was Hazel.

'Tomorrow?' She scribbled on her jotter, *Have they cancelled reconstruction???*

'Exeter Airport. You're picking us up at 7.30 — right?'

'I thought — a taxi . . .' Hadn't she already organised the money for that?

'Total waste of money. And a good excuse for you not to be on time.'

'With the A303, Hazel, one doesn't need excuses.'

'Well, start out earlier then. Come on, Fran, with Pa in hospital, you can't look for excuses to mess around.'

'I don't think a possible murder enquiry is a mere excuse. But what's this about Pa?'

'A fall. I emailed you. Nothing serious, and the doctor was actually at the bungalow when it happened.'

'A fall when you're his age is always serious.'

'Have you booked us a hotel as we asked?' Hazel continued as if she hadn't heard.

'I understood you were to sleep at the bungalow.' Why was she always on the back foot with Hazel? 'In any case, I've had no time to—'

'Do you spend your entire life finding reasons not to fulfil perfectly reasonable requests? I asked you to book us into an hotel, on account of Grant's allergy to household dust.'

Even to her own ears, she sounded stupid. Or mulish. 'I don't know any hotels.'

'You must do. You've been down there often enough.' She made it sound as if it were by choice, somehow to escape the real world.

At last Fran responded hotly. 'Indeed. But, I assure you, not to check out hotels.' But her voice was suddenly less forceful than she meant: if she went down, would Mark come too? After all those months, years, now, of doing just that, she couldn't bear to go alone. She needed his quiet presence, the warmth of his body in the middle of the night. She changed the subject. 'Why was the doctor there?'

'Oh, another of Ma's little aches and pains.'

Fran had her mouth open to demand how Hazel knew they were little, but shut it again.

'See you at the airport!'

The phone went dead.

* * *

'Of course I shall come with you. Where else would I want to be?' Mark interrupted her hesitant enquiry over supper, which they'd picked up at a take-away and were eating at his house. 'In fact, we'll take the afternoon off to be sure of being there in time. You've more than earned it, Fran. And in a case this old half a day isn't going to matter.'

'Two and a half,' she said pettishly.

'Come on, even a few days won't really matter.'

'And I don't see why I should go at all since Hazel's going to be there. I'd be much better employed—'

'If Hazel's going to be there, you'll have time to show me round Teignmouth and environs,' he overrode her.

'Wouldn't you prefer to see the Marstons?'

'Sorry?'

'The Marstons — that was the name of your boating friends, wasn't it?'

He grimaced, and then appeared to make some sort of decision. 'I do have some friends called Marston, but not in Devon. The only reason I said they'd invited me down was so that I could spend some time with you. I'd have told you once I'd got you in my clutches,' he said, with an agreeable leer. 'As for your sister, you need a chance to discuss your parents' future care with her.' He lifted a hand to stop her interrupting. 'If your pa's had a fall, your mother may not be able to manage on her own.'

She stared at him in horror. 'But I can't take time off now! Not when I'm this far from Elise's murderer!'

'Of course you can't. And as your senior officer I should make that point officially. Unless,' he added, tenderly, taking her hand, 'you really want to leave Kent at this particular juncture. In which case, I'd have to move heaven and earth to make it happen. But you don't, Fran, do you?'

She bit her lip, shaking her head. 'And not just because of the case, Mark. It's us — I want to . . . I want to see what happens next.' It was strange to use the phrase out loud.

'Between us? That may take a long time to unfold. A very long time. Come on, let's go and turn the next page now. And then we'd better go to your place.'

'Mine?'

'So you can pack for tomorrow. And I fancy your bed's more comfortable than mine.'

* * *

If Fran had hoped to get back to the Elise case the following morning, she was disappointed. The officers questioning

Alan Pitt wanted her to talk through all her meetings with him, to make sure all he alleged was verified. She also had notes of her own to write up, and she wanted to discuss with Tom their line of enquiry for the following week. He seemed as pleased as she that they'd be working full-time together again, with no pressure from Henson.

'What I really want you to teach me, guv, is how to get these intuitions of yours.'

She smiled sadly. 'If only I could teach that, I'd be the richest women in the world. Sorry, Tom, it's something that you have to grow for yourself. I'll tell you this, though: when you get it, it'll never let you down. Not unless you stop acting on it. Come on: if I'm taking a few hours off, I don't see why you shouldn't, either.'

His face lit up: Fran could see the projects unfolding behind his eyes. 'Thanks, guv. Have a good weekend, like.'

She'd do her best. But somehow she doubted it would be the unalloyed pleasure she hoped Tom's would be.

CHAPTER THIRTY-TWO

'That's Pa's chair,' the old lady said sharply. She was so small and bent that Mark couldn't imagine that his tall, straight Fran could ever have emerged from her womb, but her voice, though cracked and reedy, was strong as a drill sergeant's.

'He won't be needing it this evening, Ma,' Fran shouted appeasingly. Was that an oxymoron? And why was the old woman's hearing aid on the table, not in her ear? 'So Mark can sit in it for a while.' He'd swear Fran had shrunk three inches since she'd stepped through the door. 'Pa's in hospital, remember. After his fall.' She slipped off her jacket and took Mark's, hugging the garments to her.

'Careless old fool. He never looks where he's going. Shuffles his feet — never picks them up properly. And then what happens to him? He goes and leaves me high and dry here.'

Mark, still trying not to breathe through his nose in what must be a hermetically sealed room, looked round for another chair. There was a huge pile of cushions on one of the unoccupied ones, and a sewing box and set of what must be corsets on the other. Two sets.

'Before you sit down, Fran, you can just mend those for me. He can make the tea.' She nodded vaguely in Mark's direction.

'Mark doesn't know where the kitchen is, let alone the tea, Ma. I'll—'

'I told you, you'll have to mend those. I can't see to do them, not in this light. He never puts decent bulbs in. And you'll have to go to the shops first thing tomorrow — I need some more stockings. That Sylvia — she's so rough putting them on me in a morning she keeps laddering them. You'll have to tell her. And she's taken my dentures and left someone else's. Look,' she said, turning to Mark and extracting her lower set, ready to plop them into his hand, 'you can see they aren't mine.'

Fran stepped swiftly forward, 'Well, just put them back for now. Poor Mark hasn't had a cup of tea yet — you can't expect him to look for your teeth.'

'Where are you going? You've only been here five minutes!'

'To make the tea, Ma. I'll do the mending when you're in bed.' She gathered up the corsets and hurried out with them.

Mark looked on, his stomach heaving with the smell of damp and urine and unwashed feet. Old people smell. He'd come across it often enough when he was on the beat, visiting pensioners when there was a sudden death. In those days he'd have found something easy to say to the old woman; now he stood opening and shutting his mouth before turning tail and following Fran, whom he found quickly enough, standing at the sink running water and tipping liquid detergent into the sink. She was humming something under her breath, over and over, as if trying to wear the tune out. After a moment he placed it. *Für Elise*.

'Sometimes I think she might be right about Sylvia,' she said, rubbing vigorously. 'These were — they weren't clean. In fact, I'll leave them to soak while I make our tea.'

And her open, confident face, brave in the face of hideous crimes, was crumpled as tight as a child's expecting punishment. He wanted to gather her up and throw her across whatever passed for a saddle-bow these days and gallop away — at very least cuddle her better. As she busied herself with tea things, washing one cup, throwing another away, he looked about him. The work-tops and the table were passably clean, thanks, presumably, to Sylvia, but the walls and ceiling hadn't seen fresh paint for years, and he would swear mould or mildew was growing in the corners.

She might have read his mind, or, more mundanely, simply followed the line of his eyes. 'Every time I arranged for a decorator, they'd quarrel with him over the price—'

'Which you were paying?'

'Well, yes. Or they'd refuse to let him in. And when I've bought paint to do it myself, they've — God, it's horrible, isn't it? But every single wall I've washed with bleach. Oh, Mark — why did I ever bring you here?' Her voice cracked.

Her hands still dripping, he took her in his arms, burying his face in her hair, the only sweet-smelling thing in the bungalow. 'How do you manage, week after week? By yourself?'

'As Pa always used to say, *needs must when the Devil drives*. And he'd always follow it up with, *what can't be cured, must be endured*.' She blotted her eyes, and turned from him, almost guiltily.

There was a strange double-thump, double-thump, as if a very large, very slow rabbit were lolloping inexorably towards them.

'I thought you were making some tea and here you are standing gossiping.'

He heard the woman's voice before he saw her. Finally she appeared in the doorway, leaning on a Zimmer.

'I can't find the kettle, Ma.'

It should have sounded like a statement of fact: even he heard it as more of a whining excuse.

'There it is. In front of your nose.'

There was indeed a kettle, bright and shiny, on the top of the stove.

Fran stared. 'What happened to the electric one?'

'The old fool put it on the red-ring to boil. We nearly had the fire-engine. But Sylvia smelt it before it got very bad. You know what, I think we should leave him in the hospital. He won't wear his incontinence pads, either.' She turned slowly on her heel and double-thumped away.

Fran was doubled up with laughter. 'Perhaps it's a good job you didn't sit in that chair!' But she was weeping when she straightened. 'Mark — what am I going to do?'

She was almost ready for the answer, wasn't she? But he'd rather she heard it from anyone but him. Tamely, he made the tea and put the plain biscuits she passed him on to a plate. Looking more carefully, he tipped them off again and washed the plate, the water dripping a pit into the foam on top of the corsets. As he dried the plate, Fran rolled up her sleeves again, pummelling the offending garments as if fighting off an assailant. The double-thump returned.

'That's right. Give them a good rub. It'll do your arms good. Get rid of the fat. We make her cook cottage pie, Mike.' Neither of them tried to correct her. 'Not because we like it, because we don't, not specially, though Pa finds it easy to chew, but because it's good for her arms. Mashing the potatoes. Look at all that fat.'

Fat? They were strong and beautifully shaped! But even as he tried to say so, the old voice ran on, 'It's because she used to play sport. The muscle's run to fat. Like those great ugly football managers you see on the telly, with their beer bellies over their knickers. I'll say that for you, you're a skinny-rib. And you've still got your hair. You know she dyes hers, don't you? In my day only tarts did that. And she wears trousers. I never wore trousers.'

Over the old woman's head, he could see Fran opening her mouth to speak. He caught her eye, shaking his head infinitesimally.

'Her bottom's too big for trousers. Well, she's too big all over for a girl. I did my best with her, but she was never pretty. Not like Hazel. You come with me, young man, and I'll show you a picture of our Hazel. Come on. She can bring the tray.' She turned to Fran. 'And try not to break anything. I heard you smash that plate. No good your pretending you didn't — I heard you put it in the bin. Come on, young man. Leave her to it.'

Seething, he looked back to Fran. She nodded, making a quick shooing movement with her suds-white hands. On impulse, he darted back, seized one and blew the bubbles into the air, kissing her nose as one landed on the tip. Somehow, the kiss tried to say, he would sort all this out.

Did she get its message? She was staring at her hands, wrinkled by the water: 'Everyone remarked on Elise's hands being work-worn. Living down here — I could become another Elise.'

He nodded. 'So desperate to escape you sell or give away everything that reminds you of your past life, tuck all the cash into your bag, grab a sexy motor — and get robbed of everything. Including the new life.'

'I have to find that murderer, Mark.'

'And,' he added, 'all her loot.'

'And see if anyone really has used all her papers to assume her ID. The Chief wanted me to get on to that especially, didn't he? And I haven't!'

He took her by the shoulders. 'Hang on, hang on: you worked every minute of last weekend on another case. You've hardly drawn breath since. You've run the abductor to earth and saved a child's life. Don't you dare start beating yourself up because you've not done something no one else managed in over two years of trying!' Was he speaking as her lover or as her senior officer? If it was hard for him to tell, what about Fran? Perhaps tenderness would push her into tears, which he suspected she wouldn't be able to deal with. 'Tell you what: could you do me a favour? Phone up and see the kid's still making good progress. It'd be good if she was back home.'

He could see how much it hurt her to swallow, but she took the phone he fished from his belt and dialled. Meanwhile, her mother was yelling for him.

* * *

Obediently, standing beside the old woman — he ought to call her something, but Mrs Harman seemed rather formal and Ma too intimate — he looked at a studio portrait of Fran's sister. Even with the contrived lighting, he thought he sensed a determined jaw and lips that would snap shut. But she was pretty, very pretty, and looked as if the academic world, as symbolised by the degree scroll in her hand, was her oyster. There was an out-of-focus snap of Fran too, looking absurd and ugly in the awful passing out stance no one ever used once they were in the force. He took a risk. 'But Fran has a degree, too. A BSc. And a PhD. Don't you have a photo of her in her doctor's gown?'

'Doctor? She's not a real doctor. In any case, it wasn't a proper university, not like Hazel. The Open University.'

'People say that's the hardest way to get a degree — tougher than going away—'

'That's rubbish. They write all their essays at home, so they can look up the answers. Not proper exams.'

Mark looked to Fran, who was now standing at the door with the tea things, for support. He shrugged helplessly. His attempts to balance the equation between the daughters had only given the old woman with her half-knowledge and twisted logic the chance to humiliate her further. Fran smiled, though whether love or gratitude or irony predominated he couldn't tell. Perhaps she didn't know herself. He stepped swiftly over, taking the tray and kissing her on the lips.

'Rebecca's safe at home,' she murmured. 'And the Rohypnol or whatever did its job. She can't remember anything that happened, beyond a vague grasp of the rules of chess. However, I gather she's doing a sort of cold turkey — he gave her enough over a long enough period to get her hooked. I wonder what the jury will make of it all.'

'Come on: I can't wait all day, young man.'

He put the tray on the cluttered table beside Ma's chair and started to pour.

'Look at this tea, half-stewed. And no strainer, either.'

'It's made with tea-bags, Ma. You don't need a strainer.'

'I've got my standards! God knows how you'll get on when you try to look after us properly. A real butterfly she is, Mike, always flitting from one job to the next and never finishing anything properly. Look at this room, Mike — did you ever see such a mess. And yet she won't put things away tidily when I ask.'

'We only arrived ten minutes ago,' he said dryly. 'Give her half a chance!'

'Where did you put your cases? I don't want to go falling over them and ending up in hospital like your father.'

'They're still safely in the car,' he said. A look from Fran prevented him saying anything more. And he acquiesced. There was no point in getting on to his high horse and announcing the bungalow was too filthy for human habitation and that he'd booked them into the best hotel he could find. It wasn't only Grant who was allergic to dust, he'd lied to Fran. And since he'd packed both lots of clothes into one case, she'd better come with him. How she was going to tell the old lady he couldn't imagine. But he had a fair idea what the response might be.

In the event, he had to admit Fran's tactics were masterly. She announced that when they'd collected Hazel and Grant, they were going to see Pa, and then would need some supper, so they would be back later than Ma's self-imposed bedtime. So if they didn't think they could get back in without disturbing her, they, like Hazel and Grant, would stay the night down the road. 'In one of the guest-houses,' she gestured vaguely.

The old lady whipped round. 'But Hazel and Grant are married. Do you two share a bed?'

'It's much cheaper that way,' Fran explained.

And to his amazement got away with it — perhaps because on the instant Fran returned to the kitchen and started preparing her mother's supper, he took a quite spurious interest in photos of children he was sure were only Hazel's by marriage but which Ma assured him had the full benefit of her genes.

* * *

He wished that holding Fran to comfort her hadn't reminded him of Tina. Physical contact, naked body against naked body, had been all she'd wanted as her illness had progressed. What would she make of this friendship, which had blossomed so swiftly, so triumphantly against all the odds of Fran's life? He hoped it had her blessing. He mustn't give a hint of his thoughts and memories to Fran, however: she was so swift to pick up nuances. So he continued to hold her in his arms, smoothing her hair and kissing her forehead. All he'd meant was to comfort her. So he was taken by surprise when she initiated love-making so frantic it left them both gasping.

* * *

They reached the airport three minutes after the plane. But he noted with amusement that Fran was looking almost ostentatiously at her watch as she strolled lazily to meet her sister, almost yawning with the tedium of the wait.

In the flesh, the sisters were so different as to be unrelated. It was easy to see why Hazel had won all the plaudits. Even though she was ten years older than Fran, she looked the same age. She was petite, with the sort of facial bones that never seem to age. Most women he knew had become scrawny or run to flesh by their sixties: Hazel had done neither, retaining the figure of a woman half her years. Her complexion was clear, and her eyes the sort of whisky-brown that looked as innocent as a running stream. Her hair, pulled into a loose bun, was dark honey, very dark, with enough white to make it almost blonde: either she was extremely lucky or she had a hairdresser as good as Fran's.

It was almost possible to overlook her husband, for all he was over six feet tall, as he hovered apologetically at her left shoulder, not quite sure how to greet anyone, and leaving a bony hand dangling in mid-air. Mark reached and shook it firmly, introducing himself while Hazel chuntered to Fran about the journey. Despite his cadaverous appearance, Grant was remarkably easy to talk too, and by the time they'd reached the car they had progressed from golf handicaps to whisky.

'You may have heard on the media about our kidnapping, down in Kent: it was Frances here who ran the perpetrator to earth and arrested him. I'm very proud of her,' he declared loudly enough to be overheard.

'Mmm,' Hazel murmured noncommittally.

Grant laid a hand on his arm and held him back. 'Don't, whatever you do, let the dear lass come down here and nurse them. There'll be a death within the month if you do — and I wouldn't know whose. That mother: I swear I always check the moment I see her for horns and tail.'

'I didn't think you'd seen her for some time,' Mark commented. It was hard to keep the note of criticism out of his voice.

'Alas, Mark, my stipend doesn't run to trips like this. It's only thanks to Fran we've ever come down. As a matter of fact, I rather think the old lady had disowned Hazel, but somehow Fran managed to win her round. Once seen, never forgotten, that old bat. And in my experience, Mark, people don't become saintly with age. They merely become more themselves.' He shot a glance at his wife, for some reason fingering the fabric of Fran's jacket, and dropped his voice. 'These days Hazel can do anything with them — in her they've undoubtedly met their match — but I swear Ma will end up in some circle of a Dantean Hell, telling Old Nick what a poor job he's doing.'

Fran had opened the boot and as he stowed cases, he caught her eye. To his surprise — and, he had to admit, possibly to hers — he mouthed very clearly across the few feet separating them, 'I love you.'

Whatever had prompted him he was glad: the result was as if he'd switched on a light bulb behind her face.

* * *

He made a point of taking her hand and holding it very tightly as they headed from the car park into the hospital, four abreast.

'I'm afraid you'll be very shocked,' Fran said, 'not just by Ma and Pa — who are every minute of their age these days — but by the state of the bungalow. I've had it painted outside every three years, but the inside is — well, let's just say if I were a social worker seeing it for the first time I'd accuse the carer of neglecting them. I saw Mark was shocked this afternoon. He can't deny it. In fact, every weekend when I go down I'm shocked, too — but then I get the first little job to do and the bigger picture fades. I've nagged; I've begged; I've cajoled. But they simply will not permit anyone, even me, to disturb the tenor of their life by applying paint or buying new curtains.'

'Pop them into respite care while you do it.' Hazel said crisply.

'Respite care while Fran pays someone else to do it,' Mark couldn't stop himself from retorting.

'She earns in a month what Grant and I subsist on for a year, so I don't see that as a problem. And now there are two of you . . .'

'Fine,' agreed Fran. 'You get them to agree to the care, get them into the home and keep them there. I'll pay for everything. But we're getting diverted. I don't think they can survive as they are, not with Pa in hospital. Ma's just not up to looking after herself. And to be honest, I think they need a different sort of care from anything I can offer. Even if I were living in. It was seeing things through Mark's eyes today that brought it home. I'm sorry, but there it is.' Everything came out in a rush, as if she were a child confessing to breaking an impossible promise.

Which she was, of course, Mark realised. He squeezed her hand.

* * *

Mr Harman was alone in a side ward, or he had a feeling that their arrival well after visiting hours wouldn't have been welcome. The very old man, unshaven and dentureless, was propped up in bed staring at a blank TV screen. He looked up as they came in, the men standing back as the daughters ran to his bed, one either side. His face lit up. 'It's never our Hazel! It is, it is!' He turned his head towards Fran. 'But who's this other lady? I don't know her, do I?'

CHAPTER THIRTY-THREE

To his great anxiety, Fran was the life and soul of the late supper they ate in Exeter. At first he'd thought it might be drink talking, but although they'd had drinks on an empty stomach, he knew she could hold her liquor if she needed to. All the same, there was a glitter about her eyes that made him take her quips and fancies more as an indication of her hurt than of any real happiness.

Perhaps it was his fault if she were drunk. He had had no idea how the city might buzz in the evening, and, not having booked a table, was turned away by three places before a fourth promised them a table in half an hour. They could wait in the bar area. Throughout all the delays and hesitations, Fran scintillated.

Grant, hesitantly, had put himself forward as the driver, so the others could drink: 'It's nothing to do with my calling, so don't be embarrassed that I'm about to impose total abstinence on you all. I'm simply taking antibiotics, which give you a hangover on the sniff of a barmaid's apron. And I have full insurance, whatever vehicle I drive. But I shall quite understand if you don't want me to drive that gleaming beastie of yours, Fran.'

She flipped him the keys with the brightest of grins.

She'd said nothing about her father's appalling snub, all the more painful for being its being unconscious, and he doubted that she ever would. Imagine, her own father not recognising her, but making such a fuss of her long-absent sister. But it explained something he'd thought odd at the time, her request, urgently whispered as they first made love, that he call out her name when he came. He'd thought it was to do with Tina, and perhaps it was, predominantly. But now he feared it came from a deeper anxiety, only now realised.

If he hadn't been able to protect Fran from this evening's pain, there was at least one thing he could stop: a family gathering at the bungalow, and Hazel's narrow-eyed and ruthless inspection. It had been bad enough for Fran to have him see it, someone she trusted to be non-judgemental, work matters apart. But non-judgemental didn't seem to be part of Hazel's vocabulary: it was as if she had embraced Calvinism when she'd embraced a man of the kirk. Not that Grant was in any way a stereotypical minister, getting more cheerfully inebriated on sparkling water than Hazel, whose waspishness increased in direct proportion to the amount of wine she insisted on drinking. Their curries were quite excellent, better than anything he'd been able to find in Kent. He'd never subscribed to the curry and lager school of thought, and had also settled for water with the meal, but didn't propose to deny Grant what he suspected would be an enormous treat.

At a suitable moment he would announce that they had to return first thing the next morning. The Rebecca case was the obvious reason. Maybe Fran could think of another. Much as he wanted to protect her, the thought of telling her what to do and more specifically what not to do was abhorrent.

It wasn't until — at his apparently romantic suggestion — that Grant parked the car under the fairy lights on the almost deserted Teignmouth seafront, so they could take in the sight of the moon over the surprisingly calm sea, that he managed to get Fran to himself for a moment.

'Shall we paddle?' he asked, taking her hand and running between the flowerbeds on the prom towards the beach.

'In these clothes?'

'Why not?' But he contented himself with walking along the sort of sand that brought back memories of hours of beach cricket. He drew her close so that they faced each other. 'Fran: will you indulge me in something?'

'Of course.' But the moonlight showed her puzzlement.

'I don't think a big family reunion in the bungalow tomorrow would be a good idea. Do you?'

'Ma's heart, you mean, with all of us thronging round? No?'

'I was thinking it wouldn't be pleasant for you—'

'But—'

'I know you don't expect life to be pleasant, but there's no need to make it worse. My suggestion is that I find a police reason to be away early. We pop in to see your Ma to say goodbye, and thence to the hospital to see your Pa, so your filial duty will be done.' He hadn't meant to give such a curl of the tongue to the words. But he couldn't call the intonation back, could he? 'That way Hazel gets some idea of what you've been up against. If she's in charge, there's no reason why we shouldn't make a leisurely journey back — remember the M3 and M25 traffic.'

'Why is this indulging *you*?'

'Because I don't like to see anyone treated the way your mother treated you today. And the fact she didn't mean any harm made it worse in my book. It looked as if it came with practice. And don't forget I've seen you when you've just got back from your weekend's labours down here. Why did you never say what a strain it was?'

She shook her head as if genuinely puzzled. 'She's just being Ma.'

'Will you do it? Indulge me?' He surprised himself again with his earnestness. He might have been proposing marriage, it mattered so much.

'OK. Yes, OK.' She said it as lightly as if he were suggesting poached, not scrambled eggs. She was perching on one leg to strip off her popsocks and roll up her trouser legs.

She was only going to paddle!

He had an idea that Grant saw through his ploy, but since he said that they were responsible for overseeing the final details of the case against Rebecca's abductor, Hazel could make no objection.

Ma did, when they called in to see her. 'You can go back on the train now; she can drive back tomorrow,' she said. 'She always does.'

He said, with some brutality, 'That's not possible. She has to be at work tomorrow.' If the old woman remembered that the next day was Sunday, he'd have to extemporise. 'She's run out of leave, you see, with all her journeys down here. So no more days off for Fran. Sorry, but there it is.'

Ma sniffed. 'It's about time you left that place. We always said you would. You were going to live here and look after us.'

'I haven't retired yet,' Fran said.

'You'll have to speak up. You know your Pa can never hear a word you say. This Mike of yours, he's got a good voice. Doesn't mumble like you do. Now, if you're off, I'll just use the commode so you can empty it before you go.'

'Allow me to help you to the bathroom,' Mark said firmly, having painfully tangled with the sitting frame and supports designed to make loos more accessible to the old and now determined that the apparatus support the person for whom it was meant.

Ma took a firm grip on his arm. Her hand was almost devoid of flesh. 'And you can get out my pink dress,' she said over her shoulder. 'I want to make a bit of an effort for our Hazel.'

* * *

Mark thought Pa was noticeably frailer, although he'd been hauled out of bed and propped in a chair. At last recognising her, he let his hand rest in Fran's, the age spots so profuse it was hard to tell the original colour. His legs, vulnerable between the jaunty paisley pyjamas and slippers fastened with wide Velcro strips, were deeply discoloured, bruised as he fell, perhaps.

'They're kind. Very kind. Only I'm so thirsty. So very thirsty. Could you just nip and get me a cup of tea, Frances? You always were a good girl.'

Fran shot Mark a look: should she acquiesce? Or were there medical reasons for his lack of fluid — the possibility of an operation, perhaps.

'I'll go and ask a nurse,' he announced, thinking Fran deserved the odd affectionate pat her father gave.

Was it because it was the weekend that nurses were an endangered species? At last he cornered one, speaking to her with the easy authority he prided himself on. If constables jumped, this young woman showed no signs of moving.

'So why is he thirsty? Is it a symptom of his illness?'

She shrugged.

'Will you find out, please? He looks pretty dehydrated to me.'

'The consultant doesn't do his round on Sundays.'

'Why don't I speak to a staff nurse?' He recalled Fran recounting the battles she'd had with Michael Penn and his colleagues: what had happened to the angels who used to flit around wards making people better by their very presence? Government directives, that was what had happened.

As he strode back to Fran — surely the nurse would recognise a man used to giving orders and being obeyed by his walk — a tiny gnome of a man opposite Pa called him over. Laying an almost transparent hand on his arm, the man said, 'They leaves his tea on the side there and he can't reach it, can he? So they takes it away again. And 'cos he's mostly asleep, they doesn't ask him why he hasn't drunk it, see? Not nurses — they're just tea girls. Piece-work, I'd bet. See how many cups you can dish out and collect in again. Tell you what — they say I can get up tomorrow: I'll look out for him.'

But by now there was a bustle across the ward: Pa's curtains were being drawn and Fran expelled, heading towards him hands spread. 'I ran a junior doctor to earth as she was prowling along, trying to be invisible. They're going to fit a drip, he's so dehydrated! Why didn't I notice, Mark?'

'Because you and your Pa were sharing a tender moment and — hey, what's up?'

Fran? Weeping? He drew her out into the corridor.

'He's dying, isn't he? He won't come out alive, will he?'

Mark shook his head. 'Is that what you think or what he thinks?'

'He says he's had enough. He wants to give up.'

If you thought of the state he'd been living in, you could hardly blame him. But Mark asked quietly, 'Isn't a man his age entitled to say that? When did he last leave the house? When did he last enjoy himself? Life's for more than enduring, Fran. It's for living.'

God help him, he was already working out how the old man's death would affect Fran. And was that because he loved her and wanted to save her further exertion or because he loved her and wanted her to himself? As for Fran, her face was inscrutable: perhaps she was speculating in exactly the same way.

CHAPTER THIRTY-FOUR

'Check out every Marjorie Gray in the country! You're joking! Wherever do I start, guv?' If she felt Monday-morningish, Tom looked and sounded it.

'Perhaps I exaggerate, Tom. Start with the obvious — DVLA, NHS, things like that. And we're looking for someone who's changed address within the last two years, so that should narrow it down. Especially if Elise's solicitor can remember where she said she was moving to. I'll check him out and also look in on the poor Draytons — see if they've got over their shock.'

He shuffled. 'I did rather wonder why you hadn't got someone from Family Liaison to check up on them if they were so upset.'

'How did you know? Tom, you organised Family Liaison yourself, didn't you? Thank you. You're a good officer and a kind young man. In whatever order.'

* * *

As she had permitted herself to hope, the Draytons were in mid-flight. This time a trip to France as Christmas shopping called. Christmas! What could she do about Christmas? She had to go to Devon, and Mark had his family, who would expect him. How could she survive Christmas without him?

But she pulled herself up short and swiftly thanked them, hoping they'd got over their ordeal. Only when they'd talked themselves breathless about the kindness of the young lady she'd been thoughtful enough to send them did she mention Elise's possible destination again.

'It really is quite important, you see. After all, there may be people somewhere wondering why she never turned up.'

'Oh, no. You see, she said she was making a completely fresh start. Somewhere with no old people, she said — we remembered that the other day, didn't we dear?' Mrs Drayton looked adoringly at her husband for confirmation.

'So she wouldn't go to Spain — too much of the old Costa Geriatrica,' he agreed. 'But she didn't want to be anywhere cold. And she wanted to avoid the small-town yobs — you've seen the pictures on TV, Chief Superintendent.'

'I've locked a few up in my time,' she agreed cheerfully. 'Now, I won't hold you up any more, but if you do think of where she might have been heading for, you will let me know, won't you? It's really very important.'

* * *

Fran then tracked down Marjorie's solicitor. He was a young man with very short hair and a suit so sharp he might cut himself, who confirmed the number of Marjorie's First Direct bank account, and intimated, with considerable boredom, that he had no idea where his client might have been intending to live. Fran had a fugitive impulse to slip him a tenner to see if it improved his memory. 'Come, you must have picked up hints!' she said as sharply as a schoolteacher.

'I don't know. Bath? Bradford?'

'Or Bolton or Billericay!' Fran suggested tartly.

* * *

First Direct were noticeably more helpful: in fact, Fran got the impression that the obliging young Leeds lass at the end of the phone would have walked down the street with a message herself if she'd been able. But even she felt unhappy to divulge information without authority, so Fran faxed a formal request.

She also had time to review all the work Tom had done tracing car-salesmen: it seemed to her only right that he should be allowed to go and question the young man he had in his sights.

She sat back, letting the chair support her middle-back, and stretched. There was a gratifying crunch from her spine. But her head didn't clear. She felt as she always did after a weekend in Devon, drained of any initiative — which was why Tom should have been spared the menial task she'd set him that morning and done the ones involving skill and judgement, like questioning the car salesman.

The phone rang. Mark? But it was only First Direct — goodness, their employees had a price above rubies. They had an address for Miss Marjorie Gray — in Birmingham.

* * *

'What a fortunate coincidence we have a Chief Constables' meeting up there tomorrow,' Mark said, joining her outside the canteen. 'The Chief wanted me to go in his stead. I was going to tell him no, it but it means I can give you a lift.' He squeezed her hand reassuringly. 'You might need some local support and I—'

'I trained the ACC (Crime) up there,' she interrupted, laughing. 'She owes me! So I can grease my own wheels, thanks! But as a driver — oh, Mark,' she continued, dropping her voice, unable to sustain even this mild banter, 'it'd be so good to go up with you. If you can be spared.'

'Spared! The Chief asked me to represent him, I told you! And yes, I was going to say no because I was worried about leaving you on your own. After the weekend to end all weekends,' he said.

'Not much worse than usual. Oh, the complaint about my fat arms wasn't nice. But they always did have a thing about my size — I must have been a total cuckoo in their nest. And Pa not recognising me — that was really painful.' Tears welled. 'After all this time, recognising Hazel, but not the daughter who trims his fingernails and holds his hand at the dentist's. Ah, well — prodigal daughter time!'

'You don't think,' he said tentatively, 'that all that criticism of you was designed to make me think again? That Ma sees me as a rival for your affections and attentions?'

'Surely she wouldn't . . . No, I can't imagine she sees me as anything other than an old maid glued to the shelf.'

'How did she get on with your fiancé?'

'Loathed him on sight. But,' she added with a grin, 'he did rather ask for it. White hair and a beard. He looked a bit like an Old Testament prophet. You, on the other hand, have kept your hair colour and are a skinny-rib.'

'So she doesn't disapprove of me *per se*, but does disapprove of our relationship?'

She shrugged. 'She would, wouldn't she? But no, it's nothing personal. I'd say you'd actually made a bit of a hit.'

'You won't . . . you wouldn't think of ditching me to suit her?'

There was a note she didn't recognise. 'How could I? Oh, Mark — never!' But then she remembered the real world, in which every weekend was taken up and Christmas — yes, Christmas was already spoken for. Her reassuring smile, the joy in her eyes, faded. She bit her lip. 'But it's not going to be easy. Juggling everything.'

'Once they're in a retirement home it'll be easier,' he said, as if their move was an established fact.

'You're right. Even if I moved down tomorrow, I couldn't nurse Pa. Or live with Ma for more than a week without going crazy. But Ma will want Plan B. Which was them moving into a home and my going down to live in their bungalow to keep an eye on them.'

'No one can live in that place till it's been taken apart and fumigated! Can they?' he added more gently. 'And, Fran, you still have to put in your resignation and that involves three months' notice. They may not survive that long.'

'But they're as tough as old boots! Oh, they've had a succession of minor ailments, but you know what they say about creaky gates.'

He put a gentle hand on her forearm. 'Are you quite sure your Pa's not a bit more than creaky?'

'My God, I've not phoned the hospital yet.' She reached for her mobile.

'After lunch. Please, leave it till after lunch. Your getting an ulcer won't help them.'

* * *

'What does "poorly but stable" mean?' Fran asked the voice with the Devon burr.

'He's a very old man, Dr Harman, isn't he? And that fall shook him up proper.'

Fran smiled at the precise medical terminology. She also enjoyed his use of her civilian title, the one only Alan Pitt ever used. One day she might tell the medics that she wasn't really one of them. Meanwhile, their spurious professional respect was useful. 'How's the rehydration going?'

'He *will* keep pulling his drip out, Dr Harman. It frets him something shocking. We're not getting him up today — let the poor old soul have a bit of peace and quiet. Now, our Dr Ahmed would like a word with you later — what's the best number to call you on?'

'Why should he need to speak to me?' She took a deep breath.

'It's about something we have to consider. He's terribly old, Dr Harman. If his heart gives out . . .'

'Are we talking about resuscitation? Because' — her throat hurt as she swallowed — 'I don't think you should force him back. Not if he's — going. But you should talk to my sister as well.' She reeled off the bungalow phone number.

‘She and her husband will no doubt be visiting today. So you can do it face to face.’

Tom came in as she cut the call. Not at all to her surprise, he reached for a couple of tissues from the box on her desk and passed them across. ‘Bad news, ma’am?’

‘Expected. They want permission not to resuscitate my father. That’s all.’

‘That’s enough for anyone. A big decision. I’ll get you some water, shall I?’ His kind deed done; he was evidently keen to escape.

‘Water would be great, thanks.’ She took several deep breaths and was relatively under control, if not composed, when he returned. ‘I’m off tomorrow, Tom, to check out the flat in the centre of Birmingham. Elise told her bank she was moving there.’

He sat heavily opposite her. ‘In that case you may find the new Miss Gray — only this one’s very much a “Ms” — alive and well and living in it. I did what you said, and found as many Marjorie Grays as I could. And one’s living in Birmingham.’ He read the address from his notebook.

‘Bingo! Same address. Tell you what, just on the off-chance, let’s see if she’s got a criminal record. What wonderful things computers are!’

‘They sure beat carrier pigeons,’ he agreed, coming to stand at her shoulder.

‘Wow! Speeding, non-payment of parking fines: she’s not a lot like Elise, is she?’

‘They’re pretty trivial, though. Nothing juicy.’

‘That doesn’t mean she’s clean. Our friends in Brum may have private suspicions they’ll share with me.’ She rubbed her hands in glee.

‘I suppose,’ he said, the expression on his face like a puppy hoping for a walk, ‘I couldn’t come too?’

What a cow she was to deny him this. But she, no more than Mark, would want a third person with them.

‘I’d love you to. But I want you to chase up our missing salesman and haul him in.’ She rubbed her face. ‘Tom: what did you say his name was? I’m losing the plot here!’

He cringed as if expecting a reprimand. 'Actually it may be me, like. I don't know that I ever told you, did I?'

'I'm sure you did. Anyway, remind me, as it were, and tell me a bit about him. And take a seat: you look untidy stuck up there.'

'He's one Dean Roberts. Born and bred in Chatham — well, I suppose someone's got to be. Got a few GCSEs. Didn't stay on at school or go to college. Started as a car valeter or whatever you'd call it, and used to chauffeur people back home when they'd taken their cars in for service. Very charming to old folk — very popular. Anyway, he must have had a good break, because he got into sales — commission only, to start with. If his lifestyle's anything to with it, he must be very good at selling — fantastically good. He's got his own flat, his own car, even a boat down in Hythe. Not bad for twenty-five.' Tom sounded wistful.

'You'll get that student loan paid off one day,' she said, wishing she could help with a discreet bag stuffed with fivers. 'And Car Crime have their beadies on him too?'

'Only as a contact of a contact: they've never thought of him as a big player. But they're dead interested, like, in what we're doing.'

'Why not take one of them along with you? It's always good to build bridges. You see, I don't want our new Ms Gray to be able to communicate with him and if he's in for questioning — oh, any pretext, Tom: you don't like the ring-tone of his mobile, anything! — she won't be able to.'

'What about you? You won't be doing this on your own?'

'I shall have half of West Midlands Police backing me up, never fear. Courtesy,' she added, with an encouraging grin, 'of an ex-sergeant of mine, who's now an ACC. Good role model for you, Tom — except, of course, she's a woman! Sorry! Now, off you go and talk to Car Crime and set up your sting for about midday.'

He dawdled, and then seemed to make up his mind: 'It's better, isn't it, to keep busy when things are bad? You were very good to me when I was worried about Dad, guv — you know you only have to ask, like, if you need . . . well, anything . . .' He blushed but didn't drop his eyes. 'And I'm sure that goes for half CID out there.'

'Thanks, Tom.' Damn it if her eyes didn't well with tears again. 'I won't hesitate. If only,' she added, with a watery grin, 'you're not kind to me. You know how it is.'

He flapped a hand, smiled, and left, returning as she called him back.

'I just wanted to know if you'd sent your mum her model car.'

'I did better than that. I sent her one of those Day Out vouchers. She's going to drive a rally car. And have a little Burago model of the car afterwards to sit on her fireplace, as a memento, like.'

CHAPTER THIRTY-FIVE

If only they'd all been wearing uniform, the braid and buttons would have been dazzling. As it was, both Fran and her one-time protégée, the West Midlands ACC, were in mufti, though both as smart in their own trouser-suited way as Mark, resplendent in his full rig. When she'd started in the force, the idea of senior officers greeting each other with hugs would have been unthought of. Now it was as natural to greet Emma that way as to salute the West Midlands Chief Constable when they passed in the corridor as Mark went off to the CCs' meeting.

Emma, eyeing Mark, would clearly have liked some girls' talk, but she had her own schedule: crime didn't stop in a city like hers just because two senior officers wanted a gossip. She introduced Fran to a charming Asian detective sergeant called Farat, from whose eyes intelligence positively radiated. Fran rebuked herself firmly for the tiniest moment of surprise she felt at the sight of a detective wearing a hijab: what a difference between shire counties like hers and a truly urban force.

If Farat was tiny to the point of petite, Fran towering over her, she was as steely as Fran could have wished, sharing intelligence with gusto: 'Keeping a disorderly house, prostitution—'

'Prostitution! Our Marjorie Gray's in her sixties!'

'Ours isn't. Forty — well, fifty at most. So we may get her for using false documents too. If you wouldn't mind coming into the CID office, ma'am, I can show you what we've got so far.'

Fran pulled a face. 'Couldn't you call me guv?'

'I'd call you gaffer if you were one of our officers.'

'Gaffer?'

'It's what foremen and senior workers used to be called in factories and so on round here. Actually it sounds like someone from Hardy, doesn't it? A yokel chewing a straw. We did Hardy for A Level, in the days before they dumbed down. Do you know, my sister says her students want to see the video of a set text, not read it for themselves! Would you mind stepping this way, ma'am?'

Fran stopped dead, hands on hips. 'Farat, you're doing everything except curtsey. Drop the formality, would you? I'm not bloody royalty.'

'Sorry, ma'am.'

'Or even gaffer? What have people been saying about me? Am I such a dragon?'

'You've . . . you've just got such a reputation, gaffer. I mean, anyone who taught our ACC has got to be good. And when she does training sessions, your name always comes up. You're something of a legend.'

'The living dead, more like. No, I'm not quite joking. I've been — still am, come to think of it — under a lot of personal stress at the moment and I've got a bit sloppy. I've missed things, let things slide. So I need you to brief me and work with me as a colleague, someone as fallible as the next woman. Tell you what, let's find the loo — see what I mean? — and a coffee, in that order, and I'll tell you what we've done so far, and then you can fill me in on the new Miss Gray . . .'

* * *

Fran settled herself at the visitor's side of Farat's desk. 'Let's get this straight. We have one genuine Marjorie Gray — our poor

Elise. Her documents were stolen, so another woman could take her identity. But now you think she may be one of several clones, as it were. Surely, though, there's a limit to how many middle-aged to elderly woman you need passports and other papers for. Young people of either sex, I can understand that.'

'Madams, ma'am.' Farat's eyes were full of fun.

'My God — someone to keep an eye on the young prostitutes brought in from — where did you say? Eastern Europe?' Fran slapped her head in irritation. 'And, of course, once you've got a good original, you can make excellent forgeries of documents for people of either gender. And you have bank references to back them. All kosher.'

'Or indeed,' Farat laughed, 'halal! The Muslim equivalent,' she added, when she saw that Fran was nonplussed. 'Was this Elise of yours — you obviously think of her as that, rather than as Marjorie — a confiding soul? The sort that would spill the beans to anyone prepared to listen?'

'Who knows? But she probably was lonely, living almost exclusively amongst the very old — and if you found, say, a car salesperson, with an open engaging manner, you might start talking about why you wanted the car and where you were going to take it. But why a car salesman from Kent should be helping sex traders defeats me.'

'Drugs, I'd say. There's usually a connection somewhere. Not to mention all the ports you've got there, both passengers and freight. Now, here's the file we're preparing on the new Marjorie. We think she started life as one Sonja Kranic, sister of what was effectively a little warlord, so she was spared the worst risks attendant on being a poor girl in a poor country. If anyone made attempts on her virtue, he'd be cold meat, his genitals stuffed down his throat. She did have a husband at one point, but he seems to have disappeared — we're not sure how. She arrived in Birmingham about two years ago, and has kept a fairly low profile.'

'Apart from the odd speeding offence.'

'And non-payment of fines. She's never without a male protector, and if she is a prostitute, she's a very high-class one. We've never had enough of a case to take it any further, not even hopefully to the DPP. My suspicion is that she isn't in fact a tom herself, but, as I said, a madam.'

'Does she live on the premises then?'

'Goodness no! She's too fly for that. She lives in a very chic area; the brothels are in the poorer parts of Edgbaston, though we have noticed a couple of much more upmarket affairs sprouting up under the guise of private clubs or casinos. We've been waiting till we could put together a cast-iron case.'

Fran sighed. 'So many threads to pull together. All I ever wanted to do was identify Elise and find her killer. Now I seem to be dabbling in international crime and leaving young Tom to pick up the murderer all by himself.' She didn't regret leaving all the ensuing paperwork to him, but she did wish she could have been involved. But that was modern policing and modern crime. You had to delegate or die. Or let the case die.

'A simultaneous swoop seems a good bet,' said Farat hesitantly, as if unsure of the older woman's mood.

'Of course it does.' Her phone rang. 'Excuse me. Tom? All well with you?'

'We've just picked him up, guv. Guess what — his call tone is that tune you keep humming under your breath.'

'I don't hum tunes under my breath.'

'You always do when you're worried — didn't you realise? Anyway, it's that.'

Puzzled, she wished him well and cut the call. Did she hum under her breath when she was worried? Ma always used to do that — it drove them all mad. A few bars, here and there. Often the same few bars. Over and over. And when you taxed her she was offended and insisted you were hearing things. Of all the things to inherit . . .

'Right,' she said brightly. 'The sun's shining out there and I always take that as an omen.'

Farat looked intently at her but simply said, 'Now, we could drive to Gray's flat or walk: it's only a step and probably quicker.'

'And that way I'd see something of the new Birmingham. Is it true you have a Selfridges and a Harvey Nicks . . .'

* * *

Their route took them nowhere near such shopping heaven, however. But they actually walked through the Convention Centre that was home to Symphony Hall, and found themselves in a canalised complex more attractive than anything Fran remembered of Birmingham. Then Farat struck out across a broad piazza, stopping at last outside a set of what appeared to be extremely bijou flats.

'Number thirty-three. What a prime site,' Farat observed, looking around. 'Walking distance from the city centre and all its shopping, Symphony Hall and the indoor sports arena over there if you fancy Davis Cup tennis. I wouldn't mind living somewhere like this myself.'

'Is there secure parking? Because our Miss Gray had just bought herself a Lotus.'

'Had she indeed! Not your average pensioner then.'

'I think she was trying quite desperately not to be. In fact,' Fran reflected, 'almost all the retired people I've come across in this investigation have been trying desperately hard not to be average. Perhaps there's no such thing as average anymore.'

'My mother's decided to take her GCSEs,' Farat volunteered. 'She only mastered English a couple of years ago, but now she's really motoring. English and Arabic she's going for. Before that I really thought she was going to be a traditional Pakistani granny. Must be something in the water,' she concluded lightly.

'There must be something pretty special in Birmingham's water to take twenty years off Marjorie's age! Oh, Farat, you should see the poor woman whose identity we think she's stolen. A living death for the latter part of her life at least — we may never get the entire picture of her life — and now in persistent vegetative state.'

Farat nodded in sympathy. 'It makes one see the advantage of a living will.'

'But for the will to be implemented people have to know who you are. OK.' Fran braced herself. 'Let's do it, shall we?'

The new Marjorie Gray was, as Farat had said, in her forties, with the expensive face, body and clothes of a woman used to pampering herself. She had cultivated a sexy, rather gravely voice. Behind the clear enunciation, however, lay, Fran was sure, an Eastern European accent. Disorderly house? Prostitution? There were countless innocent girls smuggled over from the former Soviet Bloc and forced into the most degrading sexual slavery. Miss Gray did not look as if degradation had entered her personal vocabulary: if it had, she would surely be meting it out, not enduring it. Well, presumably that was what the sister of a warlord, however minor, would do.

She was politeness itself to the two officers, however, offering coffee or tea and seating them in the sort of leather-upholstered chairs that didn't come from a down-market chain. They suited the décor of the rest of the apartment, which involved a great deal of pale wood, colour-washed walls and a couple of what looked like good paintings. Would this really have been the choice of a sixty-year-old from St Mary's Bay? After the clutter of a parental home, would she have found acres of space healing or as intimidating as the new car?

'You have a most wonderful view from here,' Fran observed. 'I didn't know Birmingham could be so attractive.'

'There has been a lot of investment,' Miss Gray said.

'Do you remember what it was like before?' Fran asked. Then warming to her theme, 'Intent on putting up the ugliest buildings it could, pedestrians at the mercy of the car — quite a laughing stock to us Southerners.'

Miss Gray's polite inclination of the head suggested that they could talk about regional geography if they liked.

'Which do you think is the most impressive change?' Farat asked.

'I don't have an opinion.'

'Ah! So you're a newcomer too,' Fran said, as if delighted. 'Where do you come from?'

'London.'

'From the Smoke! Oh, a fellow exile! Which part?' Fran continued her girlish enthusiasm.

'Hendon.' She rapped off an address, which Fran noted. 'I have yet to understand why you are here, Detective Harman and Detective Hafeez.'

'Detective Chief Superintendent Harman and Detective Sergeant Hafeez,' Fran corrected her. 'We don't use "detective" as a title here — only in America.'

'Wonderful country,' Farat observed. 'All those vast spaces. Have you ever been? Before I grow old I want to tour the world,' she continued, an impassioned sweep of the arm encompassing myriad opportunities. 'Even the former USSR and China!'

'I am happy to put down roots,' Miss Gray enunciated clearly.

'So if you want to put down roots in Birmingham, where were you from originally? It's not a Hendon accent, is it? I was at college there long enough to know the accent well,' Fran beamed. 'The police college.'

'Do you live here alone?' Farat chipped in. 'It's a really good investment, isn't it? I remember the prices of these flats when they were first on sale: prices have gone through the roof, now, haven't they?'

'What made you choose one here? And why did you move to Birmingham? Work? What line of work are you in? Do you have a work permit?' Dimly Fran remembered seeing a Pinter play with Ian, where the characters cross-questioned an entirely innocent man — she thought! — in this apparently haphazard way. All she wanted to do was rattle the woman, and between them she and Farat, who joined in the game with gusto, seemed to be succeeding.

'I don't need a work permit! I am a British citizen.'

'You have some evidence? Your driving licence? I notice you have several unpaid fines, Marjorie. Your birth certificate? Yes, I'd like to see your birth certificate. Yes, I'll wait while you find it. I'll wait all day, Marjorie. As will the Chief Superintendent here.' Farat settled herself comfortably and started to flick through the copy of *Vogue* lying on the coffee table.

'You have no right — leave my property immediately!' Sonja-Marjorie made a gesture at home on the opera stage.

'We have every right, Sonja, when we're investigating — a serious crime.' Fran had been afraid Farat would blow it by being too precise, but the pause seemed to create even more tension in the elegant room.

'My papers are in the bank. If you require it, I'll bring them to your police station.'

'Let's go and get them together, shall we? Or would you like to think a moment: you might have meant to take them to the bank, but actually have them safe and sound here. Why don't you go and have a look?' Farat asked. 'No, you won't need your mobile, not if you're looking for documents.'

Fran nodded agreement, and reinforced the point by picking up the handset of the landline phone and laying it on the elegant table. 'Now,' she said, 'why don't we go and look for your documents together?' She stopped short. Warlords had guns, didn't they? And knives? She'd bet Ms Kranic kept other things than papers in a safe place. She and young Farat were putting themselves at unnecessary risk.

'Where shall we look?' Farat asked.

'In — in my bedroom. I have a safe place there. This way,' she added, leading the way.

You bet she had a safe place. Fran stepped in. 'In that case you will lie on your bed, face down, hands spread while we check. I said face down, Ms Kranic! Down. Now.'

* * *

As before, she let the younger officer take credit for the collar. And — necessarily — all the subsequent paperwork. In the past, forces might have bickered about who got the credit in a big case like this. Now both were likely to hand over all their paperwork and information to the Serious Crimes Squad, who could pull everything together. Fran felt, now the adrenaline was subsiding, enormously tired: it must be her weekend catching up with her. Or the quick dive into a couple of shops she and Farat had indulged in before Farat and her colleagues embarked on preliminary questioning. Possessing an unlawful firearm would be added to the charge sheet, which listed several counts of possessing forged documents, an immigration offence — and her speeding tickets. The firearms offence should be enough to have bail denied until Birmingham CID could put together all their other evidence. The gun crime alone would carry a five-year mandatory sentence; with luck, she'd get even longer and then be deported.

Now what? She had time to kill before Mark's meeting finished. It would have been good to retire to a hotel room to sleep, but, not knowing how long either would be tied up with work, they had kept their options open: an early finish meant they could head for home; a late one meant a stop-over and a very early start the following morning. How about a spot of retail therapy?

More to the point, how about taking up Farat's offer of the use of her desk to phone Tom to see how things were progressing in Kent? What he'd said about the music she hummed under her breath worried her. What could a phone ring-tone and her humming possibly have to do with each other?

If she knew she hummed, she should be able to recall what she hummed.

If anyone knew, Mark ought to.

He'd never said anything, never joked about it. But perhaps their relationship as lovers was too fresh and delicate to include the joshing that was routine to long-married couples. Unbidden, thoughts of their times together stole into her mind, and she found herself smiling at them. They weren't all sexual: there was one where Mark had been complaining about the way a tune could pop up all over the place — how they dinned into your ears when you were put on hold by call centres, how even mobiles used them as—

'*Für Elise*!' she said aloud. Her fingers found Tom's number by themselves. The moment he replied, she yelled, 'You've got him! You've got Elise's killer!'

CHAPTER THIRTY-SIX

'Dying?' Mark repeated, 'Pa's dying?'

Fran's voice, as much as he could tell from the phone, was calm. 'That's what they say. I've just taken the call. That's why I've interrupted — you know I'd never have interrupted the meeting otherwise. So I'll get my overnight case from the car and hop on a train to Devon. I'll see you back in—'

'My dear girl, you don't hop anywhere. Stay right where you are. I'll excuse myself now—' He cut the call. Was it natural to make the announcement as flatly as if she'd heard — no, with less emotion than if she'd heard a meeting had been cancelled? Was it a sign of resignation or terrible stress? Biting the inside of his lip, he returned to the seminar room, apologising for the interruption, and adding that he'd been called away. 'A domestic emergency, I'm afraid. My fiancée's father is dying.'

The term came well to the lips. He'd been worrying about 'partner' — which sounded as if he shared a squad car with her — or 'girlfriend'. This word had simply erupted. What on earth did that signify?

How, in a crisis like this, did he come to be worrying about the choice of words? He thanked the chair for his understanding, and, gathering his papers, nodded his goodbyes to his friends and acquaintances around the table.

He prodded the lift button, much less cooperative than his colleagues, again and again. God help him, all he could think of how much easier this ought to make Fran's life. Her mother certainly couldn't survive on her own in that place. Until Fran could work out her notice, Ma would simply have to go into respite care. After three months she might well have been so institutionalised she wanted to stay: he'd seen it often enough. An aunt of his had had to be persuaded into sheltered accommodation; within six months, she was demanding to be up-graded into truly residential care — or down-graded, whichever way you looked at it. The question was, how much support Grant would give him: the common conception was that clergymen were not worldly, but despite having chosen Hazel as a wife, Grant struck him as being pretty clear-sighted. But it was only under cover of others' conversation that Grant had begged him not to let Fran nurse her parents: he'd been much less forthright when he'd thought Hazel might be listening. All the same, Mark must look on him as some sort of ally, for want of any better. Would it be too much to hope that his kirk would spare him long enough to oversee Pa's funeral?

At last a remarkably silly ping announced the lift, and Mark was heading for the foyer and Fran.

* * *

'The trouble with Lloyd House being right in the city centre is this traffic,' she said, looking at the solid metal in front of them.

'Do you want to try to join the rush hour and sit it out, or have a bite and try later?'

She reflected. 'I didn't have any lunch. The DS I was working with — a lovely girl — was fasting for Ramadan, and it seemed a bit self-indulgent to sit munching away while she watched. She said she didn't mind, that it was part of the fast to be tempted by other people, but I just couldn't. So I suppose a quick bite would make sense.'

'There's a good pub not so far from here. Come on.'

She was still so calm. Did it mean she had also worked out the consequences of Pa's death or that she was so full of emotion she didn't dare let any of it out? He took her hand, warm skin to warm skin, and squeezed encouragingly. She pulled up short and turned to him, burying her face in his shoulder. But only for a moment. As soon as she'd regained her composure, she straightened. He was hardly surprised when she wanted to talk shop.

* * *

It was just after nine thirty when they reached the hospital.

'Of course you can see him,' a cheerful, old-fashioned sister declared. 'He'll most likely be asleep, Miss Harman.'

'Is it genuine sleep? Or is he unconscious?'

'He drifts in and out. Mostly out. He kept tearing the drip out, and — look, sit down, I'll make you both a cup of tea and I'll tell you what I think.'

They sat, Mark taking Fran's hand and holding it firmly.

Sister Giles might almost have had the kettle on the boil, she reappeared so quickly. 'The fall was a great shock to his system. As you know, the body reacts in many ways. Some old people fight, and we can fix the broken parts and send them home again, good as new. Some people develop pneumonia, which carries them off. We're not sure exactly what's happened in your father's case, but I for one wouldn't want him put through the trauma of an MRI scan, say, just to find out there's nothing we can do for him.'

Fran looked her in the eye. 'You're sure it's his interests, not financial ones at work here?'

'Have you ever had an MRI scan? It's noisy, confusing — half an hour that a fit person can deal with, but an old man . . . I promise you, Frances, I wouldn't put my own father through it, not without a clear outcome in sight. And — I have to tell you this, though you may find it unpalatable — there comes a time when we have to allow folk to die.

Malformed babies, kids mangled in motorbike crashes, the frailest old people: there comes a point when death is the kindest thing. And I think, even though he may linger a couple more days, even a week, your dad's reached that point.' She paused, sipping her own tea. 'Would he have pulled out the drip otherwise? We tried reinserting it half a dozen times, Frances, each time explaining what we were doing. Each time he pulled it out. He won't drink; he won't eat. The man's eighty-seven. He's had his time.'

'But Ma . . .'

Sister Giles smiled. 'Women often have a few more years in them than men, as I'm sure you know. Your sister and her husband brought her in a wheelchair. It's clear she thinks the poor old man a poor specimen.'

'Did she tell him so? Oh, my God.' Fran sounded as exasperated as if one of her rookie constables had been tactless to a victim of crime.

'I don't think he could hear by then.'

'But they say that hearing is the last of the senses to go,' Fran countered, her voice breaking.

'We don't know. He's very deaf anyway, isn't he, without his aid? And that finished up the far side of the ward when we tried to get him to use it. Poor Alf has had enough, Frances. Say goodbye and let him go. That's the kindest thing, believe me.'

'But—'

What stopped her short in her protest? One moment she was angry, ready almost to shake the woman with frustration; the next she was calm, nodding acquiescence. 'You're right. Don't prolong Pa's suffering, not if there's truly only one way he can go. I'll just say goodbye, if I may.'

Mark held her hand as far as the side ward. There was some light, enough for the nursing staff to see and if necessary work on their patient, but it was dimmed, so as not to trouble the dying man. He held back, not wanting to intrude.

It seemed to him the old man stirred and murmured as Fran knelt beside the bed and took his hand. 'It's me, Pa, Fran,' she said.

There was no response. At last, she got to her feet, and put her hand on his shoulder. 'Pa? It's me, Fran. Your daughter.'

Did the old man speak simply to her or was it to the world at large? His words were faint, but clear enough for Mark to hear. 'Leave me in peace.'

'Pa?'

'Bugger off and leave me in peace.' And he hunched his shoulder away from her.

For a moment, Mark was afraid Fran would scurry to the far side of the bed and try again. But with simple dignity, she laid her hand on Pa's head and said, 'God bless you, Pa. Goodbye.' She dropped a kiss on his forehead and turned and walked away without a backwards glance.

* * *

Mark didn't trespass on whatever thoughts might be troubling her. Instead he simply drove to the Teignmouth seafront and walked with her in what was a remarkably balmy night.

'You may think I'm terribly callous,' she said at last. 'But he hasn't been my Pa for years. Not really. You've never known him, of course. And you couldn't tell from the sad old body you saw at the weekend and tonight that he was once a young man full of vigour. It was he who taught me badminton and drove me from tournament to tournament — he bought a car just for that reason, I think. He never enjoyed driving. He was never the same after he came down here, though. It was as if he gave up and became old. Very old. Crotchety. Bad tempered. Whatever I did was the wrong thing. That was when I started mourning him, except he was still alive and I couldn't. Many was the time I hated him, for the cruel things he said. But that wasn't my Pa. It was just some grumpy old man. Let's find a hotel. Ma'll be in bed. So there's no point in disturbing her. I'll check in with her and with Hazel and Grant tomorrow, and then we'll go back home.'

Despite himself he was shocked. 'Won't you stay till he actually dies?'

'Why? We've said our goodbyes. At least I have. And I'm simply doing what Pa wanted. Leaving him in peace. He only ever wanted me to work. I've got a case to wrap up, Mark. And then perhaps another human will be allowed the dignity of death: poor Elise.'

* * *

Predictably Mark wasn't the only one to feel disconcerted by her decision.

'Will you be staying down here with her, Mark?' Grant asked, peering over rimless half-moons that made him look remarkably like Alec Douglas-Hume. He'd already said he could extend what he quaintly called his furlough as long as he was needed in Devon.

Mark shook his head. 'I'll have to go back today and come back for the funeral. I promise I'll be back for that, Fran.'

She said crisply, 'So will I, of course. But meanwhile, I'm going back to my job too.'

'But surely you can't — not with Pa—' Hazel began, shaking her head. 'He's only just—'

'Ma doesn't need me if she's got you. She'll only try to play one of us off against the other, as she always did. I'll arrange a hire car for you, if you like, or set up an account with a taxi company, so you don't have to depend on public transport, which is intermittent down here. I'll place the decision about where Ma goes next in your hands. It's clear she can't manage on her own.'

'But you promised to look after her.'

Grant coughed. 'There's more than one way of looking after someone. And I think you should recall the parable of the talents, all of you. When God gave us our various abilities, I think He gave Fran an extraordinary capacity for hard work and helping others, and perhaps a little less for domesticity and geriatric nursing. Let's face it, that's what

Ma needs. And were Fran never so free, I don't think she's the one to offer it. Go your ways, Fran. If anyone knew the ins and outs of death and bereavement, it's me. I can do all that's necessary without turning what little the Lord's left me in the way of hair. It'll make Hazel very happy to care for Ma now she has the opportunity, which my occupation has denied her till recently.' Grant smiled at them all.

Perhaps only Mark detected his wink. Well, if it had taken him a mere weekend to get the measure of the older daughter, he was fairly sure Grant must have it after all those years of marriage. Mark winked back.

The ensuing silence was interrupted by the double-thump of Ma's Zimmer.

'You're supposed to be making me a cup of tea, not standing here gossiping. And I'd like to know why it takes four of you to make it. Fran, you should be emptying his wardrobe: he won't be needing his clothes again, though he'll want to be buried in his best suit, I suppose. Such waste: it could do some African good,' she added, obscurely. 'And Hazel, you can get the dining-room curtains down and give them a wash — we can't have people coming to his funeral seeing all those splashes — he was such a messy eater. As for you men, there's a week's work in the garden: she really neglected it, as you can see. All those leaves piled up. And the weeds! That tree by the bird-table — if you get it out, the council will take it away. I've always hated it but he said it attracted the birds . . .'

* * *

Grant leaned on the driver's window as they prepared to leave. 'Believe me, it's best you go like this — while you and Hazel are still on speaking terms, Fran, and while I've still got some novelty value. Off you go. No, Mark — remember what the good Lord told His disciples: "Let the dead bury the dead".' He gave the top of the car a valedictory pat and perforce Mark drove off.

CHAPTER THIRTY-SEVEN

Back at her desk, Fran worked as hard as her mother would have wished, if at different tasks. Though Farat Hafeez had the lion's share, there was still a great deal of paperwork to complete for the Birmingham business, plus an in-tray that threatened to buckle.

Top of the heap was a note from Henson, inviting her to join him and the rest of the team in a drink that evening. To build bridges, to cement bonds, such activities were essential. She ought to be there. But it was one thing to hurtle from your father's death-bed to work, and quite another to get raucous with your colleagues. Or was it? In any case, she was hardly dressed for letting her hair down, and truth to tell the height of luxury would have been beans on toast in front of the TV and a candle-lit bath. Which brought Mark into the scenario: would he be invited to the shindig, or was he too senior? In any case, wasn't it a booze-up for CID, not management? How would he feel about slumming it with a load of half-pissed underlings simply because he was sleeping with one of them?

As a new couple they had so much to work out, and this didn't seem the moment. She ran tense hands through her unkempt hair — another item on tonight's list — and found herself crying.

Furious with herself, she scrubbed at her eyes and balled the tissue into the bin, narrowly missing Mark, who had opened the door without knocking.

'I just don't know what to do about this,' she said by way of explanation. She passed him Henson's note.

Mark looked from her to the note and back again. 'A simple note thanking him and saying you couldn't be there because you were down in Devon, I'd have thought.'

'But I'm not in Devon: I'm here!'

He touched the date at the top of the note. 'I think you'll find that was yesterday's.' Was he concerned or amused or both?

'I really am losing it, aren't I? Oh, Mark, what I'd give for a nice, normal week, one in which one day followed the next in an ordered fashion.'

'When did you last have one?'

She snorted with sudden laughter. 'Not since I joined the police! OK, my demands are too great. Just a *fairly* normal week.'

* * *

The shuttlecock flew higher and higher: surely it must fall out! But it swooped in just this side of the baseline, and now she was a clear point ahead. The sports hall bulged with spectators. Most were cheering her on, falling respectfully silent when either player served. But as she prepared herself for the vital point, her father stood up.

'You'll have to hurry up, Fran — I can't wait all day for you.'

'I'll catch you up!' she shouted, serving and — yes! — winning. But as she picked up the trophy, one at least as large and grandiose as the FA Cup, she couldn't see her father.

She slipped out of bed and padded off to the bathroom. The alarm clock told her it was three, almost to the minute.

* * *

'You're entitled to three days' bereavement leave, aren't you?' Mark asked, over the muesli.

'Yes. It depends on what time they can organise the funeral how many days I'll need.'

'How do you feel now you're properly awake?'

'Am I ever properly awake these days? I know there's no comparison, Mark, but how did you feel when Tina died?'

He put down his spoon, counting on his fingers. 'Guilty: for being alive. Angry: at the waste of a life that should have gone on much longer. Terrified: I had to tell the kids. Exhausted: I'd got to the point where I couldn't physically carry on much longer. Guilty: I was almost relieved it was over. Panicky: I had so much to arrange. Lonely: someone who had been part of my life for so long had left me, taking shared memories with her. Christ, Fran, what more do you want me to say?'

'Anything else that will help me. I feel like an Easter egg, you see: strong outside but completely hollow. I ought to feel something more than I do, clearly. Guilt, mostly, because — because I'd stopped loving him. I'd started to see him as a problem, a chore. The case I couldn't solve, and one I couldn't pass on to anyone else. But today,' she said, trying for a smile and pulling herself up straight, 'it's time to turn to a case I think we can solve. I want to update Tom on the Birmingham side of the case and find out how he's got on. It's weird, Mark: you'd have thought after all this time I was used to sitting listening to reports on crimes, or even reading laboured reports, but I really resent that it was he who tied all the loose ends, not me.'

'You didn't do so badly on the Rebecca case,' he said.

'And up in Brum it'll be young Farat toiling away, pulling all the threads together.'

'And you think it ought to be you doing everything, and organising the funeral and sorting out your mother's accommodation. Fran: was what you did ever good enough for your parents?'

She bridled. 'They've always been very supportive. I told you: Pa even bought his first car so he could run me round the country for badminton tournaments. Which is why I dreamt of one last night, I suppose — the very moment he was dying.'

'What did he say when you won — which I presume was quite often?'

'Well, he'd often point out ways I could have finished off my opponent more quickly, I suppose.'

'Exam results?'

'Well, I wasn't ever the brightest lamp in the fairy lights.'

'So how are you now Detective Chief Superintendent Doctor Harman? Fran, your parents seem to me to have set intolerably high hurdles for you to jump, and when you leapt them with ease simply raised them a bit more. Did you hear your Ma this weekend — even yesterday? Before either of us had our coats off she was issuing orders, and complaining about how you carried them out. I don't expect you to take it aboard at the moment, but one day you might wonder why you're never satisfied with your performance and trace it back to them. Come on, it's time we were on the road: you've got to hear Tom tell you what you've enabled him to do. And I bet if you criticise him, it'll be so gently he thinks all the improvements are entirely his own work.'

* * *

'Tom,' she confessed, almost truthfully, 'I don't even know what day it is today, what with one thing and another, so you'll have to talk me through this very, very slowly. Take your time — use that whiteboard if necessary — and tell me everything we need to know to pass on to the DPP.'

'You're sure, like, you ought to be in today?'

He spoke as if they were equals: she replied in kind. 'What earthly use would I be down there? I'm not domesticated, Tom, like my sister, and she'll be dashing round sorting things out all the more efficiently for my being elsewhere. As for Ma: she's become an old bat, Tom, like I'll be in a few years' time if I don't watch it — she never stops nagging and giving contradictory orders. So though it looks bad, I shall stay here at my desk until the funeral.' And come back to it with gusto, she added, under her breath. 'Fire away.'

'Right. Marjorie Gray — would you mind if I called her Elise while we're talking about her, like?'

'I rather think she might have preferred it.'

'Elise looked after her parents until their deaths, one three years ago, the other just six months later. She sold or gave away all her possessions, apparently trying to shed her old life and try another for size.' He looked at her with something like panic in his eyes. 'Would she have liked it, Fran, or would she have ended up dead lonely?'

She tried to sound bracing, but wasn't sure if it might not have come across as callous. 'Hard to tell, isn't it? But dead lonely's better than plain dead, anyway.'

He managed a grin to acknowledge her effort. 'Then she sold her parents' house, and, since she inherited a tidy packet from them — I checked out their Will, Fran: they left well over four hundred thousand, nearer the half million — she bought a flat in Birmingham. Not where I'd have chosen myself, but there you are.'

'It's a lovely flat, Tom, and within walking distance of the city centre and all its amenities.'

'But *Birmingham*!' He might have said, 'Outer Mongolia!'

She raised a mock-minatory finger. 'Think about St Mary's Bay.'

He grimaced. '*A hit! A palpable hit!* As it says in the play.'

She still hadn't talked to him about Scott, and here he was quoting Shakespeare.

He took her grin as encouragement to continue. 'Anyway, she decides to buy a new car, and falls into the clutches of one Dean Roberts who persuades her to splash out on a Lotus. He's a really nice guy, Fran — you know, you'd get chatting to him in a pub, and before you know it you've told him your life story. And Elise does just that. She tells him everything: how she's given up her life down here and is going to start a brand-new life in Birmingham, where she knows no one. She hates her St Mary's Bay life so much she's shedding it like a snake its skin, and converting everything into cash. Now, nice as he appears, Dean is actually a career criminal, involved with car theft. He steals top-of-the-range models to order. Usually he gets duplicate keys made of the cars he sells so they can be stolen from people's drives. But this time he doesn't know where she's going, so he does something else. I've checked the records of the emergency calls on the day of the assault. Two people called in to say they'd seen an accident on the B2067, and indeed, officers reported tyre tracks that suggest a vehicle ended up on the grass verge. But Roberts admits the accident was faked, so that Elise would get out of her car to see what she could do to help, only to be whacked on the head and left on the verge for dead. He said he only meant to knock her out, but claims that she must have a thin skull.'

'So it's her fault that he basically killed her!'

'Quite. They load her Lotus into a horsebox and drive off.'

'The sexual assault?'

'Now, he didn't have a problem with killing her but the assault really revolted him. He denies it on his mother's grave. And his DNA confirms he's innocent. But he's fingered a mate, who's now living in Spain. We've contacted Interpol for help here. But I think he knew about it, one way or another, because he swears he felt so guilty he went straight for a while. Eventually he ran out of money and his bosses were putting pressure on him — the people he stole the cars for, not those at the showroom, who had no idea what was going on. His bosses also got him hooked on cocaine, he says, though he was very vague about that, and he ended up couriering for them. Drugs and people. He says he's only had contact with scrotes pretty low down the food chain, never the boss. But he thinks she's a woman.'

'Which is where I come in. We found the new Marjorie Gray, complete with documents for a whole series of Marjorie Grays. The people-trafficking seems to have been even more profitable than the car theft. So it's not just poor Elise's life they've destroyed: it's those of a lot of poor young women, raped and buggered and misused as only humans can hurt their fellow humans. Between us, we've unearthed a lot of nasty people, Tom.'

'But we'll put them behind bars, Fran — don't forget that. It's not just rooting out evil: it's helping the courts punish it.' As if inspired, he sprang to his feet. 'I'll get on to any dotting i's and crossing t's now, if you'll excuse me: the sooner this lot satisfies the DPP the happier I shall be. What about you?'

Fran got up too, stretching so that her back cracked. 'I'd better get on to the hospital authorities and tell them we've nailed Elise's murderer. Then they can set about the case that should put the poor woman finally out of her misery.'

He was looking at her as if unsure how she'd take his next words.

'Go on: spit it out.'

'That Alan Pitt. Will you tell him? Because he really cared for her, didn't he? And for you, actually. He told Sergeant Simpson that he's left a pair of concert tickets for you in his house and would you be allowed to take advantage of them? Talk about weird, Fran. That man should be in hospital, not jail.'

'Let's hope the courts take that view,' she said quietly.

CHAPTER THIRTY-EIGHT

'It seems really strange, seeing you in here, in the chapel of rest, looking just like you did in your bed on the ward all those months. But now I know you're dead, quite dead. That's why my psychiatrist got permission for me to come and say one last goodbye. Yes, I have a psychiatrist now, because they decided I wasn't bad but mad and put me not in prison but in hospital. No, you won't place the allusion — I wonder if you ever would have done. I doubt it: they tell me they've found out more and more about you. Once you had your own little business, running a shop specialising in wools and embroidery silks, but of course, people lost interest in old-fashioned crafts and skills, and you had to sell up and work in a variety of other people's shops. You must have hated it. And then your parents grew old and ill, and you became their carer. Because it was your job, you didn't get much in the way of respite care for them. Every day must have seemed like the last, only worse, because you knew they would only deteriorate. Their deaths must have come as a huge release! Selling up everything, and giving away what you couldn't sell — did you hate your life that much? I suppose you must have done. It must have been as if your own possessions were tainted so that you couldn't love them anymore. I wonder how I shall feel when I live in my own home again. It won't be the one I've lived in for years. Like you, I've got to start again. The bungalow's sold, and all my books and china boxed up and in store. Oh, the local vigilantes of course — the fear was

that they'd decided I was a paedophile and needed rougher justice than the courts could mete out.

'But I was mad, they said, not bad. They said it was post-traumatic stress disorder, that the balance of my mind had been disturbed by finding you in the state you were and failing to save you — indeed, perpetuating your suffering by trying to resuscitate you. I've had hours of therapy, and enough drugs to make me rattle if you shook me, so in my head I know I'm not responsible for what happened to you. In my heart — that's another matter. But I have to agree with them, or they'll probably section me.

'So it's not my fault, what happened to you. But what about that child? Whatever they say, what I did to that Rebecca was plain wicked. She may remember nothing of her ordeal, and of course, I never touched her, but she had three months of cold turkey coming off the drugs I'd foisted on her. It was all so easy: I simply moved a workman's shelter, those red and white little tents, from one place and put it in another. MacDonald's was so crowded no one noticed me sitting at Rebecca's table. Oh, I'd met her through the Internet, in one of those chat rooms. Her parents wouldn't let her have a computer of her own, so she simply used a friend's. Music, that was what we spoke about. Anyway, I put the stuff in her orange juice, and waited till I could see her getting woozy, and simply left her too it. As she came out, swaying a bit, I helped her sit down in the shelter, and then brought my car round and popped her in. It's always chaotic in Ashford on market day, with those huge white vans of the traders obstructing the CCTV cameras. They've tightened things up now.

'I wonder if Frances has been to visit you. She wouldn't talk to you as she has to me. Oh, yes, she's been to see me in hospital several times, just as if we were friends. No, she's not interrogating me, nothing like that. She tells me about her everyday life, and I tell her what little there is to tell of mine. She didn't take up my offer of tickets for the Brodsky Quartet — legal problems, she said. But she did go, and she said they hadn't lost any of their brilliance and energy. She herself seems to have a new lease of life, now she's not hurtling around the country. Yes, her father died: it was all quite sudden in the end. She thought that would make her life more complicated, but it seems there was some sort of reconciliation between her mother and her elder sister,

with the result, would you believe, that her mother's gone to live in the Hebrides or somewhere. She did say, but I'm sure one of these damned pills is wreaking havoc with my memory. It doesn't matter anyway, does it? Anyway, as Frances herself said, it solved her dilemma for her, rather than her having to make the decision. Dea ex machina, I said, and I must say I was surprised that she not only knew the term but also understood why I'd changed it. She has to retire from her present post soon, but seems resigned to that: she says you can get too old. But I doubt if she'll be unemployed, should she want work: at least two universities want her, and the Home Office is head hunting her too. And there's some body that looks into miscarriages of justice. I should think she'd be most at home in that.

'Any dreams I had of courting her have evaporated, I fear. Not just because of what I did either, she assures me of that. She's in what looks like a very sound relationship with another officer, very senior. No, no wedding bells yet. But there's something about the way her face changes when she speaks of him, and she wears this lovely ring. Victorian, I should say.

'Now, is there anything else? Of course! They've found both the men who — who did this to you. The man who cracked your skull and the man who raped you so terribly. Life sentences, I'm glad to say. They tried, unsuccessfully, to have their sentences reduced by turning Queen's Evidence and shopping their bosses — an unsavoury group by anyone's standards. They're looking at long sentences and deportation — see how police lingo has affected my own vocabulary!

'Ah, Elise — it's no good, I simply can't think of you as Marjorie Gray! — it's time for me to say goodbye. I shall be allowed to come to the funeral, of course, but I wanted one last word with you alone. So, goodbye, my dear: I wouldn't have had this happen for the world.'

THE END

THE JOFFE BOOKS STORY

We began in 2014 when Jasper agreed to publish his mum's much-rejected romance novel and it became a bestseller.

Since then we've grown into the largest independent publisher in the UK. We're extremely proud to publish some of the very best writers in the world, including Joy Ellis, Faith Martin, Caro Ramsay, Helen Forrester, Simon Brett and Robert Goddard. Everyone at Joffe Books loves reading and we never forget that it all begins with the magic of an author telling a story.

We are proud to publish talented first-time authors, as well as established writers whose books we love introducing to a new generation of readers.

We won Trade Publisher of the Year at the Independent Publishing Awards in 2023. We have been shortlisted for Independent Publisher of the Year at the British Book Awards for the last four years, and were shortlisted for the Diversity and Inclusivity Award at the 2022 Independent Publishing Awards. In 2023 we were shortlisted for Publisher of the Year at the RNA Industry Awards.

We built this company with your help, and we love to hear from you, so please email us about absolutely anything bookish at: feedback@joffebooks.com.

If you want to receive free books every Friday and hear about all our new releases, join our mailing list: www.joffebooks.com/contact.

And when you tell your friends about us, just remember: it's pronounced Joffe as in coffee or toffee!

ALSO BY JUDITH CUTLER

FRAN HARMAN MYSTERIES
Book 1: COME TO HARM

DETECTIVE KATE POWER MYSTERIES
Book 1: MURDER THE BOYS
Book 2: MURDER BY THE CANAL
Book 3: MURDER BY ARSON
Book 4: MURDER BY FRAUD
Book 5: MURDER IN DEVON
Book 6: MURDER ON THE JOB

Printed in Great Britain
by Amazon

44981395R00162